Tom Clancy's Duty and Honour

Tom Clancy's Duty and Honour

GRANT BLACKWOOD

MICHAEL JOSEPH
an imprint of
PENGUIN BOOKS

MICHAEL JOSEPH

UK | USA | Canada | Ireland | Australia
India | New Zealand | South Africa

Michael Joseph is part of the Penguin Random House group of companies
whose addresses can be found at global.penguinrandomhouse.com.

First published in the USA by G. P. Putnam's Sons 2016
First published in Great Britain by Michael Joseph 2016
002

Text copyright © The Estate of Thomas L. Clancy, Jr.; Rubicon, Inc.;
Jack Ryan Enterprises, Ltd.; and Jack Ryan Limited Partnership, 2016

The moral right of the author has been asserted

Set in 12.32/19.61 pt Berling LT Std
Printed in Great Britain by Clays Ltd, St Ives plc

A CIP catalogue record for this book is available from the British Library

HARDBACK ISBN: 978–0–718–18194–9
OM PAPERBACK ISBN: 978–0–718–18195–6

Tom Clancy's Duty and Honour

ALEXANDRIA, VIRGINIA

Jack Ryan, Jr., would later wonder what exactly had saved his life that night. One thing was certain: It hadn't been skill. Maybe the heft of the bok choy had bought him a split second, maybe the mud, but not skill. Dumb luck. Survival instinct.

The Supermercado was neither in his neighborhood nor near his frequent errand stops, but it did have the best selection of fruits and vegetables in Alexandria—so Ding Chavez had told him eight months ago, yet it had been only recently, since his forced leave of absence from The Campus, that he'd become a believer. Being unemployed had given him a lot to think about and plenty of time to broaden his horizons. The one frontier he'd so far refused to explore despite his sister Sally's exhortations was binge-watching *Girls* on HBO. That was his Rubicon. No crossing the river for the Roman legions, no chick TV for Jack Ryan. Soon, though, he'd have to make a decision about his loose-ends lifestyle. Another couple weeks and his probation would be over. Gerry Hendley would want an answer: Was he coming back to The Campus, or were they parting company permanently?

And do what? Jack thought.

He'd spent most of his adult life working at The Campus, aka Hendley Associates, first as an analyst and then as an operations officer—a field spook. The off-the-books counterterror organization had been created by his father, President Jack Ryan, and had since its inception been overseen by former senator Gerry Hendley. So far they'd had a lot of success going after some of the world's "big bads" while still managing to make a decent profit not just for their clients, all of whom knew Hendley only as a financial arbitrage company, but also for The Campus's covert operational budget.

"Seventeen fifty," the cashier told him.

Jack handed her a twenty, took his change, then collected his brown-paper sack from the glum teenage bagger and headed for the door. It was just past eight p.m. and the store was almost deserted. Through the broad front windows he could see rain glittering in the glow of the parking lot's sodium-vapor lights. Accompanied by a cold front, rain had been falling in Alexandria for three straight days. Creeks were swollen and the DIY stores nearest the Potomac were seeing a jump in sandbag sales. Perfect weather for home-made slow-cooker chili. He'd just put in a solid eight miles on his gym's indoor track, followed by a twenty-minute circuit of push-ups, pull-ups, and planks, and he hoped to turn his bag full of ground beef, beans, peppers, onions, to-matoes, and bok choy—his mom's most recent superfood recommendation—into a reward for all his sweat. The chili wouldn't be ready until tomorrow; tonight, Chinese-takeout leftovers.

The automatic door slid open and Jack used his free hand to pull his sweatshirt's hood over his head. It was a short walk to his car—a black Chrysler 300 and the first sedan he'd owned in a long time—and then a fifteen-minute drive back to his condo at the Oronoco. The parking lot's surface was new and its fresh coat of asphalt shimmered black under the slick of rain. Moving at a half-jog, feeling the chilled rain running down his chin and into his shirt, Jack covered the thirty yards to his car, which he'd parked trunk-first against the guardrail. Old habits, he thought. Be ready to leave quickly; know your closest exits and highways. Months of "civilian" life and still a lot of the fieldcraft rules John Clark and the rest had taught him hadn't faded. Did this tell Jack something? Was this just a shadow of a habit, or inclination?

As he neared his car, he saw a sheet of white paper stuck under his windshield wiper. A flyer—food drive, garage sale, voting reminder . . . Whatever it was, Jack wasn't in the mood. He leaned sideways and reached for the flyer. Sodden, it tore free in a clump, leaving a narrow strip trapped beneath the wiper blade.

"Shit," Jack muttered.

From behind, a voice: "Hey, man, give it up!"

Even before he turned, the tone of the man's voice combined with the time of night and location had touched off Jack's warning bells. The Supermercado wasn't in the best of neighborhoods, with its fair share of crack-driven homelessness and petty crime.

Jack turned on his heel while taking two steps backward, hoping to buy time and room to maneuver. The man was tall, nearly six and a half feet, and gangly, his head covered in a dark hood, and he came from Jack's left at a fast walking pace.

Overhead, lightning flashed, casting the man's face in stark shadow.

Break his pattern, Jack thought. Having targeted his prey and committed himself to the attack, the man—a crackhead or tweaker, Jack guessed—was laser-focused, confident this roll would go like all the others. Jack needed to change that.

He took a step toward the man and pointed. "Fuck off! Go away!"

Junkie muggers rarely saw this kind of victim aggression. Wolves prefer weak sheep.

But Jack's belligerence had no effect. The man's pace and his locked-on gaze at Jack didn't waver. His right hand, hanging beside his thigh, rose up to his waist, palm away from Jack. *He's got a knife.* If his attacker was carrying a gun he would have already brandished it. With a gun you could put the fear of God in someone at a distance; with a knife you needed to get close enough to put the blade against your victim's face or neck. And the palm-away knife grip told Jack something else: The man wasn't interested in scaring him into submission. It was easier to strip valuables from a dead body.

Jack's heart was pounding now, his breathing going shallow. He swept his right hand to his hip, lifted the hem of his sweatshirt with his thumb, his palm touching . . . nothing. *Goddamn it.* He wasn't armed; he had a CCW permit but had stopped carrying his Glock the day he left The Campus. *Keys.* His car keys were in his pocket, not where they should have been—in his hand, as a backup weapon. *Lazy, Jack.*

His attacker hadn't missed seeing Jack's flash of hesitation. He sprinted forward, right hand sweeping up and out in preparation for a cross-hand neck slash. As though passing a basketball, Jack heaved his grocery bag at the man. It bounced off his chest, the contents scattering across the wet asphalt. This broke both his pattern and his stride, but for only a moment, and did not leave enough time to create an opening for Jack's own attack. *Retreat, then. Live to fight another day.* There was no point getting in a knife fight if he had a choice.

He turned, sprinted for the guardrail, vaulted it, and landed in mush. Below him, a slope with patchy grass and cedar ground cover met a line of concrete Jersey barrier along the highway.

Behind him, Jack vaguely registered the man's footsteps picking up speed on the pavement. He started shuffle-sliding down the embankment, using the scrub brush for footholds.

His attacker was fast. A hand clutched Jack's hood and wrenched his head backward, exposing his throat. Jack didn't fight it, but rather spun hard to his right, into the man and toward what he guessed would be the descending knife blade. And it was there, arcing toward his face. Jack lifted his left arm and drove his forearm down, diverting the blade and trapping the man's arm in his own armpit.

With his right hand Jack reached up, fingers clawing at the man's eyes and pushing his head sideways. Together they fell back, Jack on top. They began sliding down, churning up mud and grinding over cedar stumps as they went.

The man was flailing, but with purpose, Jack realized. Trying to free his knife arm from Jack's armpit, the man reached across with his left hand, grabbed Jack's chin, and wrenched his head sideways. Pain flashed in Jack's neck.

One of the man's fingers slipped into his mouth, and Jack bit down hard, heard a muffled crunch. The man screamed.

Still entwined, they slammed to a stop against one of the Jersey barriers bordering the highway. Jack heard a sick-sounding thud, followed by an *umph*. Through squinted eyes Jack saw the flash of headlights, heard the hiss of tires on the wet pavement.

The man was rolling sideways, crawling on his hands and knees. Lightning flashed again and Jack could make out a bloody divot in the side of his skull; a flap of scalp drooped over his ear.

Skull fracture. A bad one.

Jack was crawling also, but in the opposite direction toward the embankment. He got to his feet and turned. The man was already up and lumbering toward him. Like a drunk trying to walk a line, the man crossed his feet and staggered, gathering momentum until he plunged face-first into the mud. Swaying, he pushed himself to his knees. He reached up to touch the side of his skull, then stared at his bloody hand.

"What is . . . ?" the man growled, his speech slurred. "I need a . . . need the . . ."

He scanned the ground as though he'd lost something.

Looking for his knife.

Jack spotted it a few feet to the man's left front. Too late. The man pushed himself to his feet and shuffled toward it.

Jack charged, feet slipping in the mud as he tried to close the distance. The man bent over for the knife, almost tipping forward as he did so. Jack pushed off with his back foot, drove his knee upward. It slammed into the man's face, vaulting him backward into the barricade. Jack's feet slipped out from under him and he toppled backward into the mud. His head bounced against the ground. His vision sparkled.

Move . . . do something, he thought. *He's coming.* An image of himself flashed in his mind—flat on his back in the mud, throat slashed open, rain peppering his open eyes, the flash of a coroner's camera—

No, no way.

Jack rolled onto his side.

Ten feet away his attacker sat half sprawled against the concrete barricade. His head lolled to one side. The gray concrete behind him was smeared with blood. The man was white, pale, in his mid-thirties, with close-cropped light hair. Jack glimpsed what looked like white skull through his lacerated scalp.

"Stay there, man!" Jack shouted. "Don't move."

Blinking as though confused, the man focused on Jack for a second, then rolled sideways and began working with his knees like a toddler trying to crawl on a tile floor. He managed to climb to his feet.

Tough son of a bitch.

Jack spotted the glint of the knife a few feet away, half buried in the muck. He crawled to it, grabbed it. It was a locking folder, almost eight inches long, and hefty.

"Just stop!" Jack shouted, panting. He tasted blood in his mouth. He spit it out. His, or the mugger's? he wondered. "The cops are coming!"

He doubted this, but maybe it would be enough to either drive the man off or make him sit back down and accept his fate. And a free trip to the ER. Chances were, in the darkness and the rain, no one knew what was happening, didn't know that Jack Ryan, Jr., America's First Son and unemployed special operator, was fighting for his life with a crackhead mugger in the mud beside a highway.

Christ Almighty.

The man was moving now, but not toward Jack. With his left hand braced against the top of the concrete barricade, he shuffled forward, stopped, kept going. A car swept past him, honking, covering him in a sheet of water. The man didn't react.

Brain injury, Jack thought. Despite himself, he felt a pang of . . . what? Of sympathy for a junkie who'd just tried to kill him? *Come on, Jack.* Still, he couldn't let the guy wander off, sit down in some doorway, and die of a brain bleed. *Ah, hell . . .*

"Just stop!" Jack shouted. "Come back—"

The man reached a gap between the Jersey barriers and his guiding hand dropped into free space. He stopped walking, looked down at his feet.

A few feet away a car swept past, horn honking.

The man turned left and stumbled forward onto the highway.

"Hey, don't—"

Jack saw the headlights and heard the roar of the diesel engine a second before the eighteen-wheeler emerged from under the overpass. The truck's horn started blaring.

Jack sprinted.

The truck plowed squarely into the man.

Jack stood rooted, staring, only half hearing the truck's air brakes wheeze and sputter.

Did that just happen?

Do something. Move.

He turned and ran back toward the embankment.

He stopped.

Above, standing at the guardrail, a man was backlit by car headlights.

"Hey," Jack called. "Call nine-one-one!"

The figure didn't move.

Jack cupped his hands around his mouth and shouted again.

The figure turned and disappeared. A few moments later the headlights retreated into the darkness.

Adrenaline was a hell of a thing, Jack thought. As was shock. He'd seen a lot of stuff, but something about this . . . The man hadn't even glanced at the truck bearing down on him.

Jack stood in the shower, eyes closed, forehead pressed against the tile wall, as hot water rushed over his head. His hands were still shaking, pulsing in time with his heartbeat.

He'd left. With the man's knife. He'd had the presence of mind to make sure he hadn't lost anything traceable— phone, keys, wallet, receipt, the larger items from his grocery bag—but ninety seconds after the truck struck the man, Jack was pulling out of the Supermercado parking lot. It wasn't until he was halfway back to the Oronoco that he heard sirens.

Was it the shock of it? Maybe, or maybe he just didn't want to deal with the ten thousand questions the cops and media would start asking not just of him but of his father, his mother, his sisters, his brother, and his colleagues at Hendley. Tabloids and A-list media outlets alike would interview his ex-girlfriends and elementary school friends. The headlines would be salacious. Anyone gunning for his father on Capitol Hill would milk the story for all it was worth. All that aside, he was the victim; it was cut-and-dried. There was a witness, or at least a possible witness. Why had the man left?

Jack hadn't escaped the assault unscathed. Despite having trapped the man's knife arm, the blade had gotten him—three shallow stabs right below his shoulder blade, none deeper than a half-inch, but enough to leave his shoulder burning and partially numb. Jack wondered, Were the wounds collateral to the struggle, or had his attacker been trying to drive the blade home?

His slide down the cedar bushes had scratched and abraded his lower back and belly so badly it looked like someone had taken to him with a belt sander. Another worry: Had he swallowed some of the man's blood? If so, he had to start thinking about hep C or something worse.

Guy tried to kill me, Jack thought. *Why?* Because he hadn't gotten his high for a couple hours? For the twenty-two dollars and change Jack had in his pocket? For his car? This wasn't the first time someone had tried to take his life, but this felt different.

ALEXANDRIA, VIRGINIA

J ack woke before dawn the next day, having slept fit-
fully. Even dozing, his mind had played and replayed
the incident, half dream, half reality, but always ending the same way: the mugger dying and Jack feeling, what?
Like he'd done something wrong?

He took another shower, mostly to reclean his wounds,
stood under the cold water as long as he could stand it, then
got dressed, put his previous night's clothes in the washer,
dumped in some bleach, and turned it on.

In the kitchen, he made a double espresso, downed it, set
the machine back to standard coffee, then went to the sink,
where he'd placed the mugger's knife. He put it in the dishwasher, started a hot cycle, then walked into the living room
and turned on the TV. He changed the channel to the local
news. This early in the morning, hours before the morning

shows, they were repeating stories frequently, so it didn't take long:

"Police say a man was struck and killed by a vehicle on North Kings Highway near Telegraph Road last night shortly after eight p.m. He is yet to be identified. If you have any information, the police ask that you—"

Jack muted the television. "Unidentified," Jack said. No mention of witnesses, which could mean something or nothing. If the figure at the guardrail had made a report, the police were just as likely to withhold the information until they could come at him with something solid. Especially someone named Jack Ryan.

For twenty minutes he paced and drank coffee, occasionally leaning over his laptop to scan online news sites for more information. There was nothing. He wanted to call someone, to confide in someone, but he resisted the impulse. He needed to think. Better still, he needed to do something.

With his mind only partially registering the pre-rush-hour traffic, Jack drove back to the Supermercado. The rain had stopped falling, but overhead, the clouds were still dark and swollen. Sidewalks and lawns were still wet, and potholes brimmed with water. Overhanging tree branches showing the first hint of green buds drooped under the weight of the moisture.

It was past seven, the sun just coming up, and an hour before the Supermercado opened. The parking lot appeared empty. Jack made a second pass, scanning for police cars. Seeing none, he made a U-turn, pulled into the lot, and parked in a stall close to the front doors. He climbed out.

With his breath steaming in the morning air, he walked to the spot beside the guardrail where he'd parked the previous night. He stopped and looked down the embankment.

Aside from a string of yellow police tape looped along the line of Jersey barriers at the bottom of the embankment, the scene seemed unremarkable. In his mind's eye he'd imagined his fight with the mugger had churned the slope into a jumble of mud, grass, and shredded cedar brush. Beyond the barriers, cars on the Kings Highway streamed past at a steady pace.

Jack glanced around. The parking lot was still empty. He climbed over the guardrail and picked his way down the embankment until he reached the flat area alongside the barriers. It was a goulash of mud and patchy, green-yellow grass. On the other side of the barriers the passing cars' tires sent up billowing mist.

Following his mental map, Jack found the barrier against which his attacker had fallen. He knelt before it. There was no trace of blood on the gray concrete. Either the rain or a first-responder fire truck had washed it away. Jack stood up and walked along the barriers, looking for any trace of what had happened the night before. There was nothing.

He headed back up the slope. Ten feet from the top, a flash of something caught the corner of his eye. He stopped, scanned the ground. Jutting from under a scrub brush beside his foot was the corner of a business card. Jack stooped over and picked it up. Not a business card, but a hotel key card.

"Hey, what're you doing down there?" a voice barked.

Jack looked up and saw a man in a dark blue suit standing at the guardrail, one foot resting on the post. "What's that?"

"I said, what're you doing? Come here." The man removed a wallet from his suit pocket and flopped it open, displaying what Jack guessed was an Alexandria Police Department investigator's badge. "Come on, get up here."

Shit. Jack took a breath, trying to slow his heart.

With the hotel key card palmed, Jack climbed the remaining distance, then stepped over the guardrail. He stuffed his hands into his anorak's pockets. Under his right forearm he felt the reassuring bulge of his Glock 26 in its hip paddle holster.

"Take your hands out of your pockets," the cop growled. He was in his mid-forties, stocky like a wrestler, with wavy red hair.

Jack did so and the cop gave Jack a practiced head-to-toe scan.

"What's your name?"

"Jack Ryan."

"ID."

Jack pulled out his wallet and handed over his driver's license. The cop studied it for five seconds, glancing from it to Jack's face several times before nodding slowly. "Huh. Are you—"

"Yep," Jack replied.

"Aren't you supposed to have a Secret Service detail or something?"

"Officially, maybe, but I complained to their boss, so they gave me a pass." Jack smiled.

The cop didn't reciprocate. "What were you doing down there?"

Jack had been mulling this over in his mind. The odds were decent that sooner or later he was going to come into contact with the police over this. He wasn't expecting it to be this soon, however. Had the witness come forward?

Jack hesitated, partially because he thought it would look right and partially because he'd started second-guessing his decision, then replied, "I was here last night."

You're committed now, Jack. Whether the lie he was about to tell was going to save him trouble or buy him more was yet to be seen.

The cop's brows furrowed. He gave Jack the kind of hard-eyed stare that seemed to come standard-issue to all cops. "When it happened?"

"I think so."

"Tell me. From the start."

"I went to the gym—"

"Which one?"

"Malone's, on Foundry, near the DMV."

"Keep going," the cop said.

"Then I came here for groceries. Must have been around eight."

The cop held up his finger and glanced down at Jack's driver's license. "This address . . . that's the Oronoco, right? Supermercado's not exactly in your neighborhood, is it?"

"They have the best fruits and vegetables. So I paid and came out. It was raining."

"About what time?"

"Eight-fifteen or so. I walked to my car and then heard—"

"Before or after you got in your car?" asked the cop.

"Before," replied Jack. "There was a flyer or something stuck to my windshield. I grabbed it, then heard honking coming from down there. It sounded like a truck, an eighteen-wheeler."

A flyer, Jack thought. The word caught in his head. Before he could think about it, the cop said, "Then what?"

"I put my grocery bag down—"

"Where?"

"On the hood of my car," Jack said.

"Peppers and tomatoes?"

"What?"

"The responding officer found some peppers and tomatoes on the ground right about here."

"Oh. Yeah, I was making chili. Anyway, I walked to the guardrail and looked down. I heard skidding, saw headlights, then heard a crash—I think."

"You think?" the cop asked. "What's that mean?"

"I mean it was raining and dark and I'm not sure what it was. It didn't sound like your standard car crash. When I got up this morning I saw the news, about the guy that was hit, and put two and two together."

"And then drove down here to . . . what? Render aid?"

Jack didn't take the bait. For cops, biting sarcasm was often an effective interview tool, a way to put people on the defensive: Find an inconsistency, the scab of a guilty conscience, then pick at it and see what happens. It wasn't personal.

Jack replied, "I don't know why. Wish I did. Guilt, maybe. If what I saw was—"

"It probably was. Why didn't you call it in?"

Jack shrugged. "I wish I had."

The cop took this in, then nodded slowly. "Well, it wouldn't have made any difference. He was dead on scene. Just parts. Did you know him?"

"I don't know. Who was he?"

"We're trying to figure that out."

"What'd he look like?"

"You mean before?" the cop said with a grim smile.

"Yeah, before."

"Tall, thin, white, mid-thirties."

Jack shook his head. "Don't think so. He didn't have any ID? Nobody's come forward?"

"Nope. So, tell me: What's it like? The Oval Office, I mean."

The question caught Jack off guard. Perhaps as planned. "Like you see in the pictures. I'm not there much anymore. Dinner once a week, parties here and there."

"You don't like being First Son?"

"It's okay," Jack replied. "I prefer my privacy. Luckily, I don't go to bars, don't forget to put on underwear, then get out of cabs in front of the paparazzi . . ."

The cop let out a belly laugh. "Yeah, that wouldn't be a good look for you. Your mom as nice as she seems on TV?"

"Every bit of it," Jack replied with a smile.

"So, tell me the truth. What were you really doing there? If it's nothing too bad I can try to keep it under wraps."

"I already told you. You think I'm lying?"

"I've been a cop for twelve years. I think everyone's lying. Except for my dog. He never lies."

Jack smiled. "Dogs are good like that. What's your name?"

"Doug Butler." He stuck out his hand.

Jack shook it. The motion set off a flash of pain in his shoulder blade.

Butler saw the wince: "You okay there?"

Jack nodded. "Weighted pull-ups. I'm starting to think I should give them up."

"What, you're into that CrossFit stuff?"

"No, just fighting the ticking clock. Listen, Officer Butler, I know it's odd, me coming here. Even if I couldn't have done anything for the guy, I should have called it in. I don't know how to explain it." This was the unvarnished truth.

"Nah, I get it. It's a form of survivor's guilt. You might not have actually seen it, but, in essence, you saw a guy die last night. That's a hard thing."

Jack resisted asking if there were any other witnesses. Cops had many different kinds of radar, including one for people who were too curious—or too helpful.

Butler said, "You know I'm going to need a statement, Jack."

"I understand. Will it end up in the media? If so, I should probably let my dad's press guy know."

"Not likely. Just between us, the truck driver said the guy just stepped out of nowhere. Didn't even look up. Probably never knew what happened. It's not a bad way to go, all things considered." Jack detected no facetiousness in the statement. Consciously or subconsciously, Butler had given a lot of thought to how people died. A cop thing.

"No idea who he was?"

"My guess is he was homeless, maybe high. It happens.

Why he was walking around in the rain . . . who the hell knows."

"Why are you out here? Investigating, I mean."

"Standard practice for an unexplained death. We have to tick the boxes, make sure we don't miss anything. Plus, we're about five miles from the White House."

"What's that mean?"

"Nothing, forget it."

Butler pulled a business card from his wallet. "Write your number on that." Jack did so, then Butler handed him a second card along with his driver's license. "I'll call you this afternoon for that statement. Over the phone should be good enough."

Jack was pulling into the Oronoco's garage when his mind again looped back to the word *flyer*. He pulled into his parking spot, climbed out, then stood, hands in pockets, thinking.

"What is it?" he muttered.

It had been blank.

The flyer on his windshield had been a blank piece of copier paper.

3

ALEXANDRIA, VIRGINIA

Muggers are opportunistic criminals, Jack knew. Their planning is limited. Their ambushes usually consist of blindsiding their victims. They don't use delay-attention tools. Another thing: Who passes out flyers in a rainstorm? Thinking back, Jack didn't recall seeing flyers on any of the other cars' windshields.

Was he overthinking this?

No. The knife.

He got up from the couch, walked into the kitchen, and opened the dishwasher. Using a dish towel, he pulled the still-hot knife from the utensil rack and laid it on the counter. He studied it, from the tip of the blade to the end of the haft, but found no markings save a lone six-digit number beside the thumb stud.

Jack pulled out his phone, took several pictures of the knife, uploaded them to his Dropbox account, then sat down at the dining table with his laptop. In his browser he went to tineye.com, loaded the images, and hit the search icon. The results appeared instantly on his screen.

The knife was made by Eickhorn Solingen, a model called Secutor. Jack Googled the company. It was based in Solingen, Germany, with plenty of online retailers. Jack clicked on several of them and found a price: $175.

What was a crackhead doing with an expensive knife? At the first sign of withdrawal a real junkie would have sold it for a couple rocks. Jack zoomed in on the knife. Along the blade's swedge was the word *Secutor*; beneath it a four-digit number. Near the thumb stud was Eickhorn Solingen's logo, what looked like an upright squirrel holding a sword.

"Same knife, different markings," Jack said to himself.

Jack picked up his phone and scrolled through his contacts until he found what he was looking for. He tapped dial.

"Shiloh River Gun Club," the voice on the other end said.

"Is this Adam?"

"Yep. Who's this?"

"Jack Ryan."

"Hey, Jack. Haven't seen you around for a while. You need to come in, put some rounds downrange."

"I know. Listen, I need a favor. A buddy of mine is looking at buying a knife on eBay, an Eickhorn Solingen—"

"Nice blade."

"—but the markings look odd. Can you take a look?"

Adam Flores was the co-owner of Shiloh River Gun Club, a private shooting club John Clark and Ding Chavez introduced him to. Outside of a military base, Shiloh River had one of the most realistic combat ranges on the eastern seaboard. He and Adam, a militaria aficionado, had become passing friends. If it went boom or was sharp, Adam knew about it.

This was normally a question Gavin Biery, The Campus's director of information technology, would field, but that avenue wasn't open to Jack. Gavin had stuck his neck out for Jack countless times when he was an employee, and he'd probably do it now, but Jack wasn't going to put him in that position.

"Sure," said Adam. "E-mail the pics and I'll have a look around."

"Thanks."

Jack disconnected. From the pocket of his anorak he pulled the hotel key card he'd found at the scene. Emblazoned on the card's blue front was a large red 6. Motel 6, Jack realized. But which one? He turned the card over, looking for markings. He found several, all number sequences. In turn, he typed each one into Google alongside the search term "Motel 6." The third sequence—1403, the franchise identifier, apparently—found a match belonging to a motel in Springfield, about eight miles west of Alexandria.

This, too, made no sense. While Motel 6 wasn't exactly a five-star hotel line, it was branded, mid-priced, with what Jack thought was a decent reputation. Assuming this card belonged to his attacker, it wasn't the kind of dive motel a junkie would choose, or could afford. And why Springfield? Why not one of the half-dozen motels within walking distance of the Supermercado?

Jack realized his scalp was tingling. Someone had tried very hard to kill him last night, and that someone was looking less and less like a crackhead mugger. Having someone hunting for his head was nothing new, but this felt different. He realized his separation from The Campus had lured him into a comfort zone.

Ysabel.

Jack snatched up his phone and dialed her number, a flat owned by her father in London. Jack checked his watch; it would be midafternoon there. Before the line started ringing, he changed his mind and disconnected. Until he knew more, he didn't want to tell her what was happening. She would worry. She would be on the next plane out of Heathrow.

He dialed Ysabel's father's direct line. He answered immediately.

Arman Kashani was no fan of Jack's. Rightly or wrongly, he held Jack responsible for an assault on his daughter. In an attempt to get to Jack, Yegor Morozov's people had nearly beaten her to death. She'd spent three weeks in the hospital before moving first to a private-care rehabilitation facility in London, then to her father's flat. Jack didn't begrudge Arman's animosity. If and when Jack had a child of his own—especially a girl—God only knew how he'd react if that child was threatened. For her part, Ysabel had been slowly but steadily working to change her father's mind about Jack. It seemed to be working.

"Good afternoon, Jack. What can I do for you?" The man's tone sounded almost pleasant. Almost.

"Mr. Kashani, I may have a"—Jack paused, searching for the right word—"problem you need to be aware of."

"Which involves my daughter?"

"Probably not, but just in case—"

"As she has been since the day she arrived, she's well protected, Jack. I have two former SAS gentlemen who are never far away."

That would do the trick, Jack thought. He hoped. If, in fact, last night's attack had something to do with Morozov and some loose end Jack had missed, he'd prefer Ysabel have all of Hereford there. Thinking of this, Jack felt a knot of anger in his belly. They came after her and now him. They'd missed him, and he was going to turn that to his advantage.

"I'll bet she loves that," Jack said to Arman.

"She does not love that, not even remotely, but I love her, and until she's fully recovered I will—"

"I wasn't disagreeing with you, sir."

"Good. You will keep me posted on this trouble of yours?"

"I will. As I said, it's probably nothing. I'd suggest you don't say anything to her until—"

"I wasn't planning to. Take care, Jack."

The line went dead.

Jack laid the phone down on the table and walked to the balcony windows and looked out. Below, the Potomac River was swollen. Its calm surface hid the strong spring current. A pair of yellow racing shells, their crews heaving and leaning in unison, glided past the mouth of the bay. Jack watched until they disappeared from view.

Who wants me dead? he wondered.

And why?

And had the mystery figure been a part of it?

He got an answer to his first question, at least a partial one, an hour later, when Adam Flores called back. "Jack, you've got yourself a pretty unique blade there. It's an Eickhorn Solingen Secutor, all right, but not a commercial model. The blade's thicker, there's a lanyard slot—"

"Give me the condensed version, Adam."

"Right. Eickhorn Solingen supplies the German *Heer*— the Army—with all its combat knives, but most of those are fixed-blade KM 2000 models. The one you've got is a special issue, a lot of one hundred issued to the KSK, probably for special commendations and whatever."

"KSK?" asked Jack.

"Kommando Spezialkräfte—Special Forces Command. In 1997 the Bundeswehr rolled all its SpecFor units into one. KSK is the cream of the elite, Jack. Think SEALs, Delta, Green Berets, and Marine Force Recon all rolled into one."

This explained a lot, but also raised more questions.

It explained why his attacker hadn't behaved like your typical mugger. It also explained, at least fuzzily, the figure he'd seen standing at the guardrail. The backup man in case his attacker failed. If so, why didn't he finish the job?

On the other hand, why a knife at all? Why not a gun and a noise suppressor? He could have dropped Jack from thirty feet away and kept walking.

Knives were silent, and perhaps the man's command to Jack—"Hey, man, give it up!"—answered this. A cover story. If anyone happened to overhear and/or witness Jack's murder, the details—from the man's appearance to his language to his choice of weapon—would fit, and for an ostensibly homeless crackhead the trade-in value of a gun outweighed its usefulness. They'd chosen the right neighborhood for the attack. Finally, though the murder of the President's son would trigger outrage and a massive law enforcement response, a mugging gone bad would, if staged correctly, lead nowhere substantial. But a professional killing would see the government turning the country upside down.

Someone had gone to a lot of trouble to assassinate him. If this had something to do with Yegor Morozov, the sophistication of the op made sense—but not the timing of it. Why wait so many months to come after him?

The choice of knife, a rare and expensive Eickhorn Solingen Secutor, was also curious. What did that mean? Jack knew plenty of special operators who felt attached to a particular piece of gear, whether it was a knife or a plastic army man his son had given him. In this business you took good-luck totems wherever you found them. Was this the case with his attacker?

Either way, one thing was certain: Whoever this was, they weren't going to stop at one attempt. And he had to assume Ysabel was in fact on their radar. He had a choice: hide and call in reinforcements or handle it himself? Hiding was a nonstarter. Even if it was in his nature, given the lengths to which his attacker had gone so far, lying low would do no good.

For now, he was taking the latter route.

He'd take the fight to them.

4

ALEXANDRIA, VIRGINIA

Like most special operators, Jack maintained a go-bag, yet another lesson given him by John Clark and Ding Chavez. In Jack's case, his rucksack, a 5.11 Tactical Havoc, was filled with the necessities of his chosen profession.

His first order of business was a Hail Mary. While he had little doubt his comprehensive access to The Campus's mainframe computer had been suspended, he wondered what might have been left available.

Jack opened a browser on his laptop and navigated to the Hendley Associates website, then to its secure backdoor portal. Fingers crossed, he plugged in his username and password. After a moment the portal's main window appeared. All of the access tabs were gray, ghosted out, save one: Level One. Jack clicked on the tab, and a new screen opened up. There was a message in his inbox. It was from Gavin Biery:

In case you meet a sketchy woman at a bar . . .

While Level One was just the tip of The Campus's information iceberg, it did give him access to basic investigation tools. Through a shell company, Hendley Associates maintained a private investigation firm that served primarily to provide useful cover for its operatives. Enquestor Services existed only in cyberspace, but its various licenses and documentation were irreproachable—including the private investigator's badge Jack carried.

"Thank you, Mr. Biery," Jack muttered.

He clicked to the tab marked "Credit Inquiries." From his rucksack he grabbed a magnetic barcode swiper, plugged it into his laptop's USB port, then slid his attacker's Motel 6 key card through it. While he knew the location of the motel—Springfield—he didn't know which room the card belonged to. After a moment, the information appeared on the screen: room 142. *A piece of luck*, Jack thought. Ground-level room with exterior access; the less interaction he had with the lobby staff, the better.

Within minutes he was on I-95 heading west. The rain was holding off. The afternoon temperatures had risen to the mid-seventies, causing the still-damp streets to steam. Fifteen minutes after leaving the Oronoco, he turned onto Springfield Boulevard. The motel, a long, whitewashed four-story building, overlooked the Franconia Road/I-95 clover-leaf. Jack did a full circuit of the building, then followed the placards to an entrance on the east side. He found a spot fifty feet away, tucked up against a line of hedges, and backed into it. He shut off the ignition.

Jack felt his heart rate pick up. While his attacker certainly wasn't coming back, the mystery man was a possibility. The chances were better than even that he'd already cleaned out the room. Jack hoped not. This room was his sole lead. There was something else tickling his mind: anticipation. He'd missed this, he realized. He missed The Campus.

He and Dom, Ding, and John Clark stayed in touch and had lunch or beers once a week or so, but it wasn't the same. Though they'd done nothing to prompt this, Jack had begun to feel like an outsider. What they all lived and breathed was Hendley's off-the-books missions. This was prevalent in the business, on both the civilian and military side—a natural by-product of being good at a job that frequently tries to kill you. That was a fair, if generalized, definition of addiction, wasn't it? Maybe. If so, months of withdrawal and he still felt the lure of it. There were worse vices, right?

He drew his Glock, eased back the slide until he saw the glint of brass in the chamber, then reholstered. He got out of the car and headed for the entrance.

With the swipe of the key card, the door gave a satisfying click. Jack used the back of his thumb to pull open the door, then stepped into the vestibule. Through the inner door he followed signs to room 142. The hallway was empty, but as he passed doors he caught strains of muffled conversation, a game show playing on a television.

He stopped before 142. A PRIVACY PLEASE placard was hanging from the lever handle. Jack pressed his ear to the door. Listened. All was quiet. He glanced down the hall again, saw it was clear, then drew the Glock, stepped closer to the door's hinge-side jamb, and swiped the key card. He used his fist to push down the lever handle, then nudged the door open with his foot.

He paused. Listened again. Nothing stirred inside the room. He counted to ten, then took a breath, let it out.

With the Glock in the compressed-ready position, Jack shouldered through the door and into the short hallway. Bathroom on his right. To his left was a closet with dual sliding mirrored doors. Both were open, and on the floor was a black hard-sided roller suitcase. Ahead he could see a chest of drawers and the foot of a queen bed, and the window. The sheer curtains were drawn, casting the interior in pale light.

As the door swung shut behind him, Jack backed up, putting more distance between himself and the bathroom door. He paced forward, checked the bathroom. Empty, door fully open, shower curtain back. He took another step down the hall and peeked around the corner into the main room. *Clear.* He holstered the Glock.

The room was like any other you'd find in a branded motel: low-pile carpet, white walls, a bed with two nightstands, and a small round table and two chairs beside the window. The air smelled faintly of pine-scented disinfectant.

Jack took a moment and stood still in the center of the room, taking it in. The space was tidy but lived in. Here and there things were out of place, the kinds of checklist details maids attend to, but the PRIVACY PLEASE placard outside suggested housekeeping hadn't been here.

There was nothing personal on the nightstands, chest of drawers, or table. No change, no receipts, no pocket detritus of any kind. The bedcovers were pulled up, but the bed wasn't made.

And no sign of drug paraphernalia.

This wasn't the room of a homeless crackhead.

Jack walked to the bathroom. Beside the sink, lined up

beside each other, were a toothbrush and a miniature tube of toothpaste. In the shower he found a half-empty bottle of complimentary shampoo and a used bar of soap in the holder. Hanging neatly from the curtain were a towel and washcloth, the latter folded once lengthwise, the former stiff from being air-dried. The trash can beside the toilet was empty.

He returned to the main room, put on a pair of leather golf gloves, and started his search. The nightstands were empty, as were two of the chest's drawers; the uppermost one contained rows and stacks of staple clothing: socks, underwear, jeans, plain cotton T-shirts in blue, black, and red. He carefully sorted through each item and found nothing—not even labels, all of which had been cut out.

He retrieved the suitcase from the closet and laid it on the bed. There were no luggage tags, either personal or airline-issued. He unzipped the suitcase. It was empty. Jack ran his fingertips around the nylon fabric inner lining. Again, no luck. Jack returned the suitcase to the closet.

This room was special-operator tidy. A place for everything and everything in its place. Functional, efficient, anonymous. It gave him nothing.

"Maybe . . ." Jack murmured.

He picked up the phone and dialed the main desk.

"Motel Six, how may I help you?"

"Hi, I'm in room 142," Jack said. "Can you get me a copy of my charges up to this point? My office manager needs it."

"Certainly, sir. I can e-mail it—"

"Hard copy would be better, actually. Just slip it under the door. I'm going to jump in the shower."

"Give me five minutes."

"One more thing," Jack replied. "When do you show me checking out?"

"Uh . . . hang on . . . Day after tomorrow, sir."

Jack thanked him and hung up.

The desk clerk was as good as his word. A few minutes later a lone sheet of paper wormed its way beneath the door. He waited for the footsteps to fade back down the hallway, then retrieved the bill. In the occupant information section, there was no address. How did his attacker manage that? Jack wondered. The vast majority of hotels wouldn't book a reservation without an address. There were ways around this, but they took finesse.

In the payment section, all but the last four digits of the credit card were X'd out.

But there was a name.

Eric Weber.

Even assuming the name was real, Weber was common, as was Eric, and without an address Jack had no way of narrowing his search. He put a pin in it and turned to his next task.

He left the room, and to kill some time he browsed through a couple used-book stores. After nightfall, he headed west toward Telegraph Road and turned off. He found a BP gas station across the road from the Supermercado and parked on the side of the building.

From his rucksack he took a gray hoodie and baseball cap. He donned both, then locked his car and walked to Lenore, then west across Telegraph to the grocery store. The parking lot was half full of cars, with shoppers, mostly Latinos and some whites, coming and going through the automatic doors. The sound of rickety shopping cart wheels echoed across the pavement. The automatic doors hissed open and shut.

It was seven forty-five, fifteen minutes before the store's shift change.

Jack couldn't help but glance at the guardrail on the far side of the parking lot. No cars were parked there. He stood in the near-darkness for a few moments and scanned the front of the store for surveillance cameras. Though there were plenty of them inside, little mirrored bubbles jutting from the ceiling, out here he saw none.

Jack pulled the cap down close to his eyebrows, then walked to the entrance and posted himself beside it. To each passerby he gave his rehearsed and, he hoped, well-acted spiel: He was looking for his homeless brother, someone said they'd seen him around here, followed by a description of his attacker. Most walked past him, either without responding or with some muttered excuse or a flat "No." Occasionally a shopper would stop, listen for a moment, then sadly shake his or her head and wish him luck.

At 7:55, a familiar face appeared, one of the regular cashiers, a short early-twenties woman with large black eyes. She'd checked him out a few times but was shy and rarely looked him in the eye.

"Hi, excuse me," Jack said. "I'm looking for my brother. He's missing."

"I'm sorry," she murmured, stepping around Jack and heading for the door. "I need to—"

"Tall, skinny, maybe wearing a dark hoodie. He's homeless. We're worried about him. Please."

The cashier slowed, then stopped and turned. She backed farther into the light coming through the front windows, putting some distance between them. A local, he guessed. She gave no sign she recognized him.

"How tall?" she asked.

"Six-five or so."

The woman hesitated, then said, "Wait. There was a guy. I seen him a few times in the last week. He was panhandling, asking for change. I gave him a few dollars but felt kinda stupid, you know."

"Why?"

"I came in early for my shift last night, about seven-thirty, and I saw him get dropped off, right down there." She pointed toward the far end of the building.

Seven-thirty, Jack thought. A half hour before he arrived. Good timing. Here was another habit he'd let slip—that of varying his daily routine to make himself a harder target for both surveillance and ambush.

She said, "It was a real nice car, not a beater or anything. I figured if he had a car like that or had a friend with a car like that, he shouldn't be creeping for money."

Jack frowned. "I'm sorry he did that. He's got problems, if you know what I mean."

"Yeah, I get it."

"What'd the car look like?" he asked.

"White, newer, like a Nissan or Toyota. Midsize, I think."

"Did you see the driver?"

She shook her head. "Wait a second. There was something on the news . . . Wasn't some guy hit on Kings Highway last night?"

"Really?" Jack replied. "Did they describe him? Did he have ID?"

"No, I don't know. Sorry. You could call the police. I hope it's not him, but maybe . . ." She let the words trail off, tilting her head in sympathy. "I gotta go."

"Thanks," Jack said as she disappeared through the doors.

White midsize car. Did the headlights silhouetting his mystery man the previous night belong to this car?

Jack drove home, parked in the garage, then took the elevator up to his floor. The doors parted, revealing the vestibule. Sitting on the leather bench against the far wall was Doug Butler.

Jack stepped out. "Hey, Detective," he said tentatively.

Butler stood up. "We gotta talk."

5

ALEXANDRIA, VIRGINIA

How did he get back on Butler's radar? He'd already given the detective a statement over the phone, one that seemed to satisfy the cop. Jack went through the possibilities: He'd contradicted his earlier statement; a witness had come forward; they'd found trace evidence on the scene that put him there. Inwardly, Jack winced. He was thinking like a criminal. He didn't like the feeling.

He unlocked his door and stepped inside, with Butler following. Jack flipped switches on the wall, illuminating the kitchen and living room. He stepped into the kitchen. "I was about to ask how you got up," Jack said, "but you've got a hell of a hall pass, I guess."

"Comes in handy," Butler replied.

"You want something? A beer, coffee—"

"Yeah, a beer'd be good. So, what do you carry?"

Jack turned. Butler was standing in the archway, hands shoved in his pants pockets. "What?" asked Jack.

"In your hip holster."

"Glock Twenty-six. I've got a permit."

"I know you do. Were you carrying when we met at the Supermercado?" When Jack nodded, Butler gave a sad shake of his head. "Can't believe I missed it. Getting old."

"I paid extra for the Holster of Invisibility," Jack replied with a grin.

Butler snorted—not quite a laugh, but as close as he got to one, Jack suspected. He grabbed a pair of Heinekens from the fridge and handed one to Butler, who unscrewed the cap and took a swig. He held up the cap. "Garbage?"

"Counter's fine," Jack replied, and took his own sip. "You want me to ditch the gun?"

"Nah. Just don't draw on me. Might give me a heart attack. Nice place. You rich?"

"Everything's relative."

"You work at a financial company, right? Hendley something?"

"Hendley Associates. Yep. Arbitrage, analysis, that sort of thing."

"Sounds interesting."

"Everything's relative," Jack repeated. "I'm on a kind of

sabbatical, I guess you could say." This was the first time he'd explained his situation to anyone outside of his family.

Sabbatical. Forced leave of absence. Each term was accurate enough in its own way, but in essence, Gerry Hendley had told him to go to his room and think about what he'd done. *Christ*, Jack thought. He realized, slightly stunned, that he was angry. He understood why Gerry had made the call, but that wasn't the same as acceptance, was it? Had he been fooling himself? Had he come to peace with the suspension, or was that simply what he'd told himself he should feel? He didn't know, and didn't feel like thinking about it.

"Got any stock tips?" Butler asked.

"Depends on what you're looking for. Legal or illegal?"

"Better give the first one."

"Good. It's the only kind I know." Jack took another swig and thought about it. "Buy low, sell high."

Butler grinned. "Dick."

"I know a few good private investment managers, if you're looking."

"Yeah, maybe, thanks. Another eight and I'm out. Unless I win the lottery or become the next Wambaugh, I'm gonna need something."

They stood there, sipping their beers and saying nothing for a bit. Jack wondered if Butler was using the silence as an interview tool.

"My grandfather was a cop," Jack said.

"Yeah?"

"Baltimore Homicide."

Butler nodded slowly. "Mine, too. Tulsa. Small world."

"What got you into it?"

"I was military police in the Army. In May of '03 I ended up in Baghdad. A month after I got there we got mortared and I took some shrapnel. Spent about six months at Walter Reed, then they cut me loose. Alexandria was hiring cops and I figured it would be an easy transition."

"Was it?"

"Mostly. If I'd stayed in, probably not. I know guys that did tour after tour. Those are the ones that have trouble."

The silence hung in the air.

"So . . ." Jack said, hoping to nudge Butler toward the point of his visit. It worked.

"So, are you in some kind of trouble, Jack?"

"You mean aside from last night?"

"Yeah."

"Not that I know of," Jack replied. "Why?"

"About a week ago a guy was killed on the 395, up near Holmes Run Trail."

"I read about it. Carjacking went bad, wasn't it?"

"Probably. The thing is, the guy lived in this building. He parked in the same garage as you do, drove a black sedan a lot like your Chrysler. And he was a fair match for your description."

Jack felt his belly tighten. "You're serious?"

"As a heart attack. The tire on his car blew out. He pulled over to the side of the road to put the spare on. As far as we can figure it, somebody stopped, maybe offered to help him, then slit his throat and left."

Jack didn't reply.

"What I'm wondering now," Butler said, "is if somebody did something to his tire, then followed along and waited until it blew."

"What time was this?"

"About two in the morning. He was coming home from his girlfriend's house—just like he did almost every Monday, Tuesday, and Friday for the past six months."

Just as he'd done with the gym, Jack thought. "Shit," he muttered. It was all he could think to say.

"That's one word for it," Butler replied. "You didn't answer my question: Are you in trouble?"

Yes, I think I am. They'd come at him twice and missed twice, leaving an innocent guy lying on the side of the road with his throat open. If he gave them a third chance they'd make damned sure he was dead. What was this about?

Jack had never put much stock in his status as First Son.

It was a shadow cast by his father, albeit an unintentional one. Plus, he didn't like the exalted sound of it all. That aside, the truth remained: Somebody was doing their level best to kill the son of the President of the United States. That took a pair of jumbo balls. What could be that important? *Not just good old-fashioned revenge*, Jack thought. Yegor Morozov and the people in his circle were dispassionate and logical when it came to violence, ticking boxes and weighing pros and cons before ordering a trigger pulled.

"Maybe it's gambling, or sex, that kind of thing," Butler said.

"No, nothing like that."

"I'm not looking to hassle you. Even if I was that guy, shaking you down would be more trouble than it's worth, you know? If you've gotten into something over your head, maybe I can help. Don't get me wrong, it's not like you'd be hurting for help if you needed it—CIA, FBI, Department of Agriculture. But if you wanna talk . . ."

"No, I appreciate it, Detective, but—"

"Doug. You sure?"

Jack nodded. "Did this guy have family?"

"Mark's his name. Mother, father, and two sisters. They own a chain of specialty bread shops—Macloon's. Anyway, Mark was the heir apparent. It's somebody else's case, so I don't know if there's anything shady on the business side.

Listen, Jack, this could be all coincidence. It happens more times than you'd think. Just keep an eye out, yeah?"

"I will."

"Might as well keep that Glock handy, too."

Jack nodded. "Anything more on my guy from last night? Witnesses? Did anyone come forward to claim the body? How about an autopsy?"

"No and no. As for an autopsy, there really wasn't much left to cut on. I'm sure the M.E. will run a tox screen and his fingerprints, but that's about it. Chances are, unless some next of kin show up, he'll end up a guest of the city."

"What's that mean?"

"In the city cemetery. After a month, unidentified bodies are classified as destitute. The taxpayers foot the funeral bill. Anyway . . ." Butler downed the rest of the beer and set it on the counter. "Thanks for that. Gotta run."

"Thanks for stopping by."

"Yep. And Jack, one more thing: Maybe think about calling that Secret Service detail, huh? At least for the near future."

6

ALEXANDRIA, VIRGINIA

For the second morning in a row, Jack awoke before dawn.

He'd slept in fits and starts, glancing at the clock and getting up to stare out the window before lying back down and trying again. He was restless and there was no outlet for it. No action to take. Somebody was hunting him. The first time his survival had depended on mistaken identity; the second, the luck of the roll. Tumbling down that slope with Weber, it could have just as easily been Jack's head that had smacked into the concrete barrier. Weber would've had no trouble finishing him off.

Pure chaos and chance.

———

Short of waiting for them to try again, Jack had one card left to play, and it was at best a long shot. Assuming the mystery man was Weber's accomplice, the man would have three options: Leave the area, make another try for Jack, or tidy up and then go to ground. Jack was counting on option three.

They knew he'd survived. They would assume he now knew about both attempts on his life. They would assume Jack had reported this to the Secret Service. They would assume the full investigative might of the federal government was being mustered. With Weber gone and an untraceable John Doe in the morgue, there was only one fragile investigative thread left to pluck: Weber's belongings at the motel. If anyone was coming to collect these, it would be Weber's accomplice.

After stocking up on food and water and a few paperback mysteries from his wanna-read shelf, Jack drove back to Springfield and used another item from his rucksack—a fake driver's license—to check into the Motel 6. Citing a "very special anniversary" with his soon-to-arrive girlfriend, Jack asked for room 144. The vaguely goth, nerdy teenage girl behind the reception desk gave him a sotto voce "Whatever, dude . . . have fun" and handed him the key card.

Jack drove back to the side exit, parked, and went inside. At the door to room 142 he paused to listen. The PRIVACY PLEASE placard was still in place. Hearing nothing, he swiped the key card and went inside and made a quick inspection. The room was unchanged.

He left and entered the room next door and settled in.

Jack's gambit depended largely on the accomplice. Why he'd failed to intervene on Weber's behalf was a mystery. Had he gotten spooked? It was possible. If so, how likely was it that kind of man would show up to collect Weber's belongings? Maybe, if the decision wasn't his to make. Jack had found nothing of use in the room; perhaps there was nothing of use to find. Did the accomplice or whoever was pulling his strings know this?

The morning passed slowly. Jack, afraid he'd miss hearing the double beep of Weber's door lock, had assembled a reading nook of bed pillows on the hallway floor. The maids and their squeaky-wheeled carts slowly but steadily made their rounds, tapping on doors and softly calling "Housekeeping" before either stopping to clean or moving on to the next room. Out of boredom, Jack timed them. They averaged twelve minutes per room. *Was this good, bad, or average?* he wondered. Finally one of the maids reached his door.

"Housekeeping . . . Do you need anything? Clean towels or soap?"

Jack didn't answer. His PRIVACY PLEASE placard was in place. Did management make them ask anyway, just to cover their bases? Maybe the maids got a secret thrill from interrupting the occasional carnal union. The job was probably boring; you took fun where you found it.

After five seconds the maid and her cart continued down the hallway.

B y midafternoon he'd finished one novel and started a second. He alternately dozed, snacked on trail mix, and drank bottled water. There was a better-than-average chance he was wasting his time here. But he had nothing else, no other lead. Perhaps it was time to call Gerry, maybe Clark. Bringing his dad—and thereby the FBI and the Secret Service—into the loop would create more problems than it would solve, especially for The Campus.

S unset came and then faded into night.

Shortly after nine, Jack's eyes fluttered open. He reached for the Glock beside his leg. He'd heard a double beep. Or had he? From where? He rolled to one side and pressed his ear to the wall in time to hear the door to room 142 click shut.

I'll be damned.

For a full minute there was only silence—then a voice, male and heavily muffled through the wall. Jack couldn't make out any words. He crawled into the bathroom, grabbed a glass off the sink, then crawled back. Did this work any-where outside of the movies? he wondered. He felt idi-otic. He pressed the rim against the wall, then his ear to the bottom. The sound was no better. He moved the glass a few inches left, tried again. The voice, though still faint, was clearer.

". . . don't know. Nothing that I can see." The man sounded agitated, hesitant. "Uh, clothes . . . toiletries, a suitcase . . . Yes, okay. I will."

Something banged against the wall beside Jack's head. He jerked away, then thought, *Closet*. It was on the other side of the wall. *Collecting Weber's suitcase?* he wondered.

Jack stood up, put on his jacket, grabbed his duffel, then holstered the Glock and slipped out of the room. *Which way?* Whoever was inside Weber's room had come in either through the lobby or through the same side entrance Jack had used. Jack flipped a mental coin and chose the latter. Once outside, he headed for his car, scanning the parking spots as he went. In the fifth stall was a white late-model

Nissan Altima. As he passed the trunk he ducked into a crouch. He took out his cell phone, snapped a picture of the license plate, then stood up and walked the remaining distance to his car.

Five minutes later a man emerged from the side exit. In the glow of the sconce, Jack caught a glimpse of thinning gray hair and jowls. Jack judged him to be in his mid-fifties. The man was gone, heading toward the Nissan, pulling Weber's black suitcase behind him.

A minute later the car backed out of the stall, turned, and headed for the lot's exit. With his headlights off, Jack followed at a distance until the Nissan turned east onto Springfield Boulevard, then sped to the stop sign. He waited until another car had passed, then turned on his headlights and followed.

7

ALEXANDRIA, VIRGINIA

The Nissan headed east, away from Springfield and up 495, then took the South Van Dorn exit south. At Franconia the Nissan turned again and once more headed east. *Is he dry-cleaning, looking for tails?* Jack wondered. Another ten minutes of driving brought Jack to the Rose Hill area, where the Nissan turned into a residential area. Finally, on Climbhill Road, the Nissan slowed and pulled into the driveway of a rambler with sage-green paint, white shutters, and a line of squared-off yew bushes bracketing the front steps. A lone porch light burned beside the door. Across the street, instead of houses, there was a park with playground equipment.

As Jack drove past the house he glanced out the side window and saw the Nissan disappearing into a detached garage. Jack continued to the end of the block, then pulled to the curb and shut off his lights.

The man's destination was confusing. Rose Hill was a well-established lower-to-middle-class neighborhood of single-family homes, parks, and elementary schools. How did Eric Weber, the man who'd butchered Mark Macloon on the side of a highway and then tried to do the same to him in a grocery store parking lot, cross paths with the man behind the wheel of the Nissan? *Hell, not just cross paths. Conspire to murder.*

Make a decision, Jack. He couldn't sit here for long and risk a visit from the police. Any cop who regularly patrolled the neighborhood would immediately pick out his Chrysler as an anomaly. He had the plate number and the house address; with his Enquestor access, those were enough to get a name. But he wanted more.

He checked his watch. Five minutes. It was worth the risk, he decided. He dug into his duffel, grabbed the items he needed, then made sure the car's dome light was off and climbed out.

Keeping a slow but purposeful pace that he hoped gave off an "I belong" vibe, Jack walked back down the block. As he drew even with the house, he turned left off the sidewalk and followed a line of overgrown shrubs down the side of the house and into the backyard. To his left sat a gray, dilapidated shed, the kind you buy as a kit at a home-improvement warehouse. To his right were the rear of the house and a raised wooden deck abutting a door. A window to the right of the deck was lit. Kitchen, Jack guessed. Directly across the lawn from him stood the garage; there was a side door, its upper half mullioned glass. Sitting beside the garage's wall was a redwood picnic table.

Jack returned his attention to the lighted window. There was no movement. *Don't think. Just walk.* Jack stood up and trotted across the lawn, eyes alternating between the lighted window and the deck's sliding doors. When he reached the garage he crouched down and put on his gloves. He tried the door. It was locked, but the knob looked ancient and on its last legs.

Jack pulled out his multi-tool, levered open the flathead screwdriver, and slipped it into the keyhole up to the haft. Simultaneously he slowly turned the tool and the knob in opposite directions. With a clunk, the knob gave way, spinning freely in its socket. Jack eased open the door and slipped inside.

He clicked on his red penlight and scanned the interior. It was what Jack expected: exposed wood walls, cardboard boxes stacked on makeshift rafter shelves, a tool-laden pegboard and cramped workbench tucked against the wall, its drawers almost touching the bumper of the Nissan, whose engine ticked as it cooled in the night air.

Jack checked his watch. Almost two of his five minutes

had passed. Two more for a search, and a minute to get back to his car. Jack made his way to the passenger side, opened the door, then leaned in and switched off the dome light. He popped the glove compartment and sorted through the contents: owner's manual, insurance card, car registration. The man's name was Peter Hahn. *Huh. Another German surname*, Jack thought. He photographed the insurance card and registration, then returned everything to the glove compartment. He opened the center console. Inside, along with a few packs of chewing gum, an Altoids tin full of quarters, and a bottle of new-car-smell air freshener, was a Nokia cell phone.

"That'll do," Jack whispered. Clearly Mr. Hahn was not a technophile who needed his phone nearby at all times. Jack's dad was the same way.

From his pocket Jack pulled a small canvas case and unzipped it. He sorted through the contents until he found the micro USB adapter, which he slid into the phone's charging port. Into the adapter itself he plugged his thumb-size DRS—data recovery stick—a commercial and less versatile version of the tailor-made models Gavin Biery produced for The Campus's personnel. This version would skim only the most basic info from the phone—contacts, text messages, call and browser history—but no DNS (domain name system) data that could tell him more about the sites the owner visited and people he e-mailed.

Jack powered up the phone. A light on the DRS started blinking green. When the light flashed red Jack disconnected and returned the phone to the console. Finally he planted a GPS tracker, a commercial model about the size of a deck of playing cards, Velcroing it around a cable cluster beneath the passenger-side dashboard.

He gave the car a quick once-over, making sure everything was where and how he'd found it, then eased shut the door and left the garage.

From his left side a flashlight beam blinded him.

Cop. He resisted the instinct to reach for his gun.

"If you move, I will shoot you," a voice said from the darkness. Jack detected a faint accent, perhaps German. Was this Peter Hahn? Jack had checked left; the man must have posted himself at the corner of the garage wall and waited. *Crafty.*

Jack took a gamble: "Hey, man, I was just looking for a little cash. I'll put it back, okay. It was just some quarters."

"Turn around," Hahn ordered. His voice was even, without the slightest trace of anxiety. This wasn't the first time the German had held someone at gunpoint.

"C'mon, just lemme go. I won't come back, I swear."

"I said turn around. Slowly. Hands out to the side."

Dammit. Rusty, Jack. You've gotten rusty.

Slowly Jack turned around. He squinted against the glare of the flashlight and lowered his head slightly so the brim of his cap would shade his face. He could see nothing of Hahn behind the beam of his flashlight.

Hahn muttered, "You little assholes, why don't you just stop . . ."

Jack felt a tinge of relief. Definitely not a cop.

". . . wait," Hahn said. "Take off your hat. Let me see your face."

You're done, Jack. He took off his cap.

"Look at me," Hahn ordered.

Squinting, Jack turned his face into the light and lifted his chin.

There were a few seconds of silence before Hahn said, "You know, it would make my life much easier if I shot you right here." If Hahn was surprised to find Jack standing in his backyard, the man betrayed none of it in his voice.

"You didn't kill me the other night when you had the chance," Jack replied. "Why do it now?"

Hahn didn't reply.

Jack pushed on: "Killing me wouldn't solve your problems. They'd only get worse. I assume you know who I am." Even in this context the phrase tasted sour in Jack's mouth, but he was arguing for his life.

"Yes, I know who you are. Still, it might solve my biggest problem," Hahn replied.

Good. Still talking, Jack thought.

"Which is what? Dealing with whoever ordered you to clean out Weber's hotel room?"

"You followed me."

"You and your friend tried to kill me. I want to know why."

Again Hahn was silent for a moment. "He's not my friend."

Jack said, "Mr. Hahn, can you take the light out of my eyes?"

"Lift up your jacket with your left hand and slowly turn around." Jack complied and Hahn said, "Remove the gun and place it on the ground in front of you." Jack did so and Hahn ordered him to back up and sit down at the picnic table.

Hahn stepped forward, his gun never wavering, and picked up Jack's Glock, stuffed it into his belt, then lowered the flashlight beam to Jack's chest.

"I have questions," Hahn said.

"That makes two of us."

"Why do they want you dead?"

"I was hoping you could tell me. I don't even know who *they* are. Why did you leave the parking lot? Why didn't you finish me?"

Jack's eyes adjusted so he could now see Hahn's silhouette. In the side glow of the flashlight he made out a snub-nosed revolver in Hahn's right hand.

"I'm not sure," Hahn replied. "I'm not that kind of man, not anymore. I never was, I don't think. What they were asking . . . it made no sense. It's just murder."

"Were you there when Weber killed that kid on the side of the freeway?"

Hahn exhaled heavily. He lowered the revolver to his side.

"I tried to tell him he had the wrong person." Hahn sounded weary, resigned. "He didn't listen. Such a waste."

"Who ordered it?"

"That I won't answer. As it is, I don't know if I've done enough to save her. I hope so." Before Jack could ask the logical question, Hahn added, "They'd never made the threat plain, you know? But I know him. He just might do it."

"I might be able to help."

"No."

Jack realized Hahn hadn't asked the obvious question: Why was the son of the President of the United States here in his backyard, rather than the Secret Service or FBI? If Madonna showed up to repossess your car, you'd want to know why her of all people. Jack suspected Hahn just didn't care. Whatever mess he'd gotten into had pushed him to his limit.

"I can make some calls," Jack said, immediately recognizing the absurdity of the statement. He couldn't begin to explain any of this.

Hahn chuckled. "Calls. You can make some calls. How nice of you. No, what's going to happen next is . . ." Hahn hesitated, as though searching for the right word. "Necessary."

Jack felt his chest tighten. He kept his eyes on Hahn's gun hand, waiting. He had little chance of reaching Hahn in time, but he'd be damned if he was going to be killed sitting at a picnic table. Nor was he going to allow Hahn to take him anywhere. Secondary locations were graveyards.

What Hahn said next surprised Jack: "Loyalty is an odd thing, isn't it?"

"Sometimes. Tell me what's going on. I'll do what I can."

"Not possible. I can't tell you. But I can point you in the right direction."

"What does that mean?"

"You'll have to do the rest. I assume you have means of following me? Never mind. Of course you do. It will happen soon, in the next day or two, so be ready."

Jack was back at the Oronoco thirty minutes later.

He'd tried to push Hahn for further explanation, for anything, but the man had simply laid Jack's Glock on the ground, then turned and walked back into his house. Jack had been so stunned he sat in the darkness for nearly a minute, mind spinning, before returning to his car.

Now he grabbed a beer, sat down in front of his laptop,

and plugged the DRS stick into the USB port. He waited until the program started downloading Hahn's cell-phone dump, then logged in to the Enquestor portal and typed in Hahn's information. The results came back in ten seconds. Jack scanned them.

Peter Hahn, sixty-three years old, naturalized citizen, emigrated from Germany sixteen years earlier. Retired from Xerox as a "facilities maintenance manager" three years ago. Widowed, one grown child, a daughter. Solid credit rating, mortgage to the Climbhill house paid off, almost no unsecured debt, no legal judgments past or pending. And so on.

With higher-level access to The Campus's system, Jack could have cross-checked both Hahn and Weber against Hendley's raw and processed intelligence databases, but that wasn't an option. Something told him the search would have turned up nothing substantial, anyway.

Peter Hahn was an average guy. No red flags. Aside from every word that had come out of the man's mouth tonight, of course. And aside from the fact that he'd handled Jack like a man who'd seen his fair share of hairy situations.

Jack's laptop beeped, signaling that the DRS had finished downloading. Jack double-clicked the text document. The data dump was a block of plain, unformatted text. Already knowing what he was looking for, Jack was able to quickly separate the data into text messages, phone usage, and Web history.

Peter Hahn didn't use his phone for text messaging or Web browsing, and the call history was brief: pizza places, theaters, the public library, a man named "Larry, Bowling Night," and someone named "BB." Jack tapped on each of these in turn. The first person, Larry Neil, also lived in Rose Hill, a few blocks from Hahn. The next name, BB, came back with a German address and phone number:

Kallmünzerstrasse 61
81664 München
011 49 89 23239779

Germany again. That thread was thickening. Had he pissed off someone in Germany? Nothing came to mind.

"It will happen soon, so be ready," Hahn had said.

What will happen?

And who is "her"?

8

ALEXANDRIA, VIRGINIA

Hahn's version of *soon* was the following afternoon.

Jack was again killing time, having spent the morning trying to piece together what he had and watching the rain clouds gather through his balcony window. By noon a steady drizzle had begun to fall.

Jack continued to wrestle with the course he'd chosen. The attempt on his life had to have something to do with The Campus. Nothing else made sense. If so, Gerry Hendley deserved to be in the loop. Especially if he wasn't the only one who'd been targeted. Ysabel was safe, but what about everyone else?

He grabbed his phone and speed-dialed John Clark's direct line. Clark answered on the second ring: "Hey, Jack, what's cooking?"

Clark's tone was untroubled. In the field, the man was impossible to read, a poker opponent's worst nightmare, but around the office as Hendley's director of operations he wore his feelings plainly enough. If someone was going after anybody at The Campus, Jack would have heard it in his voice.

"Just checking in. Making sure everyone's alive and kicking."

"All is well." If this weren't true, Clark wouldn't have said so outright, but he would have gotten his point across. Besides, if someone had come after Dom or Chavez or anyone else, Jack would've heard about it already. Though he was in exile, he was still part of the Hendley family. Clark asked, "What've you been up to?"

The question was a natural one, but Jack couldn't help but feel the absurdity of it. *What've I been up to? Busy not getting murdered.* Instead, he said, "Not much. Going to the gym, watching *Real Housewives*—you know, the usual."

Clark chuckled. "I record all mine on the DVR. Keeps me up all night. So, you're coming back into the fold soon, right? You talk to Gerry yet?"

"No. Still thinking about it."

"What's there to think about?"

Jack didn't answer. Clark said, "Ding was asking about you. Maybe let's grab a beer next week, okay?"

"Sure. I'll call you."

Jack disconnected. The conversation seemed to confirm what he suspected: This was about him specifically, not about The Campus as a whole.

Shortly after three his cell phone beeped. He checked the screen: **Tracking**. The accelerometer in the GPS unit had detected movement. Peter Hahn's car was pulling out of the garage—presumably with Hahn inside. The possibility that Jack was being lured—*invited* was a better word—into a trap had crossed his mind. Either Hahn was trying to lead Jack in the right direction or he was hoping to finish the job Weber had started, but he hadn't wanted to do it in his own backyard.

It didn't matter. This was his only lead.

He grabbed his rucksack and headed for the door.

Hahn was moving slowly, heading north and west away from Rose Hill.

After pulling out of the parking garage, Jack pulled to the curb, stuck his cell phone in the dashboard mount, and synced it to the Chrysler's onboard navigation system. On the bright, bigger screen the pulsing blue pop was easy to see.

Hahn's car reached Highway 495, where it paused momentarily before merging and heading due west. Unless Hahn exited soon, the highway would turn north up toward Annandale and Dunn Loring and Tysons Corner. Even with Hahn moving as slowly as he was, Jack couldn't catch up. For now, he'd have to settle for parallel.

He made his way to George Washington Memorial Parkway, and headed north. Traffic was light but wouldn't stay that way for long once rush hour started. His car's wipers intermittently squeaked and bumped across the windshield, keeping pace with the light rain. Jack kept one eye on the road and one eye on Hahn's blip, which was still headed north and approaching Annandale. In his mind's eye Jack ran through his options, should Hahn turn west. Once past Arlington Cemetery he could jump on the Custis Parkway and, he hoped, make up the eight-mile gap before Hahn got too far ahead.

For the next ten minutes they both continued north, Hahn still on the 495, Jack following the GW Parkway along the Potomac River, each angling toward the other. Eventually the two highways would intersect before crossing the river and turning into the Capital Beltway.

Jack's last chance to make a quick jaunt west, the Georgetown Pike, came and went, and still Hahn's blip moved steadily north. Jack picked up speed until he was going eighty miles per hour, hoping against hope a passing cop didn't spot him. Hahn's route would take him straight across the Potomac, while Jack had to follow the loop, costing him almost four miles.

Jack was halfway there, passing the midpoint of Langley Oaks Park, when the blip slowed and took the Georgetown Pike loop off-ramp, where it paused.

"What's over there?" Jack muttered to himself.

To the west lay one of the more expensive residential areas in McLean, where houses ran well into the millions. Jack used his right hand to pan and zoom the car's nav screen. To the west of the 495 was an open expanse. A nature preserve, it looked like. Secluded—and on a day like this, probably empty. The location made sense—for an isolated meeting place or for a trap. Or for whatever Peter Hahn was taking him to see.

"Come on," Jack told the blip. "Do something."

Jack was now passing Parkview Hills and approaching the Georgetown Pike/495 interchange. Hahn's car was less than a mile ahead and stopped.

The blip turned west onto the pike.

Jack sped up and reached the exit turnoff forty seconds later. Here, west of the 495, the pike was known as Cardinal Drive. On Jack's nav screen Hahn's car was a half-mile ahead and slowing at Swinks Mill Road. It turned right into what looked like an elongated, winding parking lot.

Jack took his foot off the gas pedal and coasted until he reached Swinks Mill. He stopped just short of the preserve entrance and eased ahead until he could see through the trees.

Though the temperature was in the low sixties, the rain and wind made for miserable hiking weather, and it was still too early in the season for the die-hard mushroom collectors to be out.

He saw no cars before the road curved and disappeared around a bend.

This was a damned terrible idea, Jack thought. Tactically, there were many reasons why he shouldn't be doing this, the biggest of which was exfiltration. Once inside this parking lot he would be boxed with a lone narrow road for an escape route. And he had no backup. On the other hand, if he took the time to find another entrance and Hahn left his car, Jack would never find him.

No choice. Nothing's perfect; either you adapt or you fail.

He scanned the lot for surveillance cameras but saw none.

He turned in and drove to the lot's rear section, a cul-de-sac roughly a hundred yards long. At the far end Hahn's Nissan was pulling onto a single-lane dirt access road. Jack grabbed his binoculars from the rucksack and zoomed in. A wooden sign with yellow letters read AUTHORIZED PERSONNEL ONLY. Lying on the ground beside the sign's post was a pile of chain. After a few moments the car's taillights disappeared through the trees.

"Shit." He saw no other cars in the lot. Who was Hahn

meeting? And where? This access road didn't appear on the car's navigation screen. Out his side window was a small roofed kiosk. On its wall, behind plexiglass, were what looked like a collection of enlarged historical photos. The box that should have contained maps was empty.

He rolled down both windows a couple inches and pulled ahead, scanning the trees on either side until he reached the entrance access road.

Jack's inner warning voice was talking to him: *Leave. Call Hendley.*

Not yet. His gut was also talking to him: something about Hahn, about his demeanor, that told Jack the man could be trusted. No, *trusted* was the wrong word, but twice Hahn had passed up a chance to kill Jack. Whoever was pulling the man's strings, he'd chosen a different path. What that was Jack didn't know. And he was about to find out which of his two voices was right.

Jack drew his Glock and tucked it under his thigh.

He eased the nose of the Chrysler between the posts and drove on.

9

The road wound its way north, generally following the course of a creek Jack could hear gurgling through his driver's-side window. Occasionally through the trees he glimpsed the Nissan's red taillights or the white of its trunk. Hahn was moving slowly, less than twenty miles an hour. The trees continued to thicken and soon the road veered slightly right, east, away from the river, and the grade steepened.

Ahead, Hahn's brake lights flashed, then went out. Hahn had stopped with his passenger-side tires on the dirt shoulder. Beyond the car the access road curved right, following the contour of the Potomac's banks, Jack guessed.

Jack coasted to a stop, then put the car in reverse and

backed down the road until he could barely see Hahn's car through the trees.

Hahn got out of his car. He opened a green-and-white golf umbrella. Without so much as a glance in Jack's direction he walked across the road, down into the ditch, and disappeared from view.

Jack gave him a thirty-second head start, then climbed out, pulled the brim of his cap lower over his eyes, and followed. The rain had picked up slightly and the drops pattered the loam alongside the road.

When he drew even with the spot where Hahn had left the road, Jack saw there was a narrow trail heading north and west as it skirted the base of a rocky hill. If there was high ground to be had, Jack was going to take it. And if someone was lying in wait for him, chances were good that was where they would be.

Jack continued down the road another fifty feet until he found a natural break in the trees, then hopped down into the ditch and started up the slope. The leaves were slick underfoot, but by using roots and exposed rock Jack was able to slowly pick his way upward, stopping occasionally to scan the terrain.

Another few minutes of hiking brought him to a shallow

cliff face. He picked his way up to a ledge where the rocks formed a natural stairway, then began climbing.

Jack paused. *Where is Hahn?* The trail he'd taken had to be somewhere to his left and below. He kept climbing until the stairs broadened into a rock shelf covered in scrub trees. He crept ahead until he was a few feet from the far edge, then crouched and peeked over. Below him lay a ravine bisected by the creek. To his left, at the mouth of the ravine, a waterfall plunged into a churning catch basin before emptying into a lagoon, itself spanned by a flagstone ford. Traversing the waterfall was a wooden footbridge.

Jack sensed movement to the left. He lay down on his belly and aimed the binoculars in that direction. It was Peter Hahn's green-and-white umbrella, emerging from the trail. Hahn reached the bridge and started across. At the halfway point, he stopped. He placed his hand on the railing and leaned forward for a better view of the waterfall. Rain dribbled from the edge of his umbrella.

Five minutes passed.

A lone figure wearing a khaki trench coat and carrying a black umbrella mounted the bridge from the opposite side of the ravine and walked toward Hahn. Jack zoomed in, but at this angle he could see nothing above the man's chest. His gait and build told Jack the man was younger than Hahn.

Hahn saw Trench Coat and turned toward him. He extended his hand in greeting. Trench Coat motioned to do the same. His hand came out of his coat pocket holding a palm-size semiautomatic pistol.

"What the—" Jack muttered. He drew his Glock, but too late.

The pistol's muzzle flashed orange. In the rush of the waterfall the shot was silent. Hahn took a step backward as though someone had punched him in the belly. Trench Coat fired again. Hahn's right leg buckled and he fell sideways, back against the handrail, then slid down onto his butt. His umbrella slipped from his hand, bounced off the footbridge's wooden treads, and rolled away. Trench Coat lifted the pistol and shot Hahn in the right eye. He shoved the gun into his jacket pocket, turned, and walked away. From the first shot to the coup de grâce, less than five seconds had elapsed.

Jack's natural instinct was to run to Hahn, but he quashed it. The German was dead, without a doubt. Next, run down Hahn's killer. This, too, he resisted. Had Hahn brought him here to witness this or to find the next link in the chain? Or both? Whatever the answer, it lay with the man walking back across the bridge.

Jack raised the binoculars and tracked him. Trench Coat's pace was unhurried, as if he were out for a casual nature walk. At the foot of the bridge he turned right onto a trail and Jack lost sight of him behind the trees.

Jack stood up and crouch-walked to the far edge of the

rock shelf, then lay down again and started scanning with the binoculars. According to his car's nav screen, this preserve's border was marked by the creek below, which meant Trench Coat had parked somewhere within the preserve, farther down the access road, or somewhere in the residential areas to the west; this seemed less likely, he judged, given the exclusivity of this area of McLean. A nonnative vehicle in a well-to-do and tight-knit neighborhood would quickly attract attention.

How much time did he give Trench Coat? Jack wondered. Ninety seconds, he decided. He started counting and focused the binoculars on the lagoon's flagstone pads.

When Jack's count reached forty, Trench Coat emerged from the screen of trees and stepped onto the bank of the lagoon. He started across the ford. Jack zoomed in. Still the man's face was blocked by the umbrella.

Jack backed away from the edge, turned around, and retraced his path, moving as fast and as quietly as possible. When he reached the ditch bordering the road, he stopped and looked left to where he guessed Trench Coat would emerge. *Clear.* He sprinted across it and into the trees beyond.

He needed to get ahead of Hahn's killer.

After fifty feet, he veered left toward the access road, slowing his pace as he drew closer. When he could see the road's berm through the trees, he stopped and crouched. He raised the binoculars and panned back along the road.

Where are you . . . ?

There.

Trench Coat was coming down the road, still strolling without a care in the world. Jack had a lead, but not much of one. He recalled his rough mental map of the preserve: Eventually this access road would have to curve south before reaching Highway 495 and heading back toward Cardinal Drive.

He stood up, backed through the trees until he lost sight of the road, then turned and started moving again, keeping the road on his left. Jack adjusted course to the south, ran for another sixty seconds, then again veered left until the road came back into view.

Ahead through the trees he glimpsed a flash of metallic-blue car paint. He crouched beside a stump and lifted the binoculars to his eyes. It was the hood of a midsize sedan. He'd found a second parking lot, this one smaller than the first, a horseshoe-shaped clearing with enough spaces for ten to fifteen cars. All but one of them was empty. The access road entered on the left and exited on the right.

He zoomed in on the car. It was a Chevy Malibu. On the upper right side of the windshield was a Hertz sticker. Jack panned down and focused on the Maryland license plate. He memorized the number.

Jack lowered the binoculars and looked left through the trees, waiting for a glimpse of Trench Coat. He had two options: intercept the man and snatch him up or try to gather more information and track him. The former was impractical for a number of reasons, the biggest of which was what to do with the man. Chain him up in the condo's pantry and torture him? No, if he wanted to get to the heart of what was happening and find a way to make it stop, he needed to know who was giving the orders.

Still, the idea of watching a murderer get in his car and drive away rankled Jack's conscience. Whatever Hahn's reasons, it seemed he'd come to this meeting knowing it would probably cost him his life. Moreover, he'd spared Jack's life twice. While Jack felt no particular affection for Hahn, the least he could do was make that sacrifice count.

From Jack's right he heard the crunch of tires on gravel. He looked that way and saw a red compact SUV pull into the clearing and turn into one of the stalls opposite the Malibu. After a few moments the SUV's taillights went dark and exhaust stopped flowing from the muffler pipe. The driver's-side door opened.

Jack scanned left, looking for Trench Coat. He was a hundred feet from the parking lot.

Jack felt a shiver of panic. What happened next depended on Trench Coat's attitude toward witnesses. Would it be worth a second murder to get away from the scene cleanly?

The SUV's driver got out, walked around the rear of the

vehicle, stopped. He looked left and right, then walked across the lot toward Trench Coat's Malibu. When he reached the rear bumper he pulled out a cell phone and snapped a picture of the license plate, then walked to the driver's-side window and peered inside.

"What're you doing?" Jack muttered to himself. Who was this? A cop, a thief? The man struck Jack as neither. He was in his mid-twenties, with shaggy blond hair and a prominent chin, and he moved tentatively, without the confidence of a cop.

This wasn't going to end well.

The man straightened up and started back toward his SUV.

The Malibu's headlights flashed once, accompanied by a muted beep and the clunk of the door locks disengaging.

Jack looked left, felt his heart lurch into his throat. Trench Coat was entering the parking lot, umbrella still covering half his face. His pistol was up and pointed at the SUV's driver. The muzzle flashed; the report was no louder than that of a wet towel being snapped. The SUV's driver crumpled to the ground.

Damn it! Jack thought. Whoever this new person was, bystander or player, he couldn't let Trench Coat kill him.

Jack drew his Glock, stood up, sprinted into the parking lot, and took aim on the man. "Freeze!" he shouted.

Trench Coat stopped walking, but his gun never wavered

from the fallen SUV driver. Slowly Trench Coat turned his head toward Jack.

"Put the gun down!" Jack called.

For a long three seconds the man didn't respond. Jack could see only his chin and mouth below the rim of the umbrella.

Trench Coat said, "This man is still alive." Jack detected no accent. "If you want him to stay that way, you'll lose the gun."

Trench Coat had already killed one man today and had just gunned down a second. If Jack dropped his weapon he'd be the third, either to silence another witness or because Trench Coat recognized him for who he was—the target they'd missed twice already.

Jack flicked his eyes toward the SUV. He could see the driver's feet poking out from behind the rear tire; one of them moved, scraping the dirt as though the man was trying to crawl away.

"No chance," Jack replied.

The man stared at Jack for a few seconds, then called to the SUV's driver, "You, there! Can you hear me?"

"Yes, I can hear you," came the faint reply. Now Jack caught the trace of an accent—vaguely European, perhaps German.

"Crawl toward me. Do it now or I'll shoot you again."

Jack said, "Stay there!" Then, to Trench Coat: "Give it up."

"You're not the police, are you?" the man replied. He sounded mildly surprised. Trench Coat was unflappable, Jack realized. He'd done this before, more than a few times.

"No, but I'm a decent shot," Jack replied. "Put down your gun. Last chance."

Trench Coat didn't bite. "Let me leave and we all live through this. Back up and I'll get in my car and drive away. You can help this man before he bleeds to death."

In reply, Jack stalked forward three paces until he was standing at the Malibu's bumper. Slowly he crouched down until only his shoulders and head were exposed.

"No."

"I'm taking his car. You have my word I will not kill him."

Bullshit.

With his eyes flicking between Jack and the SUV, the man paced forward, gun still trained on the fallen driver.

"I'll keep my word," Trench Coat said. "I just want to leave."

Jack shouted, "Not another step—"

In one fluid motion Trench Coat ducked and spun, his pistol swinging around. Jack saw the muzzle flash. He felt something pluck at the collar of his jacket beside his ear. He ducked behind the Malibu's engine block, then peeked around the bumper. *Fast bastard*, Jack thought.

Trench Coat was sprinting toward the SUV, gun coming back around toward the driver. The muzzle flashed. Jack tracked him with the Glock, leading him a bit, then fired. The bullet punched into the wet earth between Trench Coat and the SUV's rear bumper.

"Next one's in your chest," Jack shouted. This wasn't true; he needed the man alive, but shooting to wound went against all his training.

Trench Coat kept going. Jack fired again. This time the round struck Trench Coat's right calf; he stumbled sideways but regained his balance and disappeared behind the SUV. Jack sprinted forward, gun raised, looking for Trench Coat's silhouette inside the SUV.

"Get out of the car," Jack shouted. "Out of the car!"

Ten feet from the SUV he slowed his pace, scanning for movement. He ducked, looked beneath the SUV, but saw nothing but the inert form of the driver.

In the distance he heard the muffled snapping of branches. Jack reached the SUV's bumper and stopped to peek around the edge. Across the road, Trench Coat was fleeing through the trees. Jack raised his Glock, but it was too late. He had no shot.

To his right came a groan. The driver was alive.

"Can you hear me?" Jack asked him.

"Yes . . . who are you?"

"Stay still, don't move. Hold on. I need to be sure he's not doubling back."

Jack watched the trees for another sixty seconds, then

stood up, sidestepped to the man, and crouched beside him. He was lying on his belly, face turned toward Jack and in the dirt. The hair above his left ear was matted with blood, some of it running down his cheek. The rain diluted it pink.

"My head hurts," he told Jack.

"I'll bet. Can you see the trees across the road?"

"Yes."

"Watch them," Jack replied. "He's out there. Tell me if anything moves."

He holstered the Glock and leaned over the man. His blue eyes, wide with fear, were rotated toward Jack. Using his fingertips, Jack probed through the bloody hair until his index finger found a groove in the man's scalp about an eighth of an inch deep and two inches long. The man winced. "Am I shot?"

"Grazed," Jack replied, still probing. Trench Coat had fired twice. Was there another wound?

"There's so much blood," the man said.

"It's a scalp wound, they're like that. What's your name?"

"Effrem."

Jack had a long list of other questions, but they would have to wait.

"We need to get out of here, Effrem," Jack said. "Can you move?"

"I think so."

Jack helped Effrem to a sitting position, his back against

the tire, then walked around and opened the rear hatch. Inside the cargo area was a yellow hard-sided roller suitcase. Jack unzipped it and rummaged around until he found some white tube socks. He tied three of them together, end to end, then returned to Effrem.

"Hold this against your head," Jack told him. "Like that."

Jack guided his hand, pressing one of the sock's knots into the wound. He circled the loose ends around Effrem's skull and cinched the makeshift bandage with a square knot.

"My head really hurts," Effrem repeated.

"You're going to be okay. Lift up your shirt."

"What?"

Jack was already doing it, jerking Effrem's shirt and jacket up toward his shoulders. Effrem caught on and helped with his free hand. "Anything?" he asked. Jack could hear the fear in his voice now. The shock was starting to wear off a bit, replaced by the realization of what had just happened.

Jack turned him around, scanned his back. He saw no wounds.

Effrem asked, "What about my legs?"

"If he'd hit an artery, we'd know about it. Trust me. Can you drive? We need to get out of here."

"Okay, I think so. Are you the police?"

"Yell if you see him coming back," Jack replied.

He walked back to the Malibu, paused to pick up the Glock's two spent shell casings, then opened the driver's-side door. He pressed the trunk release, then walked around and searched it. Empty. He returned to the car and did a rapid search—glove compartment, center console, under the seats . . . On the floor of the passenger seat were two balled-up fast-food bags, one Arby's and one McDonald's. In each of these was a cash receipt, which he pocketed. Tucked behind the driver's-side floor mat next to the gas pedal he found a burgundy-colored passport bearing Germany's coat-of-arms eagle and the words *Europäische Union, Bundes-republik Deutschland*, and *Reisepass*. The name inside the passport was Stephan Möller. The identification picture showed an early-forties man with short black hair and a thick, hipsterish beard. Jack doubted this was Trench Coat's real name, but it was a start, another thread he could hopefully unravel.

He returned to Effrem, who had managed to climb to his feet and was leaning against the SUV on shaky legs. Jack dropped to his knees beside the rear tire and began probing the dirt.

"What are you looking for?" asked Effrem.

"My bullet." The other one was gone, either in Möller's leg or lost in the trees on the other side of the road.

It took two minutes, but Jack finally found the bullet's impact point. He got out his multi-tool, pried the bullet free, and dropped it into his pocket. He stood and faced Effrem.

"Give me your wallet."

"What?"

"Your wallet. And your passport and cell phone."

Frowning, Effrem dug into his back pocket and handed Jack a Belgian passport and a slim brown leather wallet containing a few credit cards, an EU driver's license, and one from Belgium: Effrem Likkel.

"Are you robbing me?" Effrem asked, handing over his cell phone.

Despite it all, Jack couldn't help but chuckle. "No, I'm not robbing you. Where are you staying, what hotel?"

"Uh, the Embassy Suites in Old Town."

"Room?"

"Four twelve."

"Go straight there," Jack said, handing back Effrem's wallet and passport. "Wait for me."

On Effrem's cell phone Jack navigated to the address book, found the phone's number, then typed it into his own cell phone.

"Why should I trust you?" asked Effrem, taking the phone back.

"Because you're still alive."

"Good point. What're you going to do now?"

"I don't know. Can you tell me anything about that guy? His name, where he's staying?"

"No. I was just following him."

Jack wanted to ask the obvious question—Why?—but instead said, "Can you get to your room without going through the lobby?"

"Yes."

"Do that. Get on the 495, find a gas station bathroom, clean yourself up, and then get into your room and stay there. Don't answer the door until you hear my voice."

10

Jack sprinted back to his car and, five minutes after sending Effrem on his way, was heading down Cardinal Drive. He crossed over the 495 and onto the Georgetown Pike. At the first stoplight he spotted a gas station. He pulled into a parking spot.

He had one shot at this, he knew, and it was fifty-fifty at best. Despite taking a bullet from Jack's Glock, Möller had been moving at a decent clip through the trees and the man had already proven himself cool in a crisis. Therefore Jack had to assume Möller had tended to his wound, regrouped, and either was lying low in the nature preserve or was already out of the area. The question was, Would the man go back to his hotel or did he have a fallback exfiltration plan? Things had gone very bad for Möller: There were witnesses and he'd been in a firefight. How would he react?

He dug the fast-food receipts out of his pocket, then used his phone's Yelp app to map both restaurants. Each was located within a quarter-mile of the other, off Richmond Highway. Next Jack dropped a pin on the app's screen and searched for nearby motels. There were three within walking distance of the restaurants, a Holiday Inn, a Days Inn, and a Comfort Inn, all similar to the hotel Eric Weber had chosen—mid-priced, nice, but not extravagant. Maybe that meant something, maybe not.

The outcome of Jack's scheme depended on human nature. Most people looking for a quick meal in a strange city chose restaurants close to their motel. Whether a man like Möller would allow himself such a convenience Jack didn't know, but it was all he had. He'd already made one mistake by leaving his passport in the Malibu; perhaps he'd make another. A common problem with professionals of any trade is self-assurance, the mother of complacency. It had happened to Jack before—perhaps as recently as the Supermercado. Even John Clark had once—just once, over a few beers—admitted his own occasional tradecraft blunder. The question was, What do you do after the mistake? What would Möller do after his?

Jack pulled out of the gas station and got back on the highway.

———

Twenty minutes later he reached Richmond Highway, turned south, then took the first exit. He chose the first motel he came to, the Holiday Inn, pulled in, and parked outside the lobby. Inside, using what he hoped was a decent German accent, he gave the name Stephan Möller to the front desk attendant and claimed he was a bit confused. Was he staying here? The answer was no. Jack moved on to the second motel, the Days Inn, and got the same results. At the third motel, he got lucky.

"Yes, sir, you sure are," the young Hispanic man said. "Can I help you with something?"

"Yes, please," Jack said, rubbing his eyes. "It has been a long day. I have been lost much of the time, and now I realize I have left my key in my room."

"I'm sorry to hear that. Do you have a driver's license or passport?"

Jack handed over Möller's passport. As the attendant studied it, Jack said with a sheepish chuckle, "About the beard, please do not ask. My wife is only now forgiving me."

Jack held his breath. Sans beard, Jack's appearance was close to that of Möller's. Whether it was close enough now depended on the attendant's observation skills.

The attendant laughed. "I hear you. Just a moment,

please. I'll be right back." The man disappeared through a door behind the desk.

Two minutes, Jack thought, half imagining the attendant already on the phone with the police. Any more than that and he'd leave.

The attendant reappeared. He handed back Möller's passport along with a new key card. "Here you go. Let me know if you need directions or a map."

"Thank you very much."

Jack started to walk away, then turned a short circle as though trying to get his bearings. "My room is . . ."

"One twenty-five. Out through the door you came in, then left down the side of the building."

Jack thanked him again and left.

He parked his car four stalls down from Möller's room and shut off the engine.

The room's window curtain was parted about an inch. Through the gap Jack saw a faint yellow light. He checked his watch. Forty-five minutes had elapsed since Möller had fled the preserve's parking lot. If he'd had an accomplice waiting at the preserve he could already be back in his room. Otherwise, his options were to hitchhike or call a taxi. He wouldn't risk the former, Jack decided. Taxi, then. Which meant he was probably ahead of Möller; if he was coming back here, Jack's lead was very slim.

Jack's question from earlier popped back into his mind: Did he snatch up Möller, or try to track him? He reached the same conclusion. Track him. Jack had to assume that unless Möller was working for himself he'd already reported the incident up his chain of command, regardless of whether he'd recognized Jack at the preserve.

With Möller wounded and on the run, he would be hypervigilant for any sign of pursuit. Jack thought it unlikely he could maintain a one-man surveillance of Möller without being spotted. That left him with one option: Track the man remotely, passively.

So many ifs and maybes. Too many.

Without giving himself a chance to come up with more of them, Jack got out of the car, strode toward Möller's door. It was late afternoon, heading toward twilight, and the rain was still falling. Jack glanced around. No one was about. He stopped at Möller's door, drew his Glock, and held it tight against his leg. He took a breath, let it out. He swiped the key card, pushed open the door, stepped inside, then used his heel to force the door shut. He raised the Glock.

To his right in the corner the floor lamp was on.

Jack reached back over his shoulder with his free hand and eased closed the door's cross-latch lock.

"Hello? Manager, Mr. Möller," Jack called. "Are you here? Hello . . . manager . . ."

Jack moved now, quickly clearing the front room, then the bathroom and closet.

As he'd done in Weber's room, Jack searched the room, taking care to leave everything as he found it. Like Weber's, Möller's clothes were nondescript, either tagless or bought locally at a Target or Walmart. No identification, no airline boarding passes, no scribbled notes or credit card receipts.

He turned his attention to the less obvious hiding spots— inside the chair's zippered cushion or the cover of the ironing board, taped to the underside of a drawer, or down the back of the toilet tank. Nothing.

He lifted the shower-curtain rod free of its wall bracket, gave it a shake, then tilted it downward. From inside the plastic tube came a scraping sound. Jack pulled off the rod's cap and out slid a screw-top aluminum cylinder. He caught it in his palm, then laid down the curtain rod, unscrewed the top, and checked the interior.

Bullets.

He turned to the sink, closed the drain plug, and dumped out the rounds.

They were .22-caliber short bullets, but the tips were coated black. It took Jack a moment to realize what he was seeing. These were Glaser Safety Slugs, frangible bullets designed to blow rat holes in whatever they struck. The black coating was a polymer cap; beneath this, the bullet's hollowed-out core was packed with No. 12 birdshot. Glasers had devastating stopping capacity but poor penetrative power. This could have been the reason Möller had chosen to shoot Hahn in the eye rather than in the skull.

Jack picked up one of the bullets. It felt light in his hand. He put it next to his ear and shook it. Not Glasers. In fact, most Glasers came with a blue polymer cap, not black. Here was the answer to the unaccountably soft report of Möller's pistol. These frangibles were subsonic, containing less propellant than it took to accelerate the round past the sound barrier. Without the sonic crack, all that remained was the explosion of the propellant's gas, and judging by the feel of the one Jack was holding, there wasn't much powder inside the casing. Past thirty or thirty-five feet the bullet's trajectory probably dropped like a mortar round—which made Möller's snap shot at Jack all the more impressive.

So this was a custom-made frangible. Whether there was a booming business for this kind of ammunition or it came from a niche market Jack didn't know, but it was worth a check. He pocketed the round. He hoped Möller wouldn't notice the discrepancy.

After taking a picture of the loose bullets, Jack wiped them down with a piece of toilet paper, returned them to the cylinder, and slid that back into the curtain rod.

He continued his search and struck pay dirt again a few minutes later.

Slipped into the folds of the wrapper of a bar of soap, he found a credit card in Möller's name. He photographed it, front and back, then returned it to its hiding place.

No second passport. If Möller had one, he either was carrying it or had stashed it elsewhere. If this was the case, the chances were good Möller's exit plan involved air travel and Jack would lose him. If not, Möller would be looking for an alternative route out of the country and would, Jack hoped, use this credit card to make it happen.

Time to go, Jack.

He gave the room one last quick inspection, saw nothing out of place, then left.

Once back in his car, Jack drove a few blocks away, pulled to the curb, and used his phone to log in to The Campus's Enquestor Services portal. He entered Möller's credit card information and toggled the real-time alerts slider beside the entry. He scanned for previous hits on the credit card but found none; it had never been used.

He got back on the Richmond Highway, headed north for five minutes, then turned left onto Duke Street. Effrem's hotel, the Embassy Suites, sat across the street from John Carlyle Square Park. Jack found a parking spot on a nearby side street and walked the remaining distance. The rain was coming more heavily now, blown diagonally by a cold wind.

He ducked under the hotel's awning, then through the lobby doors. He took off his jacket and shook the rain from it, using the time to consider his next step. Whoever Effrem Likkel was and whatever his reason for following Möller, the man was a lead Jack couldn't afford to ignore. The downside was he'd be entangling himself with an unknown commodity, which would bring up questions Jack would prefer not to answer. He'd have to deal with them as they arose.

Jack walked to the elevators and took one up to the fourth floor. When he got there he took the right-hand hallway, found room 412, then walked back to the elevators. He pulled out his cell phone and dialed Effrem's number, and Effrem answered on the first ring. Jack said, "It's me."

"The man from—"

"Yes. Are you in your room?"

"Yes."

"Come down to the lobby."

Jack disconnected. He drew his Glock, stuffed it into his jacket's side pocket, and left his hand there.

Thirty seconds later he heard a room door click shut down the hallway.

Effrem came around the corner. When he saw Jack he stopped short, his eyes wide. His hair was wet, probably freshly shampooed. There was no sign of the bullet graze.

Effrem said, "I thought—"

"Did you have any trouble getting back?" asked Jack.

"No, I don't think so."

"Let's go to your room. You lead."

Jack followed him back down the hallway to his hotel room.

"Stop," Jack said. "Look at me." When Effrem did so, Jack asked, "Is there anyone in there?"

"No." Effrem's reply was immediate, firm. He held Jack's gaze.

"Go in first," Jack told him.

Effrem swiped his key card and stepped inside. Jack followed. He stopped Effrem at the bathroom door, cleared that, then followed him the rest of the way into the room. It was empty. Jack ordered him to sit down on the bed.

Jack pulled the Glock from his jacket pocket and reholstered it. He pulled out the desk chair and sat down. He smiled at Effrem; the man had been through a lot. Jack needed to put him at ease before he shut down, decided to call the police, or took the first opportunity to leave town.

"I'm sorry about all that. How's your head?"

Absently, Effrem reached up and touched the side of his head. "It feels like the mother of all hangovers, but I took some aspirin. It's getting better."

"How did you stop the bleeding?"

"Superglue. I saw it on one of the survival shows."

"Any blurry vision, dizziness? Nausea? Loss of consciousness?"

"None of those. I'm very lucky, I think."

"I'd say so. If you get any symptoms, call me. I'll get someone here."

"Okay."

"Don't go to the hospital. They'll recognize that wound for what it is."

"Yes, I understand."

An awkward silence hung in the air between them. Jack was unsurprised, given the nature of their first meeting. It wasn't as if they'd run into each other at a coffee shop and realized they shared a love of the New York Jets and Aerosmith.

"Your English is very good," Jack said.

"I spent my third year at NYU. Do you want some coffee or tea?"

"No, thanks. Let's talk about what happened. I assume you didn't call the police."

Effrem shook his head.

Jack believed him. *Interesting.* Most people would have dialed 911 the moment Jack disappeared from their rearview mirror. Having already admitted to following Möller, Effrem had just told Jack the pursuit was something he preferred to keep secret.

"I am guessing you didn't call them, either," said Effrem.

"No. Listen, Effrem, if you'd like we can part company right here, right now. No harm done. Or we can help each other. It's pretty clear we were both following the same man." While this wasn't technically true, it was close enough for now, Jack decided.

Effrem said, "Perhaps so. I don't know your name."

"Jack."

They shook hands.

"Jack what?" asked Effrem.

"For now, Jack will do."

If Effrem recognized him, he gave no sign of it. Jack did a decent job of keeping out of the spotlight. Plus, since leaving The Campus he'd cropped his hair, switched to a loosely enforced biweekly shaving regimen, and put on ten pounds of muscle at the gym.

"How do I know I can trust you?" asked Effrem.

"Over the last couple hours we've both had plenty of chances to turn on each other."

Effrem nodded begrudgingly. "And there is the whole saving-my-life aspect, I suppose. Thank you for that, by the way."

"No problem."

Effrem hesitated, then started again: "You know my name, you know I am from Belgium. I'm a journalist, but only freelance right now."

This further complicated things, Jack knew. The last thing he needed was to have his name in the newspapers: America's First Son, assassins, and a murder conspiracy with international connections.

"I'm hoping to, you know, make a name for myself," Effrem said hesitantly. "I just got out of university three years ago. I've been working on this story for a long, long time."

"Involving Stephan Möller," Jack said.

"If you say that's his name, I believe you, but it's the first I've heard it. I found Möller through another man I was following. Eric Schrader."

"Describe him."

"Tall, skinny, short hair, very blond. Does that name mean something to you?"

"Maybe. Go on."

"A few days ago I followed Schrader to a restaurant in Falls Church. That's where he met the other one, this Stephan Möller. I knew where Schrader was staying, so I decided to take a chance and switch to Möller, hoping to find out more. Do you think that's why he shot me? Do you think he saw that I was following him and lured me to that preserve?"

"To your first question, probably; to your second, I don't think so," Jack replied. "He was there for another reason."

"What reason?"

"Later. Go on."

"Anyway, when I went back to find Schrader, I couldn't. He hasn't been back to his hotel. There was someone driving him around, but I lost him—an older man in a white Nissan. I don't know his name, but I have the license-plate number."

The recently deceased Peter Hahn. Two of the three people Effrem Likkel had been following were dead and he didn't know it.

"Tell me about Schrader."

Likkel shifted nervously on the bed. "No, I don't think so. Sorry. I've told you a lot; you've told me nothing. Why were you at the preserve?"

Jack had been hoping to get more information before Likkel demanded quid pro quo. He needed to keep both dialogue and his options open. "I was following the man in the white Nissan," Jack replied. "I found him through Schrader, who I knew as Eric Weber."

"How do you know him?"

"Our paths crossed briefly."

"How?"

"I don't want to answer that," Jack replied. "Not yet. You're a journalist, Effrem. That's not a bad thing in itself, but the hunt for a story makes journalists do strange things—especially young journalists looking to earn a name for themselves. No offense."

"I understand. But consider this: I know things you don't

know, and you know things I don't know. If we share information, we can get further. Besides, something tells me you are not the headline to my story."

"Instinct from years of hard-won experience?" Jack said with a grin.

"Not that, for sure. Genetics, maybe."

"What's that mean?"

"Look into me. You'll have no trouble finding plenty of information. If after that you want to talk, you know where to find me. If not . . ." Effrem shrugged. "Well, I've gotten this far on my own. I can keep going on my own."

11

ALEXANDRIA, VIRGINIA

Effrem had piqued his interest, but looking into the journalist's pedigree would have to wait a while longer. He had one more stop to make. One that he should have made earlier.

He drove back to Rose Hill and circled Peter Hahn's neighborhood, looking for signs of police activity. If someone had found the body at the preserve and called 911, the responding Homicide detective would immediately dispatch uniformed police officers to Peter Hahn's home, either looking for further victims or hoping to notify next of kin.

Seeing no police cars or anything extraordinary in the neighborhood, Jack turned onto Climbhill Road. When he reached Hahn's home he turned off his headlights and pulled to the curb. It was fully dark now and the rain had slowed to a drizzle that sparkled in the light of the streetlamps lining the block. A few houses away a dog started yipping in the backyard. A woman's voice snapped, "Snickers, get in here," and the barking stopped.

What he was about to do would be damned hard to explain if the police showed up. He hoped it would be worth the risk.

After making sure his car's dome light was off, Jack opened the door and climbed out. He didn't look around but strode up the driveway with purpose, a friend coming to visit his old friend Pete. At least that was the demeanor Jack hoped he was exuding.

Jack reached the back door and pulled open the screen, which swung back with only a slight squeal. Jack clicked on his penlight, shoved the end into his mouth, and leaned over to inspect the lock. It wasn't in much better shape than the knob to Hahn's garage had been. Maybe he'd get lucky again.

He got out his multi-tool, pried the flathead screwdriver open, then slipped it into the keyhole, wiggling and twisting as he went until finally the tool was haft-deep in the lock. Jack started twisting the knob and tool in opposite directions. The first three times he had to back off, afraid his multi-tool was going to snap, but on the fourth attempt the lock *thunk*ed open.

Jack poked his head inside and called, "Pete, you here? Hey, man, I thought we were supposed to meet up."

Hahn wasn't home, of course, and two more shout-outs suggested no one else was in the house. Jack drew his Glock, stepped into the kitchen, and shut the door behind him. He stood in the darkness for thirty seconds, getting a feel for the home. It felt cramped, slapped together in the late forties, Jack guessed, with narrow hallways and probably a chopped-up interior. When this house was built the concept of open, flowing floor plans was still decades away.

Jack didn't know what exactly he was looking for and didn't want to spend more than ten minutes inside. It seemed clear to him that Peter Hahn had been a reluctant participant in first the murder of Mark Macloon, and then in the attempted murder of Jack himself. There had to be a reason he'd participated at all. Jack recalled Hahn's words from the night before: *As it is, I don't know if I've done enough to save her.*

Who was "her"? His daughter? It seemed clear she was linked—perhaps unwillingly—to whoever was behind all this. How?

Jack walked through the kitchen and stepped into a TV room/nook. Sitting on a rectangular, linoleum-topped dining table was a desktop computer. The screen saver was running, tracing colorful expanding lines across the monitor's black face. On the table were disheveled stacks of newspapers, magazines, and sudoku puzzle books, the kind you find near the register at grocery stores. Lying next to the keyboard was a *Windows for Dummies* book. It was open to the chapter about e-mailing and Skype.

For safety's sake, Jack walked through the house to confirm he was alone, then returned to the nook and sat down before the computer. He tapped the mouse button. The screen saver disappeared to reveal an open e-mail window and Web browser. Jack clicked through the browser's tabs and found a few online crossword and word-search sites, the local cable company's TV listing grid, and a page with movie times at the Regal Cinemas Kingstowne a couple miles away. Jack opened the browser history and scanned backward. A site title: "Impeach President Ryan Now!" Jack clicked on the link, which took him to a rant blog dedicated to his father. Jack clicked backward, returning to the history list, and soon found more sites, all dedicated to anti–Jack Ryan ramblings, from complaints about the economy and foreign affairs to conspiracy posts about his father having murdered a woman in Kentucky when he was twelve years old and his being a secret Chinese sleeper agent.

Jack checked the "last visited" dates and times for each site. All had been visited over the course of six days shortly before the attempt on his life at the Supermercado.

Fallback cover, Jack thought. Eric Schrader/Weber had come at him as a junkie mugger and he'd gone to some trouble to lay groundwork for the role by panhandling outside the Supermercado. If there had been witnesses to Jack's murder, the police would have been looking for a knife-wielding crackhead. If that fell through and Schrader/Weber was somehow tracked back to Peter Hahn, the authorities would find a political nut job with a motive—albeit a clumsily assembled one—to see the President's son killed.

Peter Hahn wasn't crazy, that much Jack felt certain about. Nor did Hahn, who needed a book to work his e-mail, seem like the kind of man to check his browser history. If either Möller or Schrader/Weber had planted this Web history, Hahn would have been unlikely to discover the ruse. Either that or Hahn himself had visited the sites for the same reason he'd helped Schrader/Weber—under orders and to protect someone.

Jack turned his attention to Hahn's e-mail. There were only a few dozen in the inbox, all of them junk mail or advertisements; he clicked on the trash folders and found more of the same. In the window's sidebar was a folder labeled "BB." Jack opened this and found hundreds of e-mails dating back six months. Jack chose one at random and opened it.

Hi, Dad. I got the book you sent me. It's hilarious. My cat does so many of those things it kinda freaked me out . . .

It was signed Bee Bee. Jack clicked on sender to expand the name: belinda.b.hahn@gmail.com.

BB. Peter Hahn's daughter.

Securing his little girl's welfare would be leverage enough for any father.

Jack clicked on the most recent e-mail, from earlier that morning:

Sorry you had to cancel our Skype session today. I was looking forward to it. Before you know it, you're going to be a computer whiz. Anyway, call when you get a chance. Just want to make sure you're taking your meds and all that. I'm also sending you a new sudoku book. Maybe this one will take a little longer to finish. LOL.

Damn. Father and daughter were in close touch. Until Hahn's body was found and Belinda was notified, her e-mails would go unanswered. Jack felt for her.

Jack selected the last e-mail, clicked through until he reached the Properties/Details tab, then checked the message's full header, a dense block of text several hundred characters long. Too much to absorb now. Jack inserted his own USB drive, copied and pasted the header into a text document, and repeated the process another ten times, choosing messages that spanned the duration of Hahn's correspondence with Belinda.

Jack was about to close out the e-mail program when a thought occurred to him: If in fact Peter Hahn hadn't visited these anti-Ryan websites, then someone else had done it for him, either in person or remotely.

Jack grouped all the messages in the Belinda folder by file size and scanned down the list. All messages ranged in size from 40 kilobytes to 70 kilobytes—save one, which read as 1.2 megabytes and displayed a paper-clip attachment icon. Peter had received it six weeks earlier.

Jack double-clicked on the e-mail. Beside a thumbnail image of a woman with short, bobbed brown hair—Belinda, he assumed—was the message

---

Hey, Dad, can you check out my webpage and see if it loads for you?

Below this was a hyperlink.

This e-mail had all the earmarks of a phishing scam. There was no way the attached thumbnail image was 1.2 megabytes in size. Something else was occupying that space. Jack navigated to the e-mail's Properties window, copied the contents to his USB drive, then did the same with the link.

Jack called up the browser's history, pasted the link into the search box, and hit enter. There. Hahn had clicked on the link the same day he'd received it from Belinda.

Malware, Jack thought. But to do what? Monitor Hahn or to create a false website trail? Or both? And what about Belinda? Was she an unwitting or witting participant?

Jack was back at his condo thirty minutes later. He heated up a bowl of slow-cooker chili, grabbed a Heineken from the fridge, and sat down on the couch with his laptop. Two minutes into his research into Effrem Likkel he realized the young Belgian hadn't been exaggerating. Jack kicked himself for having not immediately recognized the name.

In Europe, Effrem Likkel was as close to journalistic royalty as you got, save his mother, who was, it seemed, the undisputed queen of journalism. Marie Likkel, now sixty-four, retired, and divorced, had been covering international politics, war, corruption, and legal abuse the world over for almost twenty years longer than Jack had been alive, and had done so across a spectrum of media from radio to television to print.

Effrem, having chosen to follow in her footsteps at an early age, was, as he'd told Jack, trying to make a name for himself, and had apparently been doing so without the largesse of his mother—and by mutual choice, most articles agreed. Both mother and son wanted the heir to the Likkel legacy to stand or fall on his own merits.

Unsurprisingly, this struck a chord with Jack. He knew what it felt like to live in a big shadow, and to be anxious to find a way into your own sun. No doubt Effrem Likkel was desperate for the same, while also being keenly and constantly aware he needed to do it better and cleaner than the next guy. Whether that meant Jack could trust him only time would tell. But did Jack want or need a partner? As had Effrem, he'd so far made decent inroads on his own.

Then again, Effrem had been working on his story, whatever it entailed, for a long damned time. Who knew how much information he'd collected?

Jack grabbed his cell phone, scrolled through his address book, and speed-dialed a number. "Alicia Dixon," the voice on the other end said.

"Alicia, Jack Ryan. I didn't know if you'd still be in the office."

Alicia was a reporter for *The Washington Post*. They'd dated briefly, but it hadn't worked out. Their schedules never meshed enough for them to form a bond, but they'd remained friends, occasionally having dinner or a drink.

"Jack Ryan . . ." She laughed. "If it's before ten, I'm usually here. Are you calling to apologize for standing me up?"

"I didn't stand you up, Alicia. I was just very, very late. And didn't I already apologize?"

"Yeah, you did, but I never did see that movie."

"I'll buy you the DVD. Listen, I need your expertise."

"Shoot."

"What do you know about Effrem Likkel?"

"The last name I know. Marie Likkel—that's her son, right?"

"Right. Give me the scoop."

"Well, Marie's a legend in Europe. She's won just about every journalism award out there—the Pulitzer, SPJ, Bayeux-Calvados, Bastiat . . . The woman's got schools named after her, for God's sake."

"No skeletons in her closet?" asked Jack.

"None," Alicia replied. "And believe me, some powerful people have dug into her, especially the bigger fish she's gone after. She's above reproach. When I was at Northwestern I kept a picture of her taped next to my computer screen. Everyone thought it was Madeleine Albright."

"So you're a fan," Jack said, deadpan.

"If she had a club, I'd be president."

"And what about her son?"

"I've never met him, but rumor is he's just like her—tenacious, righteous, all that," Alicia said. "He's a little green and maybe a little too eager, but that's more the rule than the exception with cubs."

"Has he cracked anything big?"

"Not really, but I've read some of his pieces. He's solid, got a feel for it. Jack, why are you asking? Has Likkel contacted you for something?"

Though he hadn't been prepared to answer this question, the lie came easily: "Not me, a buddy of mine. He just wanted to know if Likkel's a straight shooter."

When had that happened? While he wasn't so squeaky clean he'd never told a lie, he could remember a time when doing so gave him pause, even a tinge of regret. Lying was a necessity of the job, that he knew, and he had to wonder if Clark and Chavez ever ruminated over it. *You're thinking too much, Jack.*

Alicia replied, "It's a safe bet. Given his family name, one step out of line and the journalism world would know about it—including Mommy. And he knows that, I'm sure. But remember, Jack: 'Off the record' only means as much as a journalist's integrity weighs. Tell your friend to assume everything he says is going to end up in the papers."

12

ALEXANDRIA, VIRGINIA

Jack was up early again the next morning. Having made his choice about Effrem Likkel, he didn't want to waste any more time. After making a stop at Starbucks, he drove to the Embassy Suites and was knocking on Effrem's door shortly before seven. The Belgian answered the door in flannel pajamas. He rubbed his eyes and blinked at Jack. Effrem was sporting a severe case of bed head, his shaggy blond hair flattened on one side.

"I told you not to open the door," Jack said.

"I saw you through the peephole."

"You drink coffee?"

"Copious amounts."

He stepped into the room, handed Effrem one of the cups, then took one of the seats beneath the window. He parted the draperies slightly to let in some morning sun. The rain had stopped falling the night before and temperatures were going to reach the mid-seventies. Outside, the pavement was already steaming.

Yawning, Effrem shuffled to the table and sat down across from Jack, who said, "I checked into you. You've got some big shoes to fill."

Effrem smiled. "At least she didn't wear high heels. Of course, you're living in a shadow of your own, aren't you? I checked into you as well. I thought you looked familiar. You don't look much like you do in the official family portrait."

"You're a journalist, and pretty good, from what I gather. If you're after a juicy story, you've already got one. If you run with what happened yesterday—"

"I'm not," Effrem said, taking a sip of coffee.

"Why?"

"Will you be offended if I say I'm after bigger fish?"

"If it's true, no," said Jack.

"Plus, cliché as it is, you did save my life. What kind of man would I be if I repaid that by feeding you to the wolves?"

"There are a lot of your colleagues who wouldn't give it a second thought."

"I'm not them, Jack. You have a saying here, yes? It's not who wins or loses, but how you play the game. My mother believed that, and so do I."

In theory Jack agreed, but in his business you didn't always have the luxury of being a good sport. In journalism you certainly had that choice, though it probably tended to make the job much harder.

"So, what game are you playing?" asked Jack.

"Are we still quid pro quo?"

"Yes."

Effrem took a sip of coffee, then stared into space for a few seconds as though assembling his thoughts. "Have you heard the name René Allemand?"

"It's familiar. French soldier, right?"

"Correct, though he's far from typical. I'll get to that later. Last year Allemand disappeared from his post, Port-Bouët, in Ivory Coast. He was there as part of Operation Unicorn—a peacekeeping mission after the civil war began. Initially there were rumors he'd deserted, but they were discounted. The consensus is that he was captured by one faction or another and then executed."

"No ransom or video?" Jack asked. "No one claiming credit?"

"Not that I've found. And no unidentified bodies in the area that might match him. I've got a couple more leads I'm checking."

"You said 'disappeared.' Does that mean he wasn't on patrol at the time? He was on the base?"

"That's another point of fuzziness," Effrem replied. "I'll come back to that. Anyway, I have reason to believe that not only is René Allemand alive, but his disappearance was staged."

"For what reason?"

"Quid pro quo, Jack," Effrem replied.

Though Jack had already decided to join forces with the journalist, the absurdity of the situation wasn't lost on him. Nor were the pitfalls. But nothing was certain in life, was it?

"A few nights ago the man you know as Eric Schrader tried to kill me."

Effrem leaned forward. "You're serious."

"Yes. And the man in the white Nissan is named Peter Hahn. Both he and Schrader are dead now."

"How?"

"Schrader walked into traffic and was hit by a truck. Hahn was killed by Möller at the preserve about ten minutes before he tried to kill you. I was following Hahn."

"Go back, start from the beginning. Leave nothing out."

Jack did this, starting with the incident at the Supermercado and ending with his and Effrem's encounter with Möller at the preserve. He added Doug Butler's revelation about the murder of Mark Macloon.

"So many questions," Effrem muttered.

"That makes two of us."

"Why were they trying to kill you? Why didn't this Peter Hahn finish the job? Why—"

Jack held up his hand. "To answer your first question: I have no idea. I've looked at this from all angles. I had a hunch, but that's looking less likely all the time. In all your digging you never came across my name?"

"Never. What about Hahn? What's his story?"

"Hard to say. He could have killed me twice and didn't. My guess is he was acting under duress. I also think he went to the preserve knowing he might not be coming back out."

"Pardon me?"

"I think he wanted me there as a witness. I've got some data from his computer. Once I sift through it we might have a better sense of things."

We. He had to admit feeling a certain relief having a . . . what? Partner? Ally? It wasn't the same as having Dom or Chavez watching his back, but Effrem Likkel was sharp and, unless Jack's character radar was flawed, trustworthy. And crafty. Effrem had been swimming with sharks for quite a while and was still alive. He could have worse allies.

"I have to say, Jack, you seem very resourceful for a financial adviser. That's what you do, yes?"

"More or less."

"You're good at saying a lot but imparting nothing."

Jack shrugged. "How am I supposed to answer the question?"

"You're not. It was an observation. I'm curious by nature;

too much so, if you ask my friends. Jack, we're going to have secrets from each other, I think. It's inevitable. As long as they don't impact our mutual goal, so be it."

"Agreed. Let's get back on track: You were following Schrader—is that his real name, by the way?" When Effrem nodded, Jack asked, "How did you come in contact with him?"

"Through René Allemand—or at least I'm fairly certain it was him. He and Schrader met in Lyon, France, in the first week of January."

Jack thought: *Lyon . . . January.* "Wait. Are you—"

Effrem was nodding. "I believe Eric Schrader and René Allemand met in secret, a week before the Lyon terrorist attacks."

13

Jack had already separated from The Campus by the time the attacks occurred, so his only information had come from the media, which had swarmed on not just the similarities to the Paris attacks but also the timing; Lyon had taken place almost exactly two months after Paris. The scale and casualties of the Lyon attacks had been smaller than those in Paris, but both had involved closely timed bomb detonations and mass shootings at restaurants and in the Metro. While no group had claimed credit and French authorities had named no suspects, there was no mistaking the modus operandi, which had uniformly been seen as an attempt to rub France's nose in it: Despite all your preparations, we can attack you in the same way, in any place, at any time. In many ways the Lyon attacks had had a greater impact on the psyche of the French populace and government alike.

Jack asked, "And you don't think this was a coincidence?"

"No," said Effrem. "How exactly, I'm not sure, but I think Allemand was involved in the attacks, but perhaps not of his own volition."

"What's that mean?"

"I think he was false-flagged. That's the right word for it, yes? When you're recruited by an enemy posing as an ally?"

"More or less. You think Schrader was ultimately pulling his strings?"

"My guess is no. I think he was simply acting as a handler. For whom, I don't know. Maybe for this Möller fellow. He sounds like a big question mark for both of us. By the way, do you know where he is?"

"No, but with any luck we will soon. I'm tracking his credit card. I've got his passport, so he may be desperate for options. Back to Eric Schrader: What can you tell me about him?"

"German national, age forty-one, former *Feldwebel*—first sergeant, I think you would call him—with the *Heer*."

Jack could guess the rest. "He belonged to Kommando Spezialkräfte—Special Forces Command."

"Yes. KSK. How did you know?"

Jack told him about the Eickhorn Solingen knife he'd taken from Schrader—or, more accurately, after Schrader smashed his head into a chunk of concrete and dropped the knife.

Effrem whistled softly. "Have you considered, Jack, that you may be part cat?"

"Cats land on their feet. So far I haven't been that graceful. Just lucky. What else do you have?"

"Two apartments Schrader had visited in the past few months, one in Zurich and one in Munich. The former seemed like a . . . temporary arrangement, I think, but the one in Munich might be his home base."

"Munich," Jack repeated. "That's where Hahn's daughter lives."

"No kidding."

"What makes you think Zurich was temporary?" asked Jack.

"I tracked him there after his first meeting with Allemand in Lyon. The place was luxurious, and in a well-to-do neighborhood. Schrader's place in Munich is a far cry from that. Unless he is slumming, the Zurich apartment belongs to someone else."

"Was Schrader in Munich when he left to come here?" Effrem nodded and Jack said, "At some point I'll want to see a detailed timeline of all this."

"I have one. Great minds think alike."

"And I'll want to know how you got from Allemand going missing in Ivory Coast to him and Schrader meeting in Lyon."

"Of course. We can meet again after you've had a look at Hahn's e-mails."

Still quid pro quo. While Jack didn't blame Effrem for it, he hoped the parrying wouldn't last much longer. The sooner they put their respective puzzle pieces together on a table, the better.

However, Jack wasn't confident he could make full use of Hahn's data. Even the simplest of e-mails was an alphanumeric stew that made Jack's brain hurt. He could parse only a fraction of the available information, and his go-to expert, Gavin Biery, wasn't an option. He'd have to come up with something else.

A thought occurred to Jack. "You said you're working the story freelance. Have you got anyone looking at this?"

"An editor, you mean? No one's seen any of it—with the exception of you now. This is my story. I'm going to deliver it whole."

"Who's footing the bill?"

"I am. Through credit cards."

Jack decided to twist the knife a bit, see if he could rattle Effrem. "You're practically Belgian Fourth Estate royalty. No gratuitous allowance? No trust fund?"

"Not until I'm thirty. By then, I expect to have my Pulitzer," Effrem said with a grin. "Jack, when I graduated from university my mother gave me a box of red pencils and a card that said 'Edit in good health.' So the answer to your question is no. No allowance. Just three nearly maxed-out credit cards and a box of red pencils."

Jack laughed. He couldn't help liking Effrem. Clearly Marie Likkel and Jack's parents had gone to the same parenting school—the University of Stand on Your Own Two Feet. For Jack that had meant joining The Campus; for Effrem Likkel, chasing down a story most journalists wait a lifetime to find. The guy had balls, no doubt about it.

Jack had to wonder if his getting involved in all this would help or hurt the Belgian. At least three people were dead so far and Jack had come damned close to being the fourth. If he included the casualties from the Lyon attacks the tally skyrocketed. The players involved seemed snatched from a grab bag: a missing and possibly traitorous French soldier, a German Special Forces operator posing as a crackhead, a widowed and lonely man from Rose Hill, and a terrorist group who, despite striking the second-deadliest blow on French soil in history, had disappeared from the world terrorism stage. *Then there's me*, Jack thought. He was the outlier. Why?

"What about you, Jack?" asked Effrem. "Aren't you supposed to have bodyguards or something? Oh, wait, is there a helicopter on the roof as we speak?"

Jack laughed again. "If there is, it's not for me."

Effrem finished his coffee, tossed the empty cup into the garbage can beside the dresser. "So what now? Do we keep going together, or separately?"

Jack considered this for a few seconds. "I hope I don't live to regret this, but I vote for the former."

Effrem nodded. "Seconded."

Jack left Effrem with two chores: One, inspect his rental SUV for any trace of the second round Möller had fired. It was beyond a long shot and would almost certainly turn out to be worthless, but Stephan Möller had in front of witnesses committed murder and attempted murder on a government nature preserve. Jack had an unspent, custom-made bullet from the murder weapon, and if one of Möller's frangibles had embedded itself in Effrem's SUV they also had a spent round for comparison. The chances of Stephan Möller seeing the inside of any courtroom were virtually nonexistent, but it was an avenue Jack wasn't going to ignore.

The second chore he gave Effrem was to pack his bags and be ready to move within five minutes of Jack's call. If he got a ping on Möller's credit card they'd have to scramble to catch up.

When Jack got home he switched on the TV and surfed the local channels. When he reached WJLA, the Washington-area ABC affiliate, a news ticker crawling at the bottom of the screen read ". . . the man's name has not been released pending notification of family . . ." Jack waited, watching for the story to reappear. "A Rose Hill man was found dead at a local nature preserve. The police, who were called to the scene this morning by a hiker, have said only that the circumstances are suspicious. The man's name has not . . ."

They'd found Hahn. Jack hoped it wouldn't take them long to notify Belinda. It was going to be gut-wrenching for her, but better than waiting and wondering why her father wasn't answering his phone or returning e-mails.

Unbidden, an image popped into his head: Hahn falling back against the bridge railing, sliding down onto his butt, then staring up as Möller lifted the pistol to his eye . . .

Should he have anonymously tipped off the police? Hahn had sat dead overnight in the rain before being found. It was irrational, Jack knew, but the thought of it set his belly churning.

Now the waiting began. Waiting for Stephan Möller to pop his head up.

Waiting for the knock on his door that would answer the question of whether a witness had spotted him at the preserve.

At four-fifteen Jack's phone chimed. It was a text from Effrem:

The police were here.

Jack felt his heart thud against his chest wall. He forced himself to slow down and think. Could they still be there, looking over Effrem's shoulder? he wondered. Effrem was a decent guy, of that Jack was certain, but having the police show up on your doorstep asking hard questions about a murder could rattle anyone into submission. Or was this ingrained overcautiousness flavored with strains of paranoia?

Jack texted back: **And?**

Effrem answered: **They had an anonymous tip that my vehicle had been seen in the preserve.**

Jack had to step carefully. **Go on.**

Anonymous tip, came Effrem's reply. **No one else there. What's that sound like to you?**

It sounded like Möller was trying to slow down his pursuers. This was actually good news. If Möller had already left the country, he wouldn't have bothered with the ruse.

Effrem added, **I told them I drove past the preserve but turned around when I realized I was lost. They seemed okay with it.**

Glad to hear it, Jack wrote. **Want to grab a cup of coffee?**

Jack gave Effrem a twenty-minute head start, then left the condo, headed west on Wythe Street, and spent ten minutes driving around the area, watching for signs of surveillance before heading to Washington Street, where he turned left.

Out his driver's-side window he scanned the Starbucks parking lot for Effrem's SUV. It was there, hood pointed toward the street. Jack kept going, looking for a phone booth, a rare beast these days, it seemed. He spotted one on a corner outside a liquor store and pulled to the curb. He dropped some change into the slot and dialed Effrem's phone.

"Do you have anything you want to tell me?" Jack said when he answered.

"What? Huh?"

"Think it through."

"Oh . . . I see. I'm alone, Jack. They talked to me for about ten minutes, then left. You're a source, Jack—well, more than that, but you get the point. I don't betray sources."

"Wait two minutes, then go back to your hotel."

Jack hung up and made his way back to the Starbucks. Right on time, Effrem's SUV pulled out of the parking lot onto Washington and headed north. Jack hung back, let a couple cars get between them, then followed Effrem back to the Embassy Suites. As far as Jack could tell, neither of them was being followed.

Ten minutes later he was knocking on Effrem's door. Effrem answered, let Jack in, and shut the door behind him. "Was that all really necessary?" Effrem asked.

"Yes," replied Jack. "Don't take it personally. You're sure you weren't seen leaving the preserve?"

"There was no one. When I got to Cardinal, I turned left

and headed straight to 495. I didn't see another car until I got on it."

"Did the cops mention Hahn's body?"

"No, but I asked. It seemed the natural thing to do. I'd seen it on the news and had been near a preserve recently, and now they were questioning me."

Jack asked, "How did they react?"

"They didn't. Aren't cops the same everywhere? Stone-faced. I showed them my professional website, made up some story I was working on about McLean's rapid de-gentrification, showed them some notes, then asked if I could interview someone about the death. They told me to call the Public Information Office, then left. They seemed annoyed."

Effrem had handled himself well. He was quick on his feet and not easily shaken. Jack asked, "Is that true, about McLean's de-gentrification?"

"I have no idea. Is that even a word?"

"Smartass."

Jack hadn't taken two steps back into his condo when his cell phone chimed again, this time with an Enquestor alert. Möller's credit card had been used to buy thirteen dollars' worth of gas and five dollars's worth of "grocery items" at a Mike's Mini Mart in West Haven, Connecticut. As Möller hadn't *immediately* boarded an airplane, it now seemed unlikely he had a second passport, but perhaps he'd stashed a second vehicle.

"West Haven?" Jack murmured. "What the hell's in West Haven?"

Nothing. But due north through Vermont it was only five or so hours from the Canadian border. *Possible*, Jack thought. Vermont shared about ninety miles of border with Canada, much of it rugged and isolated.

Jack checked the route from Alexandria to New Haven on his phone's map application: three hundred fifty miles; a six-hour drive. Too long. He got on his laptop and went to a travel website, selected Washington Dulles as the departure point, and chose Hartford as the destination. No. The earliest flight was tomorrow morning. He repeated the search, this time with New York JFK as the destination.

There was one flight remaining today, a JetBlue shuttle leaving in three hours.

14

By ten-fifteen they were leaving the airport in their rental car, a Hyundai Sonata, and getting on the Van Wyck Expressway into Queens. With Effrem navigating from his cell phone screen, Jack took them across the Bronx-Whitestone Bridge and picked up Interstate 91, which they would take north.

Thirty minutes outside New Haven, Jack got another Enquestor alert. "Read it," he told Effrem.

"Uh . . . something about a motel in Hartford, the Best Western. A room charge, I think."

"How long ago?"

"Sixty minutes. Where is Hartford?"

"About forty-five minutes north of New Haven. And that much closer to the Canadian border."

"Why stop in Hartford?" asked Effrem. "Why not find a rest stop and pull in for a nap? Why advertise your location?"

"Maybe he thinks he's free and clear. I left his credit card as I'd found it. If he'd been suspicious he wouldn't have used it at all."

"I guess. What do you want to do?"

Jack thought about it. If Möller had stopped for the night, they had plenty of time to set up on the hotel before morning; if, on the other hand, Möller paid for a room and then just kept heading north, they'd already lost him. They'd never catch up.

"Let's do the legwork," Jack replied.

Shortly before midnight they pulled into Mike's Mini Mart, which was on Saw Mill Road not far from 95. Jack was relieved to see the interior lights on and a glowing neon sign that read OPEN 24/7. He pulled into a spot in front of the propane tank cage and shut off the engine. A couple teenage boys sat on the curb before the store's doors, drinking slushies and balancing their skateboards on their laps.

"They should be in bed," Effrem said. "Isn't this a school night?"

"Go have a chat with them. I'll go inside."

Jack opened his door and Effrem went to do the same.

Jack turned back. "I was kidding. Stay in the car or you might end up wearing a slushy."

Jack opened the Sonata's rear door, grabbed his jacket, and put it on. He pushed through the doors and walked straight to the counter. A teenage boy with a wispy light brown mustache and acne on his chin stood at the register. Jack's odds had just improved.

"Evening," Jack said.

"Hey."

"Wondering if you can help me." Jack pulled his private investigator's badge out, showed it to the kid, returned it to his blazer pocket. "What's your name?"

If the kid was going to balk at Jack's credentials, it would happen now.

"Uh, Nate."

"How long have you been here, Nate?"

"Eight months, I guess."

"Tonight," Jack replied.

"Oh. Since four."

"I'm looking for a guy. He bought gas here at five thirty-five." From his pocket Jack took the photocopy he'd made of Stephan Möller's passport folder. "Does he look familiar?"

"I don't know. Maybe."

Jack put a little steel in his voice. "He was here, you were here. He came in and bought snacks. Do you recognize him?"

"Yeah, I think so."

Jack gestured at the trio of tiny black-and-white video monitors sitting on the counter beside the register. "Do those work?"

"Yeah, but just the pumps. The one in here is busted."

"Show me," Jack replied. Without waiting to be invited, he walked behind the counter. The kid hesitated a bit now, so Jack nudged him. "It was about five-thirty. Which pump did he use?"

"Uh, okay, just a sec." Nate knelt before a DVD-like box on the shelf beneath the monitors and rewound the footage until the counter read *1725*.

"You're doing good. Think back. Which pump?"

"Three. No, two. That monitor on the left."

"Okay, hit fast-forward," Jack replied. "Easy, not too fast . . ."

When the counter clicked over to *1731* a dark blue or black sedan pulled up to the pump. The driver's-side door opened. Out climbed Stephan Möller.

"Hey, that's him," Nate blurted, apparently warming to the task. "It's him, right? That beard."

"Yep, that's him. You've got a good eye. What'd he buy? Don't think, just say the first thing that pops into your head."

"Chocolate milk, tuna sandwich, bag of Fritos."

"Can you enlarge that pump picture? I need the license plate."

"I can zoom in, but it's not optical, y'know. Just digital. It'll get all pixelated. It might be better on the office TV, though."

"Where?"

"Straight down that hall on the left."

"Thanks."

Jack followed Nate's directions and pushed through a swinging door bearing the scrawled words "Employees Only" in red permanent marker. At the front of the store a warning *bing-bong* chime sounded. Jack glanced over his shoulder to see Nate giving him a thumbs-up. *Most exciting day of the kid's life*, Jack thought.

He was in a storeroom. On the left-hand wall was a steel shelving unit holding rolls of toilet paper, bottles of floor cleaner, and cases of soda and water. In the corner on a small card table sat an eighteen-inch flat-screen television. Nate had already transferred the security camera image to it.

"Zooming in," Nate called enthusiastically.

"Ten-four," Jack replied.

Slowly the image enlarged, panning and tightening on Möller's license plate as it expanded.

"Hold," Jack called. The image froze.

Nate was right. The image was growing badly pixelated, but it would have to do. Emblazoned across the bottom of the plate were the words TAXATION WITHOUT REPRESENTATION, which made it a Washington, D.C., plate, but the camera angle was such that Jack could make out only the first two letters: EB. The four characters to the right of the D.C. flag icon were blurred.

Jack returned to the front of the store. Nate asked, "Get it?"

"Got it. I owe you, Nate. See you later."

Jack was halfway to the door when Nate called, "Hey, he took a map or something, too, if that's important."

"What map?" asked Jack.

"From the rack beside the chips. Behind you."

Jack turned. The rack was waist high, with vertical slots for twenty to thirty travel brochures, maps, bus and train schedules, and restaurant coupons. "Nate, did you see which one he took?"

"No. Sorry, man."

"Just one, or a bunch?"

Nate screwed up his face, thinking. "Not a bunch. One, maybe two."

Jack returned to the Sonata and climbed in beside Effrem, who asked, "Any luck?"

"I'm not sure."

"What's that mean?"

"Möller took something—a map or brochure."

"So?" asked Effrem.

"How long between the time he got gas and he checked into the Best Western in Hartford? Five hours, give or take? But it's at most an hour drive. What was he doing the rest of the time?"

Jack was missing something. He could feel it nibbling at the back of his brain like a song you can hear but can't name. He closed his eyes and mentally backtracked . . .

"Huh," he muttered.

He got out of the car and went back into the store. "Hey, Nate, you still have that picture on the office TV?"

"Yeah."

"You're the man. Be right back."

Jack walked to the office and sat down at the card table and stared at the image of Möller standing beside his car. Jack leaned in, squinted.

The car was a Ford Fusion Hybrid.

Jack walked out, gave Nate a "Dude" and a thumbs-up, then returned to the car.

"Effrem, Google this: Ford Fusion Hybrid tank size and range."

It took thirty seconds. "Fourteen gallons, forty-three miles per gallon, highway. So that makes the range . . . six hundred miles per tank."

"It's three hundred miles from D.C. to here, and he put in thirteen bucks' worth of gas. That's, what, seven gallons?"

"Yeah, half a tank," Effrem confirmed.

"Then he drives forty miles up the road to Hartford and checks into the Best Western. Why stop here? Why not push through?"

"Maybe he was hungry."

"And why use a credit card for such a small purchase? Möller's too savvy to not be carrying emergency cash."

"You think he's leading us? Leaving bread crumbs?"

"It's very possible." The idea that Möller would use the credit card Jack had found in the Alexandria motel had been a stretch from the beginning. Wanting to believe in something isn't the same as it being real, Jack reminded himself.

On the other hand, why would Möller bother playing them at all? Why not disappear? Jack had no answer.

He grabbed his phone and called up the last Enquestor alert on Möller's credit card: Best Western Hartford Hotel & Suites, 185 Brainard Road, Hartford, CT 06114. Pre-auth room charge. Jack showed Effrem the screen and said, "It's a pre-authorization, not a charge."

"Oh, man, sorry."

"Forget it. I should have caught it. Möller doesn't have a passport or he would've gotten on a plane, and you can't rent a room without showing identification."

"What now? Have we lost him?"

"Go back inside and grab brochures for Amtrak, Metro-North, and Greyhound. Nate's seen my face too much."

Effrem did as Jack asked and returned a minute later with the schedules. He handed them to Jack. "What're you thinking, Jack?"

"Greyhound allows prepaid or gift tickets. Someone else buys it and the passenger picks it up at the station with a password. As for trains, it's not as easy to get a ticket without ID, but it's doable. Once you're aboard, if you can bypass the random checks, you're set. Somebody like Möller would find a way to make it work."

Jack scanned the schedules. Greyhound, Amtrak, and Shore Line East were hubbed at New Haven's Union Station, about ten minutes to the north. But the Metro-North Railroad had a station in West Haven itself—about two hundred yards south of Mike's Mini Mart.

Jack explained his thinking to Effrem, who said, "Let's say you're right. Let's say he stopped here because it's close to the West Haven Station. Where could he go from here?"

"And why not drive another ten minutes to New Haven?" Jack added. "Union Station would give him a lot more travel options."

Jack could feel his brain spiraling as it tried to plot all the variables. He caught himself and pulled back. He'd learned the hard way that the only way to stop the spiral was to make a choice, to take action, whether right or wrong.

Jack studied the schedules again. On instinct, he dismissed Greyhound. Too confined, he decided. If pressed, it would be easier to maneuver and hide on a train. That left trains: Amtrak, Shore Line East, Metro-North.

Jack said, "Let's think it through: If Möller's goal is still the Canadian border, he'd want as straight a shot as possible. Shore Line only goes as far north as New London, so scratch that. If he takes Amtrak up to Boston, he's got a lot more destination options, but more transfers."

Effrem added, "More chances for delays and complications."

"Bigger stations, tighter security."

"That leaves Metro-North," Jack said. "And leaves him . . ." He traced his finger down the schedule grid. "The Waterbury line. Two departures: seven-thirty and ten-fifty."

Effrem checked his watch. "It left over an hour ago."

The train had left, but Jack was by no means certain Möller had been on either it or the earlier one. As reasoned as their speculation was, it was still speculation.

But maybe there was a way to confirm it.

In that moment Jack felt the absurdity of the situation crash down on him. One phone call to the Secret Service and Möller's chances of escape would drop to almost nil. Yet here he was sitting in the parking lot of a gas station posing

as a private investigator with a rookie journalist while studying train schedules.

Just hit speed-dial, Jack thought. *And it's finished.*

No.

He could sense he was locked into the same course he'd
chosen just hours after he'd been attacked. He was being
impulsive, undisciplined. Focused on the trees rather than
the forest. All the things Gerry Hendley had cited as reason
for his exile from The Campus.

Jack didn't care.

With Effrem navigating, Jack drove south down Saw Mill
Road to Railroad Avenue and turned right. The station's
parking lot, divided into north and south areas that sat astride the tracks and the red-brick and glass terminal building,
was several acres of blacktop enclosed by a hurricane fence.
Under the glow of streetlamps Jack could see that this lot,
the northernmost one, was a quarter full of cars, but there
were no pedestrians visible. It made sense. The evening's last
train had left.

"You really think he'd park in here?" asked Effrem.

"No, but I would if I were him. As long as you're paid up,
nobody'll give your car a second glance. If I were on the run,
I wouldn't bother hunting for public parking in the middle
of the night."

"A lot of cars."

"Don't kill the mood," Jack replied.

When Jack reached the lot entrance he turned in, then followed the pavement arrow into the west side of the lot.

"We're looking for a dark Ford Fusion Hybrid," Jack said.

"D.C. plates, right? EB something."

"Right, but don't key on that. He might have swapped plates."

Jack started down the first row, eyes fixed on the cars out his window while Effrem did the same on his side, murmuring to himself, "No, wrong color . . . Uh-huh, that's an SUV . . . Oh, close but not quite right . . ."

Jack had to smile. It was hard not to like the kid.

Kid, Jack thought. He didn't have that many years on Effrem—not chronologically, at least.

They reached the end of the row, turned, and started down the next one.

"Ford Fusion," Effrem called out. "Can't tell if it's a Hybrid. Maryland plates."

"Check it," Jack replied, braking to a stop. "Check the interior for a bottle of milk, sandwich wrapper, bag of Fritos." As Effrem climbed out, Jack added, "And a rental agency sticker, or what looks like the remains of one."

Effrem returned thirty seconds later. "Nothing. Not a Hybrid."

They kept going and finished the remaining two rows

without finding another match. Jack returned to the entrance, crossed over to the adjoining lot, and continued the search. More confident now, they made short work of the first and second rows and were turning into the final one when Effrem blurted, "Gotcha!"

Jack stopped the car and glanced out Effrem's window.

Black Ford Fusion Hybrid, D.C. plates, EB 9836.

"Go," Jack said.

Effrem hopped out, circled the car, peeking in windows as he went, then returned. He leaned down and said through the open window, "Frito bag, but no sign of a rental sticker."

"You're sure?"

"One hundred percent."

Jack had assumed Möller's backup car would have also been a rental. If this was a privately owned vehicle, they had another lead. "Take a pic of the VIN," he ordered.

15

WEST HAVEN, CONNECTICUT

They had a victory, but it was minor and fleeting. Möller was likely on Metro-North's Waterbury branch, but there were six stops north of West Haven, from Derby-Shelton to Waterbury, and according to the schedule the train had already passed all but the final two: Naugatuck and Waterbury itself.

Jack said, "I need a route."

"On it," Effrem said, studying his phone's screen. "Head back down 95. We're looking for Prindle Road. It's thirty-five minutes to Naugatuck. We'll miss the train by five minutes."

"Waterbury, then."

"Forty minutes. It's going to be very close."

A few miles outside West Haven, as Prindle turned into Highway 114, Jack set the Sonata's cruise control a couple miles an hour faster than the speed limit.

They drove in silence for a while, Jack lost in a game of "What if Möller does X?" and Effrem checking his e-mails. After a time he asked Jack, "Did you get a chance to sort through Hahn's e-mail data?"

"Not yet. I don't know how much I'll find. Beyond the basics, it's not my area of expertise."

"Why didn't you say so? I know a guy."

"What guy?"

"A source," Effrem said. "One of my many. Well, okay, he's a friend. He's trustworthy. I'll shoot him an e-mail and see if he's willing."

"Okay."

Jack had a list of questions he'd been compiling for Effrem, starting with how he got onto the disappearance of René Allemand in the first place. Next: How had he not only succeeded in discovering Allemand was alive, but also been able to track him down when both France's military and civilian intelligence agencies had failed at the task? And why did Effrem believe the soldier had been false-flagged?

The list went on. For now Jack decided to satisfy his

general curiosity about the man himself: "Tell me about Allemand."

"He's a lot like you and me, actually."

"How so?"

"Born into a legacy," Effrem replied. "René's a fifth-generation soldier going back to the Napoleonic Wars and the Battle of Waterloo. René graduated top of his class at Saint-Cyr, the first of his line to pull it off."

Saint-Cyr, or the École Spéciale Militaire de Saint-Cyr, was France's version of West Point. Both of them had been founded at roughly the same time, in 1802. Jack had encountered a few Saint-Cyr graduates along the way. Without exception, they were superb soldiers.

Effrem went on. "After that, Allemand had his choice of assignments, but he took the hard route, which surprised no one, from what I gather. He requested and got the First Riflemen Regiment out of Épinal."

"Standard infantry," Jack replied.

"It had been his father's last command. Whether he did it to honor his dad or to better himself is anyone's guess."

"Either way, he's not the type to desert."

"No chance. According to friends of his I interviewed, René loved the Army. He'd been wishy-washy about taking up the family business, so to speak, but once at Saint-Cyr he blossomed."

"It stands to reason if he'd been captured and then managed to escape he would have let someone know."

"I would think so. No one's heard from him; not his father, not his friends, or even his fiancée. Unless he's lost his mind, he's doing what he's doing for a reason."

"How sure are you the man you saw in Lyon was René?"

"Ninety percent. I'll show you the photos later. You can judge for yourself."

"Good," Jack replied. "And the next time we come up for air I'll want details, Effrem. All of them."

"Deal."

They weren't going to make it, Jack estimated, watching the Sonata's dashboard clock. They were ten minutes from the Waterbury station; the train was only four minutes out. Unless Möller lingered, they would miss him.

Jack pressed harder on the gas pedal.

They passed Waterbury's city limits sign eight minutes later. At Effrem's direction, Jack turned onto Freight Street, crossed the Naugatuck River, then turned right onto Meadow. A couple hundred yards down, past a red-brick clock tower and across the street from a park, lay the train station, little more than a long, raised platform covered by an aluminum awning lit by sodium-vapor lights. There appeared to be no office and no parking lot attendant.

"The lot's coming up on our right," Effrem warned.

Jack slowed the Sonata. He checked the dashboard clock. The train had pulled in five minutes ago.

Outside his window Jack glimpsed a figure—a man, based on his build and gait—passing beneath the trees bordering the sidewalk. He glanced that way, but in the darkness he could make out no details of the person's face. As far as Jack could see the man carried neither luggage nor a briefcase.

"Is it?" asked Effrem.

"Can't tell. You see anyone else around?"

Effrem was staring out his window at the train platform. "A couple people, but they're too far away for faces."

Jack pulled to the curb and watched in his side mirror as the figure continued down the sidewalk. After a few moments the person was swallowed by the shadows.

Jack made a snap decision. "You're driving. Go down the block, then left on the next street. See if you can catch him coming the other way. Be careful. If it's him, he knows your face. Stay in touch."

Jack opened his door and climbed out. As Effrem slid into the driver's seat, he asked, "What're you going to do?"

"Check out the platform."

As Effrem pulled away, Jack crossed the street to the

entrance of the dirt parking lot and paused beside a tree. He pulled up the hood on his jacket; Waterbury was a good three hundred fifty miles north of Alexandria, and Jack could feel the difference in the chill night air.

The lot before him was large, enough for a few hundred cars, but he counted fewer than ten, all in a line before the platform. The area had an industrial feel, with what looked like warehouses on the opposite side of the tracks, and beyond these the highway cloverleaf. Jack got the impression the station had been placed here out of necessity rather than for convenience. In the distance Jack could hear the faint rush of cars on I-84.

After a minute of watching and seeing no one, Jack strode into the lot and headed for the platform. He broke into a jog, playing the desperate traveler afraid he'd missed the train. Fifty feet from the line of parked cars, one of them started backing out, its reverse lights bright in the darkness. It was a white Subaru.

"Ah, man . . . !" Jack called, and stopped running. He checked his watch, then called, "Damn." At the same time he reached under the hem of his jacket and drew his Glock.

Whether his showmanship was impressing the car's occupant Jack didn't know, but he decided to err on the side of caution. If Möller was inside this car, Jack was an easy target. He had no cover.

Twenty feet ahead, the Subaru slowed its reverse course,

did a Y-turn, then headed toward Jack. The headlights pinned him. The car picked up speed, veering slightly left to take Jack down its passenger side.

As the Subaru drew even with him, the passenger window rolled down a couple of inches. Through the gap came faint strains of easy-listening jazz.

"Hey," a man's voice called from the car's darkened interior.

Jack could see nothing through the window.

"You looking for the train? You just missed it."

Jack dropped his head in dejection, shading his face with the hood, and raised his hand in thanks. "Really? No one else got off?"

"Just my wife. Sorry."

The voice didn't sound like Möller's, Jack thought. Unless he was disguising his voice, that was. It seemed unlikely. Why stop at all? Why not just drive on past?

"You need help or something?" the voice asked.

"Nah, thanks," Jack replied in his best SWNE—Southwestern New England—accent. In his own mind he sounded like an extra from the set of *Good Will Hunting*. "Ah, man, she's gonna kill me."

As the car sped off, Jack memorized the license plate, then watched it turn onto Meadow Street and head south toward the highway.

He holstered his Glock, pulled out his cell phone, and

speed-dialed Effrem. It rang four times, then went to voice mail. "What the hell?" Jack muttered. "Come on, pick up . . ."

He dialed again and got the same result. He texted in all caps: **CALL!**

Jack walked the rest of the way to the platform. Nine or so cars remained in the lot. Better safe than sorry. As he neared the compact car's parking spot something on the ground glittered under the platform lights. He pulled out his penlight and panned the beam ahead.

Sitting in the dirt was a small mound of glass that reflected green.

Auto glass. From where the Subaru's driver's door would have been.

Jack turned and started running.

The pursuit was hopeless, he knew, but realizing he might have just been talking to Stephan Möller, might have just watched him drive away into the night, overrode rational thought. He turned onto Meadow and sprinted down the sidewalk toward the next intersection, some three hundred yards away, glancing at the parked cars as he went.

Panting, his lungs burning slightly in the cold air, Jack reached the intersection and stopped. He looked left, saw nothing, looked right. A quarter-mile away, a white car sat at a stop sign, its right blinker on.

The car turned and disappeared.

Jack's cell phone trilled. He pulled it out, checked the screen: Effrem.

"Where are you?" Jack demanded.

"Uh, I don't know. A few blocks away from the train station. Just a sec . . . State Street. I thought I saw him, so I followed. It wasn't him."

No kidding. God damn it!

"Why are you breathing hard?" asked Effrem.

16

WATERBURY, CONNECTICUT

By the time Effrem had made his way back to the intersection, Jack had already logged into the Enquestor portal and punched in the Subaru's license-plate number. As he climbed into the passenger seat the results appeared on his screen:

Eunice Miller
6773 Willow Drive
Wolcott, CT 06716

Without looking up, Jack said, "Find a coffee shop or diner or something."

Using his Yelp app, Effrem located a Denny's on Division Street, about a mile to the west, and started heading that way.

Having caught his breath and cooled off, Jack said as calmly as possible, "The next time I call you, answer the phone."

"I couldn't. I was afraid I'd lose him."

Jack repeated, "The next time I call you, answer the damn phone."

"Okay, I will. Sorry."

"And I didn't tell you to follow anyone. I told you to keep in touch."

"You didn't tell me not to follow anyone, either."

Jack bit off the sharp reply on the tip of his tongue. Effrem had a point. They lived in different worlds. What Jack considered obvious or implied might be neither to Effrem. Effrem didn't have the experience to know when initiative crossed into recklessness, or perhaps even the discipline to pull himself back across the line.

A thought struck Jack: He could easily imagine John Clark or Gerry Hendley saying the same things about him. And they wouldn't be wrong.

"What's happened?" asked Effrem.

"I think I might have been talking to Möller. He was right there, within arm's reach," Jack replied, then explained the encounter.

If it had been Möller, had he recognized Jack? Back at

the nature preserve Möller's attention had been divided between Effrem and his SUV and Jack and his Glock, and Jack's cap had been pulled low. It was a toss-up.

"If it was him, why stop at all?"

"To check me out, maybe."

"Maybe, but they've tried to kill you twice. It sounds like you were an easy target standing in that lot. Why not take advantage of it?"

"Good point."

Then again, if Möller's sole focus was escape—

Jack caught himself. *Leave it.*

The world in which he and the others at The Campus moved was one where there could always be a wheel within another wheel. At some point you had to stop the recursive thinking and make a choice. For someone like Jack, who was blessed or cursed with a fertile imagination, this was often challenging. It wasn't unlike chess, a game he both loved and hated. He had read somewhere that the number of available piece positions was represented by a 1 followed by 43 zeros, and this was governed by strict rules and limited space. Neither of these factors existed in Jack's world.

Still, Möller's theft of the Subaru seemed like a departure for him. So far the man's E&E—evasion and escape—plan had felt paint-by-numbers, with little room for improvisation. He'd used a credit card to call attention to his location, a risky but often effective strategy, especially when those pursuing you are part of a larger, less nimble force like the Secret Service or FBI, both agencies you'd expect to be called on to hunt down the would-be assassin of a VIP. Perhaps Möller and whoever he was working for had planned his exfiltration based on this assumption. Schrader was ex–German Special Forces. Möller might be as well, in which case their doctrine might be steeped more in rote response than it was in flexibility.

If so, stealing a car didn't fit.

Unless Möller's calf wound had worsened enough that he went off script.

Effrem pulled into the Denny's lot and chose an open parking spot before the main doors. "Coffee? Anything to eat?"

"Just coffee."

Jack used Enquestor to pull up Eunice Miller's Department of Motor Vehicles file. The picture showed a woman with a plump face and short gray curly hair. Her birth date put her at sixty-five years old. According to Jack's map, her address in Wolcott was about fifteen minutes north of Waterbury, off Highway 69.

Effrem returned with two large cups of coffee. He handed one to Jack, then climbed into the driver's seat.

Jack showed him Eunice Miller's picture. Effrem said, "Sweet old lady?"

"The question is, was she on that train?"

"And did Möller do something to her?" Had she been in the car with Möller, alive and bound, or dead in the backseat?

Shit. Jack chastised himself for not having checked the scrub brush bordering the train platform. If Eunice Miller had been lying there dying, only feet from where Jack had been standing . . .

"I need a pay phone," he said.

"There was one a few blocks back."

Effrem pulled out, retraced their route, and did a U-turn and pulled to the curb beside the pay phone. Jack got out, mentally rehearsed, then dialed 911. When the dispatcher answered, Jack put some gravel in his voice and said, "Hey, I was jogging by the train station on Meadow. I thought I heard a woman screaming. Either on the platform or on the train, I don't know which."

He hung up.

Please don't find anything.

At this time of night the roads were largely deserted, so they made the trip to Wolcott in ten minutes. Eunice's house, what looked like a post–World War II single-story saltbox on Google Earth, sat two blocks behind a bowling alley off the town's main thoroughfare.

When Effrem pulled up to the stop sign at the head of

her block, Jack ordered him to cross the intersection and then pull to the curb and turn off the headlights.

"How are we going to do this?"

Jack didn't respond immediately. He didn't have an answer.

"Okay, let's drive past, see if we spot her car," Jack said.

Effrem turned the Sonata around, then turned onto Willow.

"Should be the fifth or sixth house on your side."

Looking out Effrem's window, Jack watched for house numbers. When they drew even with 6773, Effrem started to slow. "Don't," Jack warned.

There was no white Subaru in the driveway, and no garage.

Two houses down, there was a Subaru. The plate matched the one from the train station. Parked ahead of the Subaru was a green Rav4 SUV. The home, which was a duplicate of Eunice's except for light yellow paint instead of white, was dark save the porch light and some yellow light around the edges of the front-room curtains.

"That's not her house," Effrem said.

"No, wrong number."

"So—"

"I don't know. Keep going, turn the corner, pull over."

Effrem did so, easing the Sonata beneath the low-hanging boughs of an elm tree and then killing the headlights.

Jack punched this new mystery address into Enquestor. The deed record came back to Kaitlin Showalter.

Jack had tilted the phone so Effrem could watch. Effrem said, "Kaitlin's a younger name."

Jack went to Facebook and searched for her name, then sorted through several of them before finding the profile that listed a hometown of Wolcott, Connecticut. Kaitlin was single; her occupation: insurance agent in Bridgeport. Her last post, prefixed by a smiley-face emoticon, was from two hours ago:

Long day, but almost over! Car wouldn't start, late for work, missed lunch. Now some General Tso's chicken and an egg roll for my savior, Eunice.

Kaitlin had borrowed Eunice's car to get to the train station for her daily commute.

Effrem said, "Could it have been her boyfriend?"

"Maybe," Jack replied. Then: "No. The guy said 'wife.' He was picking up his wife."

Unless Kaitlin had failed to change her relationship status on Facebook, which seemed unlikely, given how much time she spent there, she was still single.

"So how can we be sure it's Möller inside?"

The quickest way to answer the question was also the one Jack didn't like: Break into Kaitlin Showalter's house and, if Möller was inside, snatch him up. Of course, as before, that approach left him with a captive and all the problems that came along with that. The other option was to wait until Möller moved again and follow. If the man was using Kaitlin's house as an impromptu safe house/aid station, he was likely to make it brief.

For a moment, Jack reconsidered his approach to Möller. Maybe this was one of those times when violence would solve problems. Kill Möller and be done with it. It would make it harder to find the answers he needed, and if there was such a thing as good luck, Jack had already strained his. Committing cold-blooded murder on U.S. soil would give him a constellation of bigger problems, starting with a moral line he could never uncross.

Jack turned in his seat and reached into his rucksack, rummaged for a moment, then came up with a GPS tracker, the same kind he'd planted in Peter Hahn's car.

"What's that?" asked Effrem. Jack explained and Effrem said, "Let's just hope he doesn't switch cars again. Plus, we're making a lot of assumptions about—"

"Welcome to my world," Jack said. "Wait here, I'll be right back."

17

WOLCOTT, CONNECTICUT

With the tracker in place, they found another all-night diner off Lakewood Road, ordered a late dinner/early breakfast, then settled in to wait. It was just after three a.m. If Möller didn't move before dawn, they'd go back to the house.

They sipped their coffee in silence until Jack could feel the caffeine hit his bloodstream. He took a few moments to assemble his thoughts, then said, "Ready for some questions?"

Effrem replied, "As long as they don't require deep thinking. If I don't get my usual fourteen hours of sleep a night, I'm not at my best."

"Tell me how you got onto the Allemand story."

"I got curious. Of course, soldiers disappear all the time, especially in places like Afghanistan or Iraq. Or Ivory Coast.

It's like your Old West out there. But it struck me that Allemand's disappearance wasn't getting the attention it warranted. In French military circles his family is renowned. And it's a juicy mystery story. No one, not even his father, Marshal Allemand, spoke out very much."

"Maybe the marshal simply accepted it. It comes with the job."

"Would you accept it if your son went missing? You would want answers."

"True," Jack replied. "So you got curious and then what? Went down to Ivory Coast?"

"Exactly. I tried to get some interviews through military channels but got nowhere, so I managed to track down some of René's friends that were still stationed at Port-Bouët Airport, Abidjan. That's where Operation Unicorn was headquartered. What they said about René's disappearance didn't add up; he didn't fit the profile as either a deserter or someone reckless enough to get kidnapped. They all knew the off-limits areas of Abidjan. In fact, René was usually the voice of reason, the one talking others out of straying."

Jack noted Effrem's use of Allemand's first name. It was as though Effrem was speaking about a close friend. The young journalist was invested not only in discovering the truth behind Allemand's disappearance, but also in finding the man. Did that mean Effrem had lost objectivity? Jack wondered.

"Keep going," he said.

"In the previous eighteen months two other soldiers had gone missing. One had been kidnapped by COJEP—the Young Patriots, it's an anti-UN group—and then released. The other deserted and was apprehended a week later in Korhogo."

"In other words, you found no cases of a soldier simply vanishing."

"Not one. But here's where it gets interesting. After I'd interviewed all the military personnel willing to talk, I started visiting social hangouts favored by the soldiers—most of them in Koumassi commune—"

"Which is what?" asked Jack.

"Communes are sort of like boroughs in New York City. Koumassi is one of three on Little Bassam Island in the middle of Abidjan Harbor. It's about two miles from Port-Bouët Airport."

"Got it."

"Eventually I found one local, a café owner in Koumassi named Fabrice, who claimed to have seen René kidnapped off the street by men in balaclavas."

"Did he report it?"

"He claimed to have, but I couldn't corroborate it. I believed him, though."

"Why?" asked Jack.

"One, I did a little digging into the man; and two, instinct. I assume you did something similar after we met."

Jack had indeed. He nodded. "So Fabrice gives you this story. What did you do with it?"

"Not much. Shortly after I interviewed Fabrice, I had to go back to France. When I started investigating the story, one of the first things I did was contact his fiancée, Madeline. Of everyone involved she seemed the most frustrated over René's disappearance—or, more accurately, the lack of outcry. We hit it off, I suppose you could say. Anyway, Madeline claimed to have heard from René."

"How?"

"Text message. It wasn't from his phone, of course, but she was certain it was him. His phrasing, his punctuation, a few words here and there convinced her it was René."

"What did he say?"

Effrem pulled a small brown leather notebook from his jacket pocket, opened it, then flipped to a page. "His first message was, 'Am alive. Tell no one. Trouble. YIA, R.'"

"What's that mean, 'YIA'?"

"Yours in all. Yours in body, mind, and spirit. It was their shorthand for 'I love you.'"

This was a credible detail. Not proof of life exactly, but it certainly had the ring of truth to it. "She got other messages, I assume?"

"Three others. One a message he wanted passed to his father, the other a time and place Madeline and he were to meet. Before you ask, she refused to tell what the message was. She did give me the details of the meeting, though."

"Why trust you with that but not the message to Marshal Allemand?"

"I don't know," replied Effrem. "At any rate, I went ahead of her to the meeting place—Parc de la Feyssine in Lyon. I kept my distance and took pictures. Here." Effrem slid his phone across to Jack. "The first two pictures are of René before his deployment to Ivory Coast, then during. The last three are of him meeting with Madeline."

Jack scrolled through the album. Each picture showed a young man in his late twenties with a lantern jaw and thin lips. In the first two images his black hair was buzz-cut; in the last three, longer, almost to his shoulders. Effrem was right: If these most recent images were not of René Allemand, then they were of his clone.

"I'm convinced," Jack said.

"Good. René and Madeline met for about ten minutes before parting. I followed him to a brasserie near Claude Bernard University. That's where I first saw Eric Schrader. I figured I already had a strong enough link to René through Madeline, so I decided to follow Schrader."

"Which is how you eventually got here," Jack finished.

"Correct. After Zurich and Munich."

"Where Schrader did what?"

"In Zurich, he went to an office building in the business district. I don't know which office specifically, however. I have a list. And he also stayed at that apartment I mentioned—"

"The one you don't think belongs to him."

"Yes. As far as Munich goes, aside from his apartment, Schrader went to the gym, a couple nightclubs, and a restaurant and market near his place."

"Have you and Madeline talked since you left Lyon?"

"A few times, but she's cooled off on me. Evasive. I think whatever René said to her scared her badly. And believe me, she's no mouse. You have to be tough to get accepted by the Allemand clan—especially the marshal."

Jack was nodding, but his mind was elsewhere, assembling a tentative plan of action. Once they'd taken the Möller pursuit as far as it could go, Jack would want to reinterview everyone Effrem had talked to, starting with Fabrice the café owner in Abidjan and Madeline in Lyon before scouting the locations in Zurich and Munich. So all he'd been doing was walking in the dark, grasping at whatever came into reach and hoping it would lead him to a light switch.

Jack realized he'd become so engrossed in the saga of René Allemand that he'd momentarily lost sight of his overriding objective: discovering who was trying to kill him and why. The truth was, the only direct connection between himself and René Allemand was Eric Schrader. Beyond that, were the attempt on Jack's life and the disappearance of Allemand interwoven, or were they simply a coincidence? If the former, how, exactly?

Jack had already asked Effrem this very question, and now he put it to him again. Effrem replied, "If there's a deeper connection, I haven't found it. As I said, you can study my notes. Maybe I've missed something."

"You told me you thought Allemand might have been false-flagged. What makes you think that?"

"Madeline let slip something the last time we talked. She said René had told her, 'He isn't who he claims to be.'"

Jack's cell phone beeped. He checked the screen, then said, "Möller's on the move."

18

O nce in the car, Jack watched his phone's screen as the red blip that represented Möller's car—or what he hoped was Möller inside Eunice Miller's car— left Willow Drive and slowly made its way to Highway 15, where it headed north. Jack let Möller get a mile's head start, then followed.

Möller headed almost due north, making his way first to 84 before picking up I-91 at Hartford. An hour later they crossed the border into Massachusetts. An hour after that they were into Vermont, following 91 along the Connecticut River, which separated Vermont and New Hampshire. Soon swaths of snow began to appear in the ditches along the highway and in crescents around the bases of pine trees. City-limits signs for distinctly colonial-sounding towns passed outside the Sonata's windows—Putney, Walpole, Charleston—and with each passing mile the terrain grew more rural until each side of the highway was hemmed in by thick forest.

"Where the hell is he going?" Effrem asked. "Canada?"

"I don't know, but I'm thinking about ending this," Jack replied.

"What's that mean?"

"Deserted rural road in the middle of the night," Jack said. "Force him off the road and—"

"And what?" Effrem blurted, clearly alarmed. "Drag him into the forest and tie him to a tree? You're kidding, right?"

"More or less."

At five a.m. Jack's phone trilled. Effrem checked it. "Google news alert?"

Jack felt his heart drop. "I set one for the Waterbury train station and the Metro-North. Read it."

Effrem scanned the story. "It's from WTNH. Let's see . . . Oh, God, Jack."

"What?"

"Unidentified woman found in bathroom of an out-of-service Metro-North train. Badly beaten, airlifted to Hartford. Police investigating."

Jack clenched his hands on the steering wheel. "Bastard."

Twenty minutes later Effrem said, "He's slowing down. Getting off the highway. He's stopped. Turning east."

Jack pressed down on the accelerator and soon the Sonata's headlights panned over a sign: EXIT 8 / VT-131 / ASCUTNEY-WINDSOR. "That's it," said Effrem.

"Where is he?"

"Half-mile ahead, turning left onto . . . I don't see a label. I'll let you know when."

Jack took the exit, then turned east. Another couple hundred yards brought them to a north-south intersection.

"Turn left."

Jack did so. A sign beside the road reading CONNECTICUT RIVER BYWAY was followed shortly after by one reading ASCUTNEY—POPULATION 540.

Now they were paralleling the river, heading north along Ascutney's main thoroughfare. Where they'd seen little traffic on Highway 91, here there was none. Ahead, what few traffic lights existed all glowed green. At each intersection Jack looked left and right and saw only darkened roads and the occasional lighted window or porch light.

"Slow down," Effrem said. "He's only a few hundred yards ahead."

Jack took his foot off the gas pedal and let the car coast until the speedometer fell below fifteen miles per hour.

"He's turning left onto . . . Black Mountain Road. There's a campground up here; the turn is just after that. Okay, you can pick up speed a bit."

Jack did so, and soon his headlights flashed over another sign. To the right, STAFFORD CONSTRUCTION; to the left, BLACK MOUNTAIN ROAD. "Effrem, do a search for Stafford Construction."

"Checking on it. He's going very slow, Jack. You think he's lost?"

Jack doubted this. Men like Stephan Möller rarely got lost. Jack flicked off his headlights, turned onto Black Mountain Road, and again dropped his speed. The moon was partially obscured by clouds, and the trees crowding the road left Jack almost blind. He concentrated on the yellow center line and kept going.

They drove in silence for two minutes.

Effrem said, "My data connection is getting spotty. I think he's turning again. Right this time, about a hundred yards ahead. Looks like a quarry, maybe? What's he want with a quarry?"

"Hell if I know."

To their right, the shoulder sloped away into a shallow draw choked with knee-high weeds. At the bottom Jack could make out what looked like a curving road, its dun-colored gravel bright in the moonlight.

"Not this one," Effrem said. "The turn-in is just ahead."

"I know."

Jack stopped the car, then put it into reverse and backed up until only the hood was exposed beyond the ridgeline. They watched the road.

A few moments later, headlights panned over the gravel, and then, as Möller's white Subaru came into view from the left, the headlights went dark. The car disappeared from view behind the trees.

Jack asked, "Are you on map view or satellite?"

"Map. It's all my phone's connection can do to keep up. It looks like the bottom of this draw is the entrance to the quarry."

"Switch to satellite view and tell me what you see."

"It's going to take a minute."

Jack put the car in drive again, then turned onto the shoulder and down into the draw, carefully picking his way between the scrub bushes. He put the transmission in neutral and shut off the engine, letting momentum carry the car forward. Jack steered right until they were almost brushing the draw's slope, then braked to a stop and put the car in park. He rolled down both their windows and listened for a few moments. He heard nothing but the croaking of frogs. He asked Effrem, "You still have him?"

"Hold on, the satellite view is resolving . . . I'm seeing what looks like construction equipment; bulldozers, excavators, trucks . . . You think he's meeting someone?"

"Either that or he's picking up another vehicle."

"I don't see anything but heavy equipment down there."

"That overhead view could be months old," Jack replied. "Come on, let's go have a look."

Jack grabbed his binoculars from his rucksack, opened his door, climbed out, then headed left toward the slope. Effrem followed a few steps behind. When they reached the edge of the gravel road, Jack stopped, knelt down. Across the road was a mound of dirt as tall as a two-story house.

Jack whispered to Effrem, "Step where I step, stop when I stop." Effrem nodded firmly, but Jack could see the barest glint of fear in his eyes. "You'll do fine."

Jack crept toward the edge of the road, then peeked right into the quarry. The entrance road they were standing beside opened into a tiered pit divided into navigable tracts by mounds of gravel and sand. Here and there dirt berms covered in stubby trees were backlit by the night sky.

Jack saw no sign of the Subaru. He checked again through the binoculars—nothing.

Hunched over, he crossed the road to the dirt mound and made his way around its back side, where he again stopped. He felt a tap on his shoulder and turned. Effrem mouthed something to Jack, then handed him the phone. Jack took it and studied the screen. In Jack's ear Effrem whispered, "Stafford Construction. It's just over that hill. Do you see what I see?"

Jack zoomed in on the image. The compound of Stafford Construction was sandwiched between Black Mountain Road and the Connecticut River on a swath of land about a quarter-mile wide and a mile long. Along the western edge nearest this quarry sat a collection of outbuildings. To the east beside the river, the compound was bisected by a long paved road bordered by what looked like construction trailers and elongated storage containers.

Something was off about the image, Jack realized, trying to pin it down.

From the darkness came the slamming of a car door.

Startled, Effrem looked over his shoulder. "Was that Möller? Is he moving?"

Jack ignored him. He zoomed in on the Stafford compound and began scrolling the image. Then he saw it.

Painted onto the pavement at each end of the compound road was a white X.

Jack knew the symbol: Permanently Closed Runway.

Möller was here for the next leg of his E&E plan, but it didn't involve a vehicle.

In the distance Jack heard the faint whine of an aircraft engine.

Jack said, "Stay close."

19

They continued forward, following the base of the mound until they reached the next track. Here Jack paused, then sprinted left, eyes scanning for the Subaru's white paint or for movement. Möller would be moving east, Jack guessed, toward the sloped tree line bordering the compound, but where exactly? The cell phone's satellite image wasn't fine enough to show footpaths, only roads.

From somewhere ahead Jack heard the scuff of a shoe on gravel, then the trickling of loose sand. Jack froze, crouched. Effrem bumped into him, whispered "Sorry."

Jack closed his eyes, trying to latch on to the memory of the sound. *Which direction? Left*, he decided, around the mound of sand before them. Jack stood up and kept going until he reached the mound, which he skirted to the right.

The sound of the aircraft engine was increasing now in both pitch and volume. Jack looked up, but his view of the compound was obscured by the mound. Effrem tapped him on the shoulder, then pointed right. The trunk of Möller's Subaru jutted out from behind the next gravel pile.

Think it through, Jack commanded himself. Don't rush. If Möller was aware of their pursuit, this quarry would be the perfect ambush point; the terrain was ideal, as was the timing. When better to tie up loose ends? If Möller was lying in wait, he would be either on forested high ground along the quarry's east edge or behind them, waiting for them to make their way toward the compound.

It wasn't lost on Jack what kind of man he was dealing with. Möller was ruthless and cool, that was a given, but Jack had a hunch that Möller and Eric Schrader shared similar backgrounds: German Special Forces. This knowledge didn't make him feel any better about the task before him.

Doesn't matter, he thought. Ambush or not, they had to reach the airstrip, and their time was dwindling. Monitoring GPS beacons and credit cards was one thing; actively tracking an aircraft was beyond Jack's resources. It was time to grab Möller and figure out the sticky logistics later.

He leaned back and whispered to Effrem, "Keep your eyes on our six until I tell you otherwise. Stay close. We're going for Möller."

"What's our six?"

"Behind us."

"Got it."

Jack drew his Glock, raised it to ready-low, stepped out from behind the mound, and headed east. He used what little cover they had the best he could, moving from gravel pile to dirt berm in hopes they would shield the two of them from any watching eyes. If Möller lay behind them, Jack could only hope Effrem's eyes were faster than the German's trigger.

Ahead lay the last gravel pile; past it, fifty feet of open ground to the eastern edge of the quarry.

"It's coming closer," Effrem whispered.

Jack heard it, too: the plane's engine, somewhere to the north. Making its final approach. Jack glanced that way but saw nothing moving in the sky. "Eyes on our six," Jack warned.

Jack reached the mound, circled left, stopped, scanned ahead. Nothing was moving. The trees on the slope were so thick they appeared as a solid mass, only their serrated crowns identifying them as having individual trunks.

Jack spotted an anomaly at the base of the slope, a thumb of dirt disappearing into the trees. It was a trail. And a perfect bottleneck. Moving from the relative light of the quarry into the darkness of the forest they would be temporarily blind. Easy targets.

Stop. He was, as John Clark would say, spiraling into paralysis by analysis.

"Effrem, directly ahead, you see that trail that leads to the trees?"

"I see it."

"We're going for it. Stay directly behind me. If shooting starts, run back, find cover, and stay out of sight. I'll come for you."

Jack didn't wait for an answer, but rather stood up and headed for the trees at a fast walking pace. He kept his eyes scanning the tree line, never settling in one place, letting his peripheral vision do the work; movement was easiest to spot on oblique angles. Something about the cones and rods in your eyes, Jack thought absently.

Jack spotted movement out of the corner of his, but far to the left and above. He glanced that way and saw a single-engine plane skimming over the trees to the north, bleeding altitude as it lined up with the runway. It disappeared behind the roof of the northernmost outbuilding.

Jack started trotting now. Heart pounding. He raised the Glock to shoulder height, making sure he still had a ready lock on his sight picture, then lowered it slightly.

Behind him, Effrem stumbled. "I'm okay, I'm still here," he said, panting.

"When we get into the trees, step left off the trail and stop."

"Right. I'm scared."

"Don't think. Just move."

The tree line loomed, and then they were into it, the darkness enveloping them. Jack stopped, crouched, side-stepped right into the foliage. If Möller was hiding somewhere on the trail above, their ploy wouldn't fool him, but it would give him dispersed and obscured targets.

Effrem whispered, "How long do we wait?"

"We don't. Stay close."

Jack stood, pushed off, and charged up the trail. The grade steepened and soon his legs were burning. Branches snagged his clothing. Leaves slapped his face. The trail snaked left, then right in a switchback. Jack bounced off a tree trunk, corrected his course, and kept going. Ahead he saw a roughly oval gap in the trees; through it, the corrugated steel wall of a building.

Five feet before the gap Jack said, "Dodge left," and again they separated and crouched off the trail. Jack peeked out, saw nothing.

"I don't hear the engine," Effrem said.

"Me neither."

Now doubt slipped into Jack's mind: If they failed to stop Möller before he reached the plane, what then? Open fire on the plane? What if the pilot was an innocent by-stander? And what if that innocent bystander spotted their kidnapping of Möller?

While Jack was ninety-nine percent sure it'd been Möller behind the wheel of Eunice Miller's Subaru, neither he nor

Effrem had actually laid eyes on the man since Mike's Mini Mart in West Haven. Moreover, if they'd managed to track Möller this far without alerting him, doing so now would be a mistake. *Damn it!*

Don't spook him, Jack. Best to let Möller go about his business and hope they could pick him up later.

Effrem said, "Jack, what're we doing?"

To the east, the plane's engine began idling up.

"Jack . . ."

"We're letting him go."

"What! You said—"

"I changed my mind. How're your eyes?" Jack said, handing the binoculars across to him. "You've got one job: Grab that plane's tail number before we lose it."

"And while I'm doing that, you're doing what?"

"Making sure Möller isn't getting ready to snap shut the bear trap."

Before Effrem could protest or ask another question, Jack got up, covered the last few feet to the trail opening, and stepped through. Before them was a line of eight outbuildings arrayed from north to south. Between each, a narrow alley led to the tarmac.

Which way? The plane had landed north to south, which meant the pilot's takeoff would be on the reciprocal.

"Follow me."

At a trot, they moved along the buildings, Jack clearing

each alley before they proceeded across. As they passed the sixth intersection Jack glanced right and saw the plane taxiing north along the runway. It was picking up speed, the engine spooling up for takeoff. Despite being a single-engine prop aircraft, this was no Cessna or Piper Cub, Jack realized. It was bigger in both fuselage and wingspan.

"Keep moving," Jack ordered, and started sprinting.

They reached the last building and Jack skidded to a stop, peeked around the corner. It was clear. "Go," he told Effrem, who scooted past him, sprinted to the building's front corner, and knelt down. He lifted the binoculars.

The plane swept past, its navigation lights flashing against the gray tarmac. Then it was gone, out of sight behind the trees.

"Effrem?" Jack called. "Tell me you got it."

"I got it."

20

With his head resting against the window seat bulkhead, Jack dozed, occasionally opening his eyes to see the darkened landscape below had changed, until finally he saw in the distance the twinkling lights of Munich. He yawned and stretched. Beside him, Effrem was typing on his laptop.

A Lufthansa flight attendant's voice came over the intercom and announced the plane's descent to the airport, first in German and then in English. Well familiar with the procedure, Jack was already returning his seat to the upright position.

"Tray table," Jack told Effrem.

"Huh?"

"Before you get scolded by Dagmar."

Their attendant, a statuesque blonde with an easy smile, had been downright Teutonic in her cabin management. The way Jack had caught Effrem staring at her, he guessed Effrem was either attracted to her or frightened of her. Or both.

"Shoot, sorry." Effrem powered down the laptop and stowed it in his messenger bag beneath the seat. "Did she catch me?" he asked.

"Do you want her to catch you?"

"Shut up. So what's our first order of business when we land?"

"Hotel, sleep, coffee, then strategy."

They'd been running hard for almost forty hours, first from Alexandria to Vermont and then, with the departure of Möller's plane, from Vermont to JFK Airport and finally back to Dulles. By ten a.m. they were back at Jack's condo and looking for flights to Munich. They found one, a nonstop Lufthansa leaving out of Dulles that afternoon. Once aboard the plane, Jack had promptly buckled his seat belt, then drifted off to sleep.

Effrem's capture of the plane's tail number tightened Jack's focus on Germany and Switzerland, but it also raised more questions. According to Switzerland's Federal Office of Civil Aviation website, the plane in question, a Swiss-made Pilatus PC-12 NG, registry HB-FXT, belonged to a private citizen, a Zurich resident named Alexander Bossard. Both Jack's and Effrem's initial research into plane and man turned up little aside from the fact that Alexander Bossard could afford a $4 million private jet and dispatch it across the Atlantic to rescue Möller from a defunct airstrip in rural Vermont. Was Bossard also the owner of the luxury apartment Eric Schrader used while staying in Zurich? It seemed a reasonable hunch.

Jack's larger concern was for Belinda Hahn's safety. Her father had intimated she was in jeopardy but hadn't gone any further. With her father dead, a tied-up loose end, presumably, was she slated for the same fate? Or did he have it wrong? Though her e-mails to Peter had been those of a loving daughter, Jack couldn't discount the possibility that she was a willing participant in all this—whatever "this" was. Whatever the truth, reaching out to Belinda Hahn was at the top of Jack's to-do list.

Having vacationed in Munich, Jack returned to what he knew: Hotel München Palace in the city's Bogenhausen Quarter, a long stone's throw from the Luitpold Bridge and the Isar River, which split the city into east and west. Jack had spent hours walking the river trails and parks along both banks.

Thirty minutes after clearing customs and picking up their rental car, a Citroën, they were pulling to a stop outside the München Palace's front doors. It was almost three a.m. The bellman was at their car door instantly, opening it before walking to the trunk and retrieving their luggage.

"*Danke schön*," Jack said, handing him a tip.

"*Es ist mir ein Vergnügen.*"

Jack headed for the doors. He noticed Effrem wasn't following but rather standing, staring at his cell phone. His face was drawn. Jack walked back to him. "What's up?"

"Kaitlin Showalter died yesterday afternoon."

This news changed Jack's plans. Kaitlin Showalter was dead because she was on the wrong train at the wrong time and she had something Stephan Möller needed, a car. What might he or his compatriots do to Belinda Hahn, who was much more than a target of opportunity? Jack wondered if they were already too late.

He allowed himself and Effrem ninety minutes of sleep, then left the hotel and headed west on Prinzregentenstrasse in the predawn light. The city was already coming alive, with morning delivery trucks and buses making their stops. Despite sitting just thirty miles from the northern edge of the Bavarian Alps, Munich had had a wet and hot spring, and already the trees were well into bloom.

Staring out the window, Effrem said, "So much greenery. And it's so tidy. I have been here a dozen times and I can count on one hand the pieces of trash I've seen on the street."

"German efficiency."

Once they were across the Isar River, Jack followed the

car's in-dash navigation system until they reached the Neu-aubing district. Belinda's apartment building, a five-floor quadplex, sat several blocks south of Bodenseestrasse, surrounded by boutique restaurants and pubs, all of which were closed and dark. It was not yet six o' clock. He wanted to catch Belinda before she left for the day.

Jack slowed as he passed the front door of her building. The lobby was dimly lit, but Jack could make out a two-door vestibule with an intercom system on the wall. He saw no doorman.

Jack debated whether he should simply ring Belinda's buzzer and ask to see her. He quickly rejected the idea. What would he say? *I was there when your father was murdered?* If she had any sense—and based on her e-mails to Peter, she had plenty—she would call the police. Plan B.

Jack circled the block until he found an all-night grocery store, and left Effrem waiting in the car. He came back out with a brown paper bag overflowing with vegetables. Jack climbed in and handed the bag to Effrem, who said, "I don't cook."

"You should learn. Essential skill for a bachelor."

"Who said I'm a bachelor?"

"You aren't?"

Effrem hesitated. "Yeah, I am. But I'm offended you assumed so."

Jack returned to Belinda's apartment building and found

a parking spot down the block. He shut off the headlights and the engine. "You see her front door?"

Effrem turned in his seat and looked out the Citroën's rear window. "Yes."

"Stay here and watch. You'll know what to do when it's time."

"Oh, good," Effrem replied. "Could you be a little more vague, please?"

"If you'd like."

They sat for a few minutes, watching her door until Jack was satisfied they hadn't been followed. Then he took the grocery bag from Effrem and climbed out. He walked down the block and took up station beneath a tree directly across from Belinda's door. He kept his eyes fixed on the elevator at the far end of the lobby.

Jack's ploy depended on two factors: timing and the kindness of strangers.

Ten minutes later the first of these factors fell into place. Through the vestibule doors he saw the down arrow above the elevator door light up.

He trotted across the street, opened the first vestibule door, then fumbled his grocery bag and let half the contents spill onto the floor. Jack knelt down and grabbed at a head of lettuce that was rolling away from him. Across the lobby, the elevator doors parted. He reached up and, using his own condo keys, tried to slip one of the keys into the inner door's lock. He dropped the keys, reached for them, and let a trio of oranges tumble from the bag.

"Einen Augenblick. Warten Sie ab!" a female voice called. A moment. Wait.

Jack looked up to see a woman in her early thirties in jogging clothes, her blond hair in a ponytail, hurrying toward the door.

"Danke," he called.

He scooted back so she could open the door, scattering the oranges as he did so.

"Lassen Sie mich Ihnen helfen!" the woman said. Let me help you.

She knelt down and began helping Jack collect his runaway fruit.

Jack gave her a sheepish smile and muttered, *"Danke schön."* When they finished, he stood up, thanked her again, and stepped into the lobby as she held the door for him.

"Schönen Tag." Have a good day.

"Dir auch."

Jack waved as she jogged away.

A few moments later Effrem walked up to the door and Jack let him in. They headed toward the elevators. "Smooth, Jack," Effrem noted.

"Who can't sympathize with a bumbling idiot?"

They took the elevator to Belinda's floor. Her apartment was at the end of the hall.

"Now what?" asked Effrem. "What're you going to say?"

It was a good question. Jack's grocery-bag ploy had gotten them inside, but he still faced the same problem as before: how to make contact with Belinda without spooking her. He'd already put the possibility she was involved in all this on a mental side burner. Chances were, unless she was a monster, she had nothing to do with her father's death; whether this also applied to the attempt on Jack's life was something else. One step at a time.

"I'm going to let her speak for herself," he replied.

Jack handed Effrem the groceries, then pushed the buzzer button. Thirty seconds passed. Jack buzzed again. Now he heard movement from inside, feet stomping on wood floors. He caught a flicker of movement behind the peephole.

"Wer ist das?" a woman's voice said through the door.

Jack took a breath, then said, "Fräulein Hahn?"

"Ja? Wer ist das?"

"Sprechen Sie Englisch?"

A long pause. "I speak English."

"Miss Hahn, I live in Alexandria, not far from your father's house. I have something of his. May I slide it under the door?"

Another long pause. "Yes, go ahead."

From his jacket pocket Jack took one of the sudoku books he'd found in Peter Hahn's house. Like all of the others, this one's inside cover bore an inscription: "To your good brain health. Love, Belinda."

Jack slid it under the door and waited.

"I am calling the police," she said finally.

"Please, don't," he replied. *Both feet, Jack. Dive in.* "I was there. I saw what happened to him. I want to help."

"Who's that with you?"

"A friend. Listen, dial the police, dial 110, but keep your finger on the zero. If we do something you don't like, make the call."

"I have pepper spray."

"Good. Go get it. Belinda, listen: I know the name of the man who killed your father. I came to help."

After a long thirty seconds, the dead bolt on the door clicked open.

21

MUNICH, GERMANY

Belinda hadn't been bluffing, Jack noted as they stepped through the door. Belinda did have pepper spray, not one of the pocket models, but rather a soda can–size version designed for bears. She stood at the end of the hallway, pointing the nozzle at them with one hand while clutching her cell phone in the other. Lying at her feet was the sudoku book.

"Is that thing real?" Effrem murmured to Jack. "Do they make Mace that big?"

"Yep. And it's more powerful than regular pepper spray."

Over the years Jack had been stabbed, slashed, beaten, and doused with OC, or pepper spray. He would take the first three over the fourth any day. Pain was manageable.

OC was pure, unmitigated misery so intense it made time stand still. The memory of it churned his stomach.

"Stop right there," Belinda ordered.

Peter Hahn's daughter was barely five feet tall, petite, with short dark hair and rectangular-shaped glasses. She wore a pair of gray sweatpants and a red Washington Wizards T-shirt.

"You, with the mop on your head!" she barked. "Close the door and lock it."

Effrem touched his index finger to his chest. "Me?"

"Yes, you! Do it or I'll give you a shower!"

Jack believed her. Peter Hahn hadn't raised a pushover. Jack said to Effrem, "Move very slowly."

With his free hand held above his head, Effrem shut and locked the door.

"What's your name?" Belinda demanded.

"I'm Jack. This is Effrem."

"Do you have guns?"

"No."

"Show me. Lift your jackets and turn in a circle." They both did so. She asked, "What happened to my father?"

In the hallway Jack had rehearsed a gentle answer to this question, but Belinda Hahn was tough. And angry. She deserved an unvarnished answer. "He was shot. Once in the stomach, once in the head."

"Where in the head? I know, so don't lie. The police told me."

"The right eye," Jack replied.

Belinda's hand on the OC canister wavered slightly, then steadied.

Jack said, "Effrem and I have been following the man who shot your father. His name is Stephan Möller. Does that name mean anything to you?"

Belinda ignored him. "Why didn't you go to the police?"

"Möller was working with a man named Schrader. Schrader tried to kill me, and your father had been helping him."

"You're lying! My father would never—"

"I think he helped Schrader as little as he could, and even then he didn't want to. He had a chance to kill me twice and didn't do it. Belinda, men like Möller and Schrader don't worry much about police. Do you understand what I mean?"

"Maybe."

Interesting answer. "And I think he was trying to protect you. Is that possible?"

"Possible," she replied.

Effrem asked, "In what way?"

Belinda jerked the OC canister toward him. "Flip that light switch beside you."

Effrem did so and the overhead hallway light came on.

Canister extended, Belinda took three steps forward, raised her cell phone, and took a picture of Jack and Effrem's faces. She said, "Now you're in my cloud. And my Photobucket account. The police will check it, you know, if something happens to me. They have face-scanning technology now, too."

"We'd be lucky to make it out of the city," Jack replied. "Belinda, if we meant you harm, we wouldn't have knocked on your door. You can either trust us or tell us to leave. Either way, you're in charge."

After a few moments Belinda lowered the OC canister. "You want coffee?"

Belinda's apartment was small, with a kitchen/nook, sitting room, and one bedroom. It was tidy, the decor all blond wood and stainless steel. Her tiny balcony was a hanging forest of ferns so thick Jack could barely see the building across the street.

Belinda finished making the coffee and they sat down at the nook table. Beside her Belinda placed her cell phone and her father's sudoku book. The OC canister she kept in her lap. "Trust but verify," she told them.

"Wise," said Effrem.

"Jack, where did you get this book?"

"After your father died I went to his house."

"You broke into his house."

"Guilty. I found the sudoku books, your e-mails to him, and your address."

"You said you thought my dad was trying to protect me. Why?"

Jack recounted his backyard confrontation with Peter. Belinda asked, "Those were his words, 'I don't know if I've done enough to save her,' and 'They'd never made the threat plain'?"

"Verbatim. Who was he talking about?"

"I can't be sure."

Effrem replied, "But you have a hunch."

Belinda took a sip of coffee, then absently spun her cell phone on the table, staring at it for a few seconds before answering Effrem's question. "Jürgen Rostock. He's my boss."

Jack knew the name. Jürgen Rostock was the CEO of Rostock Security Group. RSG specialized in personal and site protection—essentially, bodyguards to the rich and famous, and physical security for vulnerable business facilities. Across Europe RSG was so well regarded that it no longer sought clients; clients sought RSG, and Rostock took on only the most important VIPs.

As Hugo Allemand was in France, Jürgen Rostock was a celebrity in Germany, a dairy farmer who'd risen through the ranks of the *Heer* to *Generalleutnant*, and eventually to inspector general of the Bundeswehr. After retiring in 2004, Rostock had served under two chancellors as minister of defense, then left public service and started RSG. Twice since then Rostock had been urged to run for president of Germany, and twice he had declined. He was a fixture on the European social scene, contributing to a plethora of charities, as well as sitting on the board of half a dozen foundations whose mandates ranged from providing potable water for rural African villages to exposing child labor abuses in Indonesia.

Apparently Effrem knew the name as well. "Jack, one of Rostock's postings was commander of Division Schnelle Kräfte—the Rapid Forces Division. Kommando Spezialkräfte falls under its command."

Eric Schrader was former KSK, Jack reminded himself.

As he was with clients, Jürgen Rostock was highly selective with his employees. The vast majority of his recruits were plucked from the ranks of GSG 9, the Federal Police's counterterrorism unit, Bundeswehr Special Forces, military intelligence, and the BND, the country's Federal Intelligence Service.

Jack had no trouble imagining Stephan Möller as having come from those ranks.

Belinda said, "My father was KSM. Special Forces Marine, S2, intelligence. He and Rostock were friends. About a month after I graduated from U of V, I moved here."

"Has Rostock ever threatened you? Can you think of any reason why your father would think that?"

"No, Jürgen's never threatened me." Belinda sighed, shrugged. "My father was a smart man. Grounded. If he thought that, he would have had his reasons."

Effrem asked, "What exactly do you do at RSG?"

"I'm one of Jürgen's personal assistants. He has two, one for here in Munich, and another that travels with him. We alternate every three months. Right now I'm here."

"Has he said anything about your father's death?"

"He left me a nice voice mail yesterday and sent some flowers. He sounded sincere. Sad. Since I got the news I haven't been back to work. I don't know what to do. Mom's buried in Alexandria, but part of me wants him back here with me."

Jack called up his cell phone's photo album and handed it to her. "That first picture is of Stephan Möller, the second is of Eric Schrader."

"I don't recognize Möller, but this other one, Schrader . . . I think so. I think I saw him in Jürgen's office a few weeks ago. Is this the one that tried to kill you?"

Jack nodded. "I'm trying to find out why."

Belinda looked at Effrem. "And why are you here? What's your story?"

"I'm a journalist. I'm working on a story that involves Schrader."

"I don't want to end up in the newspapers," Belinda said.

"You won't," Jack replied. "Have you noticed anyone following you? Anything out of place here? Does anything in your life feel . . . off?"

"You mean aside from my dad being murdered? No, nothing."

"Scroll to the next picture," Jack said. She did so, and Jack said, "That's an e-mail he got from you a few weeks ago."

Belinda was already shaking her head. "I didn't send this. I mean, it's from my Gmail, but I didn't send it. He mentioned something about a link that didn't work, but I didn't think anything of it."

"How do you use your Gmail?"

"In browser, mainly at work and at home."

"Does anyone have your password at work?" asked Efrem.

"If they do, they didn't get it from me. What is that, by the way, that link?"

"Malware of some kind," Jack replied. "We're looking into it."

Belinda laid Jack's phone on the table and pushed it away as though it were a rotting egg. "This is too much. Why can't we just call the police? You can tell them about Möller and Schrader and this e-mail and they'll—"

"Eventually we might, but we need to do some more digging first."

Effrem asked, "Does the name René Allemand mean anything to you?"

"No. I can't believe this!" Belinda ran her fingers through her hair and squeezed her eyes shut. "There's no way that Jürgen ordered my dad killed. That's what you're suggesting, aren't you?"

"I'm saying there's a connection. What it is we don't know."

"You're going to have to do better than that."

"We will. Give us some time."

Belinda frowned at them. "Why are you here, anyway? What do you want from me?"

"That's up to you," Jack replied, then asked, "If you choose not to help us, we'll go away and leave you alone. Right now, though, we've hit you with a lot of stuff. Can you take some time off work?"

"Jürgen told me to take as much as I wanted."

"Good. Do you have someplace else you can stay?" When Belinda nodded and opened her mouth to answer, Jack cut her off. "Don't tell us where. I'm going to give you a prepaid phone. Keep it close by. You have a lot to think about. Call if you want to talk."

Outside, the sun had come up and a couple of the street's restaurants had opened. People sat under umbrellas and awnings having coffee and breakfast.

Jack and Effrem headed back toward their car.

Effrem said, "What're the chances she's already on the phone with Rostock?"

"She's too smart for that," Jack replied. "I hope."

In the end, Belinda Hahn had three choices: confront Rostock, call the police, or decide to trust and help the two strangers who showed up on her doorstep with a story that had turned her world upside down.

Following Effrem's directions, Jack turned the Citroën back onto Bodenseestrasse and headed west, then picked up Highway 99 and turned north.

Effrem dialed his cell phone, then said, "Mitch, I know you're there. We'll be there within the hour, so make some coffee." Effrem disconnected and said to Jack, "My IT guy. He's not an early riser."

"IT guy or hacker?"

"Either/or. He's not a black hat, if that's what you're asking. Perhaps dark gray, but not black."

According to Effrem, Eric Schrader's apartment was in the Hasenbergl district, a more run-down area of the city and home to a large immigrant population. "I wouldn't call it crime-ridden," he told Jack. "But it does have something of a reputation. It's not exactly the sylvan getaway we had in Neuaubing."

As the highway began looping east again, Effrem had Jack get off and turn south on Dachauer Strasse. Almost immediately the terrain took on a more industrial feel, with fewer trees and more concrete, side streets lined with 1960s-era row houses, and gray, blocky apartment buildings with graffiti-festooned walls.

"You came here alone?" Jack asked.

"Came here?" Effrem replied. "I staked out his place overnight. I'm tougher than I look, Jack."

"Apparently so. Maybe tough enough to handle Dagmar."

"Sylvia," Effrem corrected. "Up here, turn right, then left at the next corner."

Jack made the turns, and Effrem tapped on his window. "Here."

Out the window, across a vacant lot turned dumping ground, sat a two-story cinder-block building fronted by a set of broad concrete steps that led to a breezeway entrance. A trio of teenage boys sat on the steps, smoking and laughing.

"Schrader's place is on the second floor, third window in," Effrem said. "The one with the blackout curtain."

Jack saw it. Effrem was using the term "window" generously. Like those of his neighbors, Schrader's apartment window was more a horizontal slit covered by bars.

"Apartment or prison?" Jack asked.

Effrem laughed. "Not far off. It used to be a halfway house for recovering heroin addicts. Besides, if you had a dump for a backyard, would you want a generous view of it? What are we hoping to find in there, anyway?"

"No idea. I'll take anything."

He meant it. He could feel frustration itching in his brain, growing each time he added another entry to his "Who Wants Me Dead?" list. If Belinda was right and it had been Eric Schrader she'd seen at RSG's headquarters, they had a connection to Jürgen Rostock, but a tenuous one at best. Jack felt as though he'd put in a lot of legwork but had barely gotten anywhere.

"Is there a more secluded entrance?" Jack asked.

Effrem directed him around the block, then down a hedge-lined alley to a small parking lot that abutted the apartment's communal backyard, a cracked slab of concrete with four picnic tables. Sitting between them was a barrel-size flowerpot overflowing with cigarette butts. No one was about.

Jack and Effrem got out, walked across the yard, then down a breezeway and through a heavy wooden door on the left. They found themselves standing in a foyer with butter-yellow walls, black-and-white-checkerboard tile floors, and an elevator whose doors were crisscrossed with duct tape bearing a cardboard sign that read AUßER BETRIEB. The air stank of rotten fruit.

"It's called Merkel Punch," Effrem told him. "It caught on during the 2008–2009 recession. Cheaper than store-bought liquor, easy to make in fun-sized portions. Why they named it after the chancellor I don't know."

Jack followed Effrem through a set of double doors to a stairwell, then climbed to the second floor. Once on the landing, Jack could hear the rhythmic thump of what he guessed was German rap music. Effrem led him down the hallway to Schrader's apartment door. The music was louder now, coming from the apartment across the hall.

"How does this work?" Effrem asked. "I've never actually broken into anything."

Jack knelt before the door and studied the door's lock for a few seconds. It was a standard pin tumbler. He'd come armed with a few options, a pick set made out of a modified pair of tweezers and a paper clip, or a bump key. Jack decided to try the latter. From his pocket he pulled a pair of rubber washers, which he forced down the key's shaft and onto its shoulder.

Jack inserted the key into the lock, depressing the washers as far as they would go, withdrew it a quarter-inch, then repeated the process but faster. After ten seconds the lock let go. Jack pushed open the door and stepped through, followed by Effrem. Jack wiped the knob with his shirttail.

The interior was dark save for a thin strip of sunlight coming through the blackout curtains. Jack turned on his cell phone's camera flash and panned it across the ten-by-fourteen-foot room. Schrader's living space was spartan, with a cot and sleeping bag against one wall, a milk crate containing a neatly folded stack of clothes, a writing desk beneath the window, a kitchenette, and a bathroom that consisted of a sink and a toilet.

The place reminded Jack of enlisted bachelor quarters on a military base. Schrader was on the road a lot, Jack guessed, and didn't make enough money to afford a better place. Wouldn't an employee of Jürgen Rostock's be paid better? Maybe Schrader had been freelance, his mission to kill Jack an audition of sorts?

Jack walked to the curtains, closed them fully, then told Effrem to flip the light switch. An overhead fluorescent bulb flickered to life.

Jack said, "I take it the place Schrader stayed in Zurich was a step up?"

"Night and day," replied Effrem. "Champagne versus Merkel Punch. Okay, so do we toss the place?" He said this with a trace of glee in his voice.

Jack pulled a pair of latex gloves from his pocket, passed them to Effrem, then put on his own pair. "Let's start with drawers. You take the kitchen. Look for mail, notebooks, scraps of paper . . . anything with writing on it. Try to leave everything as you found it. Watch out for booby traps."

"Pardon me?"

"Kidding."

While Effrem started in the kitchen, Jack searched the cot, then sorted through the clothes in the milk crate before checking the desk drawers. All were empty. This place was less an apartment and more a bivouac.

"Got something," Effrem called. He was on his hands and knees, half his torso inside the under-sink cabinet. "Looks like a planner or something. It's jammed between the drainpipe and the basin."

"Check for trip wires, then pull it out," Jack said.

"Funny."

Head still in the cabinet, Effrem reached back and handed Jack the black leatherette notebook. On its cover in fake gold leaf letters was "2016." Jack paged through it. Many of the pages showed curt handwritten notations. He flipped ahead to the previous two weeks and his eye caught an entry: "U.S./VA."

United States, Virginia.

He checked the current day and found nothing, then paged ahead. An entry on the following day read "S.M./ Friedenstr. 8/2100."

Effrem, having climbed out of the cabinet, was standing at Jack's shoulder. He said, "'Friedenstr.' could be Frieden-strasse, the first number a building number. As for the other number—"

"Military time," Jack replied.

S.M.

Stephan Möller?

Effrem had Jack head in the general direction of their hotel, then directed him south onto Highway 9, parallel to the Isar River, into the Schwabing district. They were in an upscale part of Munich now, near the Englischer Garten, a 910-acre swath of lush forest, nature trails, pavilions, and outdoor eateries that abutted the river's west bank. Jack had spent his fair share of time here too, mostly on morning runs. The Englischer Garten was Munich's version of New York's Central Park, but much larger. An oasis in an already green city. Having seen the kind of houses that dominated this area of Schwabing, Jack doubted there was a sub-million-dollar house within a quarter-mile of the Englischer Garten's border.

"Your guy lives here?" Jack asked.

"What were you expecting?" replied Effrem.

Jack realized his vision of private hackers was stereotypical: pasty-faced introverts in dark basements surrounded by a crescent of glowing computer monitors. "Not this, I guess."

"Mitch has done well for himself. He's a transplant, an expat American. Used to work in IT at a Fortune 500. He retired a few years ago."

"And he does what now?" asked Jack. "Helps budding journalists?"

"Budding journalists with famous mothers," Effrem replied. "Actually, Mitch was the one and only contact she gave me when I graduated."

That said a lot, Jack decided, given how many sources Marie Likkel had probably accrued over her career.

"You trust him?" asked Jack.

"She did. He never let her down."

Mitch's house wasn't adjacent to the Englischer Garten but butted up against Schwabinger Bach, the creek that forms the park's western edge.

Jack pulled down the long tree-lined driveway until it opened into a clearing of brown and tan paving stones. The house itself was a whitewashed two-story box with an all-glass vaulted gambrel roof. A large Japanese maple shaded the front yard. Jack parked beside the walkway, got out, and followed Effrem to the front door, a chunk of wood bracketed by vertical glass slits. Effrem pushed the buzzer.

The door swung open, revealing a man in his late forties in black gym shorts and a light blue polo shirt. His face was very tan. "In, in," he said, then turned and walked away.

Effrem asked, "Did we wake you?"

"No, my bladder did. I heard your voice mail and decided to ignore it. No offense, Effrem's friend, whoever you are. I was up late playing cyber tag with some idiot in Belarus."

"None taken," said Jack.

The interior of Mitch's house was what Jack had expected: white walls, white furniture, light wood floors, and a second floor looking down on the main level. They followed Mitch into a kitchen full of white appliances. Jack's eyes began to ache.

"Anyone care for a virgin mimosa?" Mitch asked.

"Isn't that just orange juice?" Effrem said.

"Ding, ding. Momma Likkel didn't raise no dummy. Seriously, though, help yourself. Coffee, orange juice, bagels, whatever strikes you. So, do you have a name?" he asked Jack.

"Yes."

When it was clear Jack was going to add nothing further, Mitch nodded thoughtfully. "Works for me. What can I do for you guys?"

Effrem said, "A few e-mail headers and a dicey-looking hyperlink."

"Roger. Send it to me: mlakattack@hushmail.com."

Jack got on his cell phone and forwarded Mitch a Dropbox link containing the e-mail headers from Belinda and the suspicious link Jack had lifted from Peter Hahn's computer. Mitch walked over to a laptop sitting on the counter, checked his e-mail, clicked on Jack's link. He studied the material, then said, "Okay, well, nothing suspicious about these headers. Let's have a look at the link. Interesting."

From there Mitch fell into a stream-of-consciousness conversation with himself that sounded only vaguely like English to Jack:

"Have to hide my IP . . . Let's go with a proxy from Ecuador. Boot up the VM, get you sandboxed . . . Let's see how good you are. Oh, trace route, how I love you . . ."

After another two minutes of this Mitch straightened up and said, "So, Effrem's friend, did you click on this link?"

"No."

"Smart. I've got good news and bad news. Good news is I can do something with this. Bad news is it's going to take a few hours, maybe the day. I'll call you."

22

MUNICH, GERMANY

Mitch called Effrem's cell phone mid-morning the next day. Effrem put him on speaker. "Is Mr. X there, too?" asked Mitch.

"I'm here," Jack replied.

"Okay, so the computer you got this hyperlink from . . . Did you happen to check the Web browser history? Anything odd about it?"

"You could say that."

"I figured. You're right. The site it links to is down, but I was able to root out some interesting stuff. This is malware— a bot, actually—designed to insert Web history into the target computer. It's also designed to sign up the user at some discussion forums, do some troll posting, and so forth."

"What kind of forums?"

"Political crap, conspiracy stuff."

This matched what Jack had seen on Hahn's computer. "Anything else?" he asked. "Was it monitoring him?"

"Nope," said Mitch. "Just playing grab-ass with his browser history. Cleverly designed bot, too."

Effrem asked, "Any idea who created it?"

"I know exactly who created it. All the servers he used were anagrams for *Game of Thrones* characters: storkbarb, hotboarbanterer, tinylionsranter."

"You're kidding?"

"Nope. This guy's good, but everybody's got their peccadilloes. This is his."

"What's his name and where can we find him?" Jack asked.

"The name part is easy," Mitch replied. "Gerhard Klugmann. As for where, that's a bit trickier. Gerhard ain't exactly somebody you Google. I can do some digging, but he's skittish. If I don't pin him down without him realizing it, he'll pull up stakes and move on."

"Digitally or physically?" asked Effrem.

"Both, maybe. Guys like him can work anywhere."

"Find him," Jack ordered.

After running a few errands, they spent the afternoon waiting in Jack's room at the Hotel München Palace. Waiting for a call from Mitch; waiting for a call from Belinda;

waiting for a call from one of Jack's own contacts, a gun guy he had met a year earlier during a routine mission for The Campus. Given the penalties for a foreigner carrying a weapon on German soil, Jack had wanted to avoid doing so, but Effrem's search for 8 Friedenstrasse led to something called Kultfabrik. In Jack's eyes, urban ambush points didn't come any better.

A popular hangout that catered to what one website described as Munich's "bacchanalian night people," Kultfabrik was a noodle factory turned warren of pubs, discos, a skate park, gambling pavilions, game arcades, and flea markets. The twenty-acre complex was in an industrial area of Munich just east of the Ostbahnhof rail complex. Kultfabrik was closed, Effrem told him, and in the middle of conversion to Werksviertel, an office park/cultural center/apartment complex. In short, Kultfabrik was a construction zone.

This alone put Jack on guard, but in perusing Eric Schrader's day planner, Effrem had discovered a disturbing discrepancy: Over the last four months Schrader had met with S.M.—Stephan Möller—six times in Munich. However, for three of these meetings Schrader hadn't even been in the city, but rather in Lyon or Zurich. This left two possibilities: one, Schrader was bad with dates; or two, the day planner was a plant and they were being lured to Kultfabrik. By whom? The most obvious answer was Möller, but that meant either Möller had known about their pursuit of him or he'd learned of their arrival in Munich and assumed they would find Schrader's apartment.

At seven o'clock Jack's gun guy called and the meeting was set: one hour, at the Ostbahnhof.

Jack called Belinda's cell phone and got her voice mail. He left no message.

"Let's go," Jack told Effrem.

They left moments later, Jack in his Citroën, Effrem in his recently rented Audi, and found a pair of parking spots just east of the Orleansplatz, a crescent-shaped public park across from the rail station.

With night falling, the lights of food vendors' stalls were coming on, casting colorful stripes across the pathways and on through the trees. The afternoon crowds, made up mostly of parents and children, were thinning out and being slowly replaced by an early-twenties crowd of singles.

Jack stopped at one of the vendor stalls and got a small soda and a napkin, and he and Effrem sat down on a nearby bench. Jack gulped half of the soda, gave the rest to Effrem, then used the napkin to dry the cup's interior before stuffing six hundred-euro notes inside and replacing the lid.

At seven-forty they crossed Orleansstrasse to the Ostbahnhof, a wide, flat-fronted building just east of the rail hub. In the distance Jack could hear the rumble and screech of incoming and outgoing trains, accompanied by a woman's voice over the station's public address system. The station buzzed with commuters.

Once inside, they picked their way through the throngs to a coffee kiosk counter on the north side of the station. Jack's contact—actually, Ding Chavez's contact—a man he knew only as Freddy, spotted Jack and waved a rolled-up newspaper at him.

"Wait here," Jack told Effrem, and walked over.

He and Freddy shook hands. "Who's that?" Freddy asked in heavily accented English.

"My intern. How've you been?"

"*Ja*, good. I could not get exactly what you asked for, but close. They're clean." Freddy placed a brass key with a red plastic dongle on the counter. "Locker twenty-six."

This had multiple meanings, Jack knew. The guns hadn't been used in a crime, weren't stolen, and weren't traceable; the first two were easy enough to manage, but the third was trickier. Most likely Freddy simply meant the weapons weren't traceable to him.

Freddy asked, "Anything else I can do for you?"

"Maybe. I'll let you know." Jack placed his soda cup on the counter before Freddy, then palmed the key. "How're you set outside Munich?"

"I have a few friends. Depends on what kind of help you need," replied Freddy.

"Thanks. See you."

Jack walked away, nodded at Effrem to follow, then walked across the station to a bank of temporary lockers. He found number 26, inserted the key, removed the blue back-pack inside, then left.

Once they were back in their cars, Jack picked up Rosen-heimer Strasse and headed east, passed beneath the rail-road overpass, then turned north onto Friedenstrasse and slowed down to let Effrem make the turn and catch up.

Jack donned the headset/walkie-talkie rig they'd pur-chased earlier at Conrad, Munich's version of Radio Shack, then keyed the talk button. "You there?"

After a few seconds Effrem came back: "Here. These are nifty, eh?"

"That's what I asked for when I went in," Jack replied, and sped up again. "Stay close."

A few hundred yards ahead on the right Jack saw strobing colored lights and lasers crisscrossing the darkening sky. He rolled down the passenger window and the car's interior was filled with the muted thump of live German trance music.

"I thought you said Kultfabrik was closed," Jack radioed.

"It is. That's Optimolwerke. According to the Web, it's

Kultfabrik's smaller, rowdier next-door neighbor. Developers have bought it. Another couple weeks and it'll be shut down, too."

Jack kept driving until they drew even with the entrance to Optimolwerke's yellow-lighted archway, where hundreds of revelers, most of them dressed in skimpy clothes adorned with rainbow-hued glow sticks, milled about, drinking, laughing, and smoking. A pair of blond-haired girls sat on the curb, vomiting into the garbage-strewn gutter.

Jack muttered, "Hello, future Mrs. Jack Ryan."

As Effrem had described, Optimolwerke sat directly beside the Kultfabrik construction site, the border a twelve-foot-tall, barbed-wire fence that abutted a line of Bavarian-style structures housing Optimolwerke's pubs and arcades. It reminded Jack of a satellite view of North and South Korea at night: pitch blackness to one side, a sea of lights on the other.

As if reading Jack's mind, Effrem radioed, "It's like a boozy, half-naked Iron Curtain."

In his rearview mirror Jack saw a little person in a Fred Flintstone costume wave at Effrem's Audi and shout, *"Wie geht's, Schweinhund!"*

Effrem said, "I think he just called me a pig-dog."

"Sounds about right," Jack replied. "Keep moving. We're turning right at the next intersection."

Jack and Effrem had spent hours studying the Google

Earth view of Kultfabrik and its environs, but as with all satellite imagery, this gave them only half the picture. On the ground everything looked different and felt different. Especially at night. The first order of business was for them to start connecting the landmark dots.

Jack drove slowly past the gated and chain-locked entrance of Kultfabrik itself, then made the turn onto Grafinger Strasse. Like its shared border with Optimolwerke, the construction site's northern and eastern sides were ringed by a high barbed-wire fence, but here they were partially obscured by tall trees so thick Jack's view of the site was obstructed.

Jack spent the next few minutes circumnavigating Kultfabrik before turning back onto Friedenstrasse and repeating the process, this time lingering at the alleys and driveways of the nearby office parks and apartment buildings as he reconciled the area's overhead image with his ground view. Satisfied with his reconnoiter, he met Effrem in the parking lot of a closed auto body shop down Grafinger Strasse.

Effrem slowed to a hood-to-trunk stop beside Jack's Citroën and said out his window, "Well? What do you think?"

Jack thought: *I'd like to have three more shooters, a pair of L1 GPNVG-18 ground panoramic night-vision goggles, and a 3D-printed mockup of the place, but if wishes were horses . . .* Instead, he replied simply, "The sooner I get in there, the better."

It was eight-thirty, thirty minutes before the meeting time. If this was a trap, Möller and his people would probably be doing what Jack was trying to do: set up early and choose his ground. Möller's purpose would be clear, Jack knew: kill him and Effrem. But Jack's end goal was fuzzier. All he knew was, if Möller was going to be there, it was an opportunity he wasn't going to miss.

"Wish you'd change your mind," Effrem said. "You should have somebody watching your six. Did I say that right?"

"Perfect." Jack had decided to post Effrem outside the construction site as a quick-response backup, but this was only partially true. Jack couldn't afford the distraction of having to worry about the young journalist. "I'll feel better knowing you've got the perimeter."

Jack opened the backpack they'd collected from the Ostbahnhof and unzipped it. Inside were two handguns, one an HK USP45 with Gemtech Blackside noise suppressor, the other a snub-nosed .38 revolver. Better to keep it simple for Effrem. He passed the revolver to Effrem, along with three spare speed loaders.

"What's rule one?" Jack asked.

"Never point this thing at anything I don't want to kill."

"Including yourself."

Effrem gave him a withering gaze. "I have fired a gun before, you know."

"Was anyone shooting back?"

"No."

"Big difference," Jack replied. "Post yourself on the corner and we'll get started."

"Good luck."

Effrem pulled away, as did Jack, who paused at the lot's exit until he saw Effrem's Audi pull to the curb at Grafinger Strasse and Friedenstrasse and douse the headlights. From there Effrem would be able to see two of the three likely approaches to the construction site.

Jack turned left, headed south a hundred yards, then turned into the apartment complex's parking lot. The front was well lit by streetlamps, but as Jack proceeded around the building they faded and darkness enveloped the car. When he reached the back of the property he turned right and pulled beneath a squat oak tree. He turned off the car, climbed out, then eased shut the car door and locked it.

In the distance he could hear the *thump-umph-umph* of a band at Optimolwerke. Through the boughs of the tree the night sky pulsed red, yellow, and purple in time with the pumping music.

Jack took off his jacket, donned the HK's shoulder rig, then put his jacket back on and adjusted the rig so the noise suppressor wouldn't poke out the bottom of his jacket. Next he donned the last piece of gear he'd purchased from Conrad, an off-brand set of night-vision goggles that looked more like a seventies-era View-Master with a head strap than it did a military-grade pair of NVGs. Jack mounted the goggles on his head, powered up the unit, and looked around. The muted gray-green view was grainy and blurred at the edges but clear enough to keep him from bumping into bad guys. How long the batteries would last Jack didn't know. He took off the goggles.

He radioed Effrem: "You set?"

"Set. A few cars have passed down Friedenstrasse, but nobody's turned. Quiet down Grafinger Strasse, too."

"Good. I'm moving."

23

Jack ducked beneath the tree boughs and walked until he reached the construction site's outer fence, then followed it until he reached the sidewalk along Grafinger Strasse, where he headed in Effrem's direction. He could see the Audi a hundred yards ahead and across the street.

"Can you see me?" Jack radioed.

"No."

"Good."

Halfway down the block, Jack stopped and looked around for landmarks. *Almost there.* He proceeded another fifty feet, stopped again to check his location, then slipped into the trees to his left and picked his way through the foliage till his outstretched hand touched the hurricane fence.

His early reconnoiter had shown what looked like a gap in the fence. He donned the NVGs and powered them on.

He'd found the spot. A triangular section of fencing had been cut away; the tool marks were old and a cluster of vines had already pushed their way through the opening. Through the gap Jack saw a pair of backhoe scoops, and beyond these a row of construction trailers. This was the site's heavy equipment parking area and site offices. He crawled through the gap, then crept to the nearest backhoe scoop and ducked inside.

Though closed and vacant, Kultfabrik's buildings were too many to search, and the ground was too open for Jack's liking. Aside from the long, north-south line of abandoned arcades, pubs, and pool halls on the site's far side, only two buildings had survived the demolition: to Jack's left, in the center of the site, a clamshell open-air amphitheater; to his right, sitting just inside the fence at the corner of Frieden-strasse and Grafinger Strasse, an L-shaped office building. The walls of the first four floors were finished, sans windows, but the fifth floor was still mostly skeletal, with iron beams and girders backlit by the night sky. Overlapping blue plastic tarps formed the building's temporary roof. Aluminum scaffolding enclosed the building's first three floors.

This was his destination. If he were laying a trap, he'd want the high ground. At the very least it was the ideal observation post. As a sniper perch, it was serviceable.

Jack checked his watch: eight forty-five.

He scanned the office building with his NVG, left to right and bottom to top. In his monochrome view the walls appeared gray; the window openings were charcoal rectangles. He saw no shadows, no movement. He picked up a rock and hurled it over the bulldozer. As the rock *thunk*ed against the nearest trailer's roof, Jack watched the building. Again, he saw no movement. Twice more he repeated the process with the same result, then once more but this time pelting the side of the building itself. Nothing.

Either Möller's men were not set up in there, or they were too disciplined to overtly react to Jack's stone-throwing. Either way, it was time to move.

Jack slipped back to the fence and turned left, using the low-hanging tree branches to cover his movement. When he reached the building, he paused to look and listen, then continued to the corner of the fence. He looked right; through the foliage he could just make out Effrem's shadowed form sitting in the Audi's driver's seat.

"I'm at your nine o'clock."

Effrem's head turned. In the NVG glow Effrem's eyes narrowed and darted. "Yeah, I don't see you. Nothing to report. All quiet. Maybe we've got it wrong."

A small part of Jack hoped Effrem was right. Getting into a firefight on foreign soil was something best avoided. Trading bullets with bad guys in a major city was downright stupid. The cacophony coming from Optimolwerke would obscure the sounds of gunfire but that was little comfort. You never fight the war you want, Jack knew. You fight the war you have.

"We'll find out soon enough," Jack replied. "I'm going in."

He drew his HK, stepped out from under the trees, raised the gun, and stalked forward. He was facing the hollow portion of the structure's L-shape, most of which was crowded with wheelbarrows, cement mixers, and sawhorse tables. With both his gun and his eyes alternating between the windows above and the ground ahead Jack picked his way through the maze to a broad archway he assumed would eventually be the lobby entrance. He ducked right, pressed himself against the inner wall. The sounds of Optimolwerke's revelers and pumping music faded slightly. He looked around.

Though the building's exterior was nearly finished, the interior had a long way to go. The lobby was a slab of rough concrete crisscrossed with power cables and pneumatic hoses. The interior beams were exposed along with the water pipes and electrical conduits. Half-finished ducting snaked above Jack's head. Directly ahead lay an open elevator shaft and on either side of this a pair of stairwells leading upward.

Effrem radioed, "Jack, I see something."

Jack cupped his hand around the headset microphone. "What and where?"

"Light, just a flicker. Second floor—no, third floor, my side."

To my left and above, Jack thought. Instinctively he pointed the NVG that way. He answered Effrem, "Roger. Don't make me ask next time."

They'd gone over this: The more radio silence Jack maintained, the better his chances. Effrem's reports needed to be concise but thorough.

"Yeah, sorry," he said.

"I'm moving up to the second floor."

Effrem replied "Roger" with a double click.

Jack headed to the left-hand stairwell and started upward. At the first landing he stopped, leaned forward, peeked up, saw nothing, and kept going until he reached the second floor. Here there was an opening for a door, but no door. Jack stepped forward with his HK at relaxed high-ready, until he could see left through the opening.

Effrem called, "A car just pulled up to the gate. Two men getting out."

Shit.

"Car's pulling away . . . Oh, damn!" Effrem went silent for ten seconds then came back: "It turned onto Grafinger Strasse. I don't think they saw me."

"License plate?"

"Missed it, sorry. Okay, the guys are at the gate. It's not locked, Jack, they're just pulling the chain."

That tended to confirm Effrem's report of seeing light on the third floor. Möller's men were already here, and now more were arriving. Either that or these newcomers were construction-site security guards and someone had forgotten to padlock the gate.

"I'm looking for weapons," Effrem whispered. "I can't tell. Okay, they're through the gate, heading your way . . . Lost sight of them."

Jack double-clicked.

He took another step forward, peeked right, and saw nothing.

From somewhere above came the crackle of a portable radio, then in German: *"Ja . . . dritten Etage."* Yes, third floor.

Jack heard the scuff of shoes on the stairs. He looked over the handrail and saw a pair of men trotting up the stairs. Each was carrying a compact assault weapon—a FAMAS bullpup or one of its variants. These men weren't security guards. Jack stepped through the door, then sidestepped four paces down the wall and raised the HK to shoulder height. He took a breath, let it out. Slowed his breathing.

Let both of them get through the door first, he told himself.

The footsteps reached the landing, then started up the next flight of stairs.

The party's on the third floor.

Jack counted to five, then paced forward, peeked around the corner in time to see the men turning onto the next landing. Moving on flat feet, Jack stepped out and followed. He reached the landing and leaned sideways over the railing in time to see the two men disappearing through the doorway. He started up the stairs.

He was two steps from the third-floor landing when Effrem's voice came over the headset: "Jack, you there?"

Jack froze and gave the radio a double click.

"I miscounted. The light I saw was on the fourth floor. It just started moving again. I'm so sorry—"

Fourth floor. Men above me.

He spun left, brought the HK up. A darkened figure was pacing down the steps. The man saw Jack, muttered, *"Scheisse,"* and jerked his rifle up. Jack shot him twice in the chest, dropping him. The already limp body slid down the steps and landed in a heap at Jack's feet. The report of Jack's HK sounded like a phone book being whacked with a wooden mallet.

"Was ist das?" a voice whispered.

Where? Behind me.

He turned, saw a man stepping through the doorway, a second man on his heels. Jack fired once, stepped forward, fired again, then charged forward and bulldozed the man backward into the second man, who instinctively reached out to grab his collapsing partner. As he did so Jack shot him in the forehead. Tangled together, the two men crumpled. One of their rifles clattered to the concrete floor.

Jack turned again, checked the up and down stairways.

Both were clear.

He stepped through the door, looked right, then left. He checked the faces of the two downed men. Neither was Stephan Möller. He sidestepped the bodies and crouched behind a garbage can. His heart was pounding. He could taste acid in his mouth. He switched the HK to his left hand and wiped his sweaty right palm on his pant leg.

Effrem called, "Jack, what's going on? I heard—"

Jack double-clicked.

Effrem went silent.

Three men down, Jack thought. *Four rounds fired, eight left.*

Was there anyone else upstairs? Probably at least one. Möller, maybe? Three men made little sense. Paired teams seemed more likely. If so, Jack had to assume whoever was left upstairs knew something had gone awry. Jack's HK was quiet, but not that quiet, especially to someone with a trained ear.

Jack put himself in their shoes. *What's the best play?*

Stay put, prepare an ambush, and make the attacker come to you. Force him to check every room and doorway on the fourth floor. Let the fear gnaw at him. Call for rein-forcements.

Jack crouch-walked to the two fallen men, quickly

searched each one and came up with two wallets and two cell phones, all of which he stuffed into his jacket pockets. He picked up the nearest rifle he saw, a FAMAS F1, and slung it over his back. Next he returned to the stairwell and frisked the other man, but found neither a wallet nor a cell phone. He was, however, carrying a pair of car keys.

What's it going to be, Jack? He'd gotten some intel—how worthwhile, he didn't yet know—but if there was a chance Möller was upstairs, Jack wasn't going to let him go.

Jack returned to his hiding spot behind the garbage can and keyed his headset. "Effrem."

"I'm here. Are you okay?"

"Fine. Anything going on out there?"

"Nothing."

"I'm moving up to the fourth floor. Keep a sharp eye out. If any more vehicles pull up, give me as much warning as possible."

"Will do."

Jack crossed the floor to the opposite stairwell, posted himself beside the doorway, then did his peek-check before starting up the steps. Just below the landing he froze.

Somewhere above, a crackling sound. A snap, a rustle.

The wind had picked up, he realized, shifting the temporary tarpaulin roof.

Jack kept climbing until he reached the fourth floor, where he again paused. Through the doorway he could see a hallway, and beyond this an open space in the midst of being framed into offices, conference rooms, and communal work areas.

Jack scanned from left to right with his NVGs but saw nothing.

Clang!

Jack turned and cocked his head, trying to pinpoint the sound's location.

Effrem called, "Jack, I've got movement again. I can barely make him out through the trees. Hold on, I'm getting out for a better look."

"Don't," Jack rasped. "Stay put."

"I'm almost there."

Jack heard another clang and then recognized the sound: scaffolding.

Effrem whispered, "I see him. He's outside, on the scaffolding stuff. My side, uhm, the north side. What do you want me to do?"

"Get back to the car and leave," Jack ordered. If Effrem could see the man, it was safe to assume the man could see Effrem. "Circle the block and park farther down Grafinger Strasse. I'll find you."

"Okay, okay, I'm going."

Jack stepped into the hallway and turned right, heading to the building's north side. Halfway there he heard a faint *pop, pop, pop.* Gunfire. Jack started running.

Effrem called, "Shit, what was that? Uh, Jack, I've got a problem. I need help!"

Jack picked up speed. He heard the clang of feet on the scaffolding but couldn't tell from what direction. The strap to his night-vision goggles slackened, and his vision began to vibrate, the images a jumbled gray mosaic of empty rooms, hallways, framing studs . . . He charged into an open space, looked left. A figure crouched in the nearest window, half on the scaffolding, half inside the room.

A muzzle flashed orange and Jack glimpsed Möller's face; the beard was gone, but it was him.

Jack dropped and slid like a baseball player while curling himself into what he hoped would be a harder target. His momentum carried him halfway across the room, where he crashed into a sawhorse. The plywood tabletop collapsed, the wooden edge dropping toward his face. He threw his hand up, turned his head, then felt something hard slam into the corner of his eye. He rolled onto his belly, looked around, and tried to get his bearings.

To his right was the now empty window from which Möller had been firing.

He crawled out from under the plywood and stumbled that way, gun coming up.

"Effrem, you there?" Jack called.

No response.

Jack reached the window.

From below came a clang, followed by footsteps pounding on aluminum rungs.

Jack poked his head out the window, looked left, and glimpsed a figure scrambling down the scaffolding's crossbraces. Jack took aim, but the man was gone. Jack ducked back inside, hurried to the opposite window, stuck his head through. Möller was below him on the first-floor scaffolding. He looked up, saw Jack, fired, then dashed away.

Jack sprinted back down the length of the floor to the stairwell, where he took the steps two at a time until he reached the lobby. In seconds he was outside. He looked right. Möller was gone.

He went still and listened.

Faintly he heard the slow *ding, ding, ding*. Jack recognized it as the chime of an open car door.

He keyed his radio. "Effrem?"

Silence.

"Effrem, answer me."

No response.

Jack ran to the main gate. It was standing partially open. He ducked through and, gun still raised, trotted down the sidewalk to the corner.

Across the street the door to Effrem's Audi was open, the interior dome light glowing in the darkness.

Effrem was gone.

24

"... *Schweinhund!*"

The shout came from behind Jack. He turned in time to see a crowd outside Optimolwerke's entrance envelop an SUV, and in seconds all Jack could see was its taillights through the multitude of legs.

SUV, silver or light gray, Jack thought. *Maybe.*

He sprinted to Effrem's Audi, got in, shut the door, and started the engine. He pulled away from the curb and sped down Friedenstrasse. Ahead, the Optimolwerke revelers were dispersing, revealing the SUV's brake lights in the distance. Jack sped up and swerved around the mob. Angry and drunken faces flashed past his window. Fists pummeled the sides of the Audi. Jack floored the accelerator and the Audi's engine surged.

Ahead, the SUV turned right onto Rosenheimer Strasse.

If Effrem wasn't in that vehicle, Jack was screwed. If the journalist was, Jack didn't have the luxury of running a covert pursuit. Once Möller or whoever was driving got Effrem to a secure location, it was over. The only question would be whether they tortured him first or simply put a bullet in his head.

If they hadn't already.

Should have told Effrem no from the start.

He reached the stop sign a few seconds later, tapped the brakes and glanced left to make sure the road was clear, then spun the wheel and accelerated again. The Audi's tail swerved momentarily before the tires caught hold and it snapped back. The SUV was fifty yards ahead and appeared to be in no hurry. Jack let the Audi coast a bit, closing the gap but not enough to alarm the SUV's occupants, until finally he could make out the license plate: MOD ZL 292.

Through the back window he saw a figure rise up in the rear seat. There was a commotion. The passenger turned in his seat and started batting at the figure until it disappeared from view. Effrem was putting up a fight. *Lie still*, Jack thought. *Don't be more trouble than you're worth. Not yet, at least.*

Jack accelerated until his bumper was almost touching the SUV's, then started flashing his high beams. He didn't expect them to pull over, of course, but now they knew there was a witness, a thorn. If they wanted to get clear with Effrem, they'd have to deal with Jack first.

The SUV accelerated, opening a gap, but Jack countered until he was again on their tail. The SUV's brake lights flashed. Jack braked hard, swerved left, and found himself alongside the SUV. Jack didn't need to see the vehicle's window rolling down to know what was coming. He jerked the wheel, crushing the Audi against the SUV. Jack's passenger window spiderwebbed once, twice, then shattered inward. Wind gushed through the Audi's interior.

He slammed on the brakes, letting the SUV pull ahead, then slid in behind it as a train overpass enveloped them. Jack stomped on the gas pedal and smacked into the SUV's bumper. He backed off and did it again, this time angling the nose of the Audi into the SUV's quarter panel in hopes of sending it into a spin. The SUV's driver countersteered into Jack and he lost the angle.

This couldn't go on for long, Jack knew. If the police weren't already on their way, they soon would be. That might solve the issue of Effrem's rescue, but if the occupants of the SUV opened fire on the police there might be bodies in the street, and at best Jack would end up in jail. He needed to end this quickly.

The road dipped and the SUV slipped into an underpass with Jack a few feet off its bumper. Headlights flashed through the Audi's windshield. The blaring of car horns echoed through the underpass. Jack weaved right, trying to pass the SUV, but again the driver countered, swerving and shoving Jack toward the guardrail, forcing him to brake hard. The SUV surged ahead, emerged from the underpass, and turned left at the next intersection. Jack momentarily lost sight of it, but then, as he, too, made the turn, he saw the SUV fishtailing and disappearing through a gate in a long wooden fence. Jack overshot the gate, braked to a stop, then reversed and turned in.

On either side of the car, massive open-sided bays stacked with lumber flashed past the Audi's windows. A lumber-yard. Bright, pole-mounted security lights cast sharp circles of light on the pavement.

A forklift emerged from an alley to Jack's right. He jerked the wheel left, but not enough. The forklift's blades scraped down the Audi's side and shattered the rear window. Jack slammed on the brakes, glanced at the sideview mirror, and saw the forklift was still upright, its driver climbing down from the cab. He hit the accelerator again.

Ahead, the SUV turned right and disappeared behind a warehouse.

Jack was five seconds behind.

The SUV was gone.

To his right was the warehouse wall. The nearest door, lit from above by a spotlight, was fifty yards away and partially closed. *Too far.* Jack looked left down an alley bordered by tiered stacks of railroad ties. No sign of the SUV. He kept going, glancing down the next alley as he went past. At the third intersection, he saw the SUV's tail end disappear behind a lumber stack. It was running parallel to him, its lights off.

Jack jammed the accelerator against the floorboards, pushing the Audi's accelerator past fifty, then tapped hard on the brakes and spun the wheel left, slewing the car down the next alley. He let the tail end snap back, then accelerated again and reached the next intersection just as the SUV sped past. Jack didn't slow but raced to the next intersection, did a hand-brake skid-turn to the right. As he raced through an exit gate, the pavement turned to rutted dirt. Out his passenger window was a line of trees, and through these he could see fragmented light that seemed to be moving, keeping pace with him. A train, he realized.

He sensed movement out his passenger window, glanced that way. The SUV's headlights filled the Audi's interior, blinding him. He jammed on the brakes. Through the windshield he saw the SUV fishtail and its rear bumper clip the Audi's hood. Jack steered into it but overshot. A pyramid of railroad ties loomed through the windshield. He countersteered, but not quickly enough. The Audi sideswiped the stack of ties, and a pair of them crashed into the hood and spiderwebbed the right half of the windshield before tumbling over the roof and disappearing.

Jack spun the wheel, bringing the Audi back in behind the SUV.

Time to end this, he thought. *Hold on, Effrem . . .*

He eased left and accelerated. The SUV took the bait and moved to cut him off. Jack tapped the brakes, swerved right and down the SUV's opposite side, then jerked the wheel hard, ramming the Audi's bumper into the SUV's tire. The driver had no choice but to counter, but he over-did it. The SUV's rear tires, now sideways to the vehicle's momentum, stuttered over the furrowed ground. The SUV flipped onto its side, then began spinning toward the trees. Dirt and chunks of the vehicle's chassis peppered Jack's windshield. He hit the brakes and the Audi skidded to a stop.

Jack got out and paused to get his bearings. Dust swirled in the beams of the Audi's headlights. The sudden halt to the chase left him momentarily dizzy.

Which way?

He raised the HK and started jogging toward what he guessed was the tree line.

From the darkness, a lone gunshot.

A round in Effrem's head? he wondered.

He slowed down, hunched over, and tried to localize the sound, then eased left. Somewhere in the distance a train whistle echoed, then went silent. Abruptly the dust thinned and he found himself in the trees. A branch smacked into his forehead. He landed on his butt, got back up. To his right one of the SUV's turn signals blinked yellow in the darkness. He headed that way.

"Jack, he's out there!" Effrem's voice.

Jack froze, crouched, sidestepped behind a tree trunk. He assumed Effrem was referring to Möller. "Just him?" he called.

"The driver's not moving."

"Are you hurt?"

"I don't know. I've got one of their guns."

Jack didn't know if this was true, but it was a smart move on Effrem's part.

"Sit tight!" Faintly Jack heard the warble of sirens. "Police are on the way."

This was as much a problem for them as it was for Möller, but Jack hoped the German would flee before he had time to think that through. Then again, Möller was just unflappable enough to do the opposite.

"No, I gotta get out!" Effrem shouted. "This thing's leaking gas."

Jack could smell it now.

From the direction of the railroad tracks came the clank of steel wheels. A train was coming.

Jack realized his NVGs were still hanging around his neck. Using his free hand, he settled them over his eyes. The left lens was shattered, leaving him only a grayish monocular view of his surroundings. With each beat of his heart the view vibrated. He took a calming breath, then looked around, starting behind himself and moving slowly toward the crashed SUV.

He stopped.

Movement.

He panned back and focused on a bush. Something there, he thought, a straight line in the curved branches. Too much bulk in the foliage. He took aim on the shape and fired once. Nothing moved.

A branch snapped. Jack spun right. Twenty feet away, a figure was moving through the trees toward him. Jack raised the HK, laid the front sight on the figure's center of mass.

"Hallo, ist da jemand?" a male voice called. Hello, is anyone there?

Jack kept the HK trained on the man. Was it Möller?

"Wer is da?" Jack called.

". . . Holzlager," came the answer. Lumberyard.

"Polizei! Gas!" Luckily the word was the same in both languages. With any luck, the man would relay this message to the first police on scene. It might slow them down a bit.

"Okay, ich verstehe!"

Jack waited until the man had backed out of sight, then headed for the SUV. He had no time left. If Möller was lying in wait, Jack would know soon enough. Jack picked his way through the trees to the SUV, which was lying on its left side. As he approached, Effrem's hands rose through the moonroof and wagged. His wrists were secured by a zip-tie. "Jack, is that you?"

"Yeah. Can you climb up?"

"I think so."

The odor of gas was almost overpowering now, stinging Jack's nostrils. Behind him, a train rattled past, its lighted windows flashing through the trees.

Jack made his way to the SUV's windshield and peeked through. The driver lay in a heap, half against the door, half on the dashboard. His head was pointing in the wrong direction; his neck was broken. Jack photographed the SUV's VIN.

Effrem hopped to the ground beside Jack. He stumbled, then steadied himself against the car. "Whoa . . . dizzy."

Jack asked, "No gun?"

"I was lying, hoping Möller would hear me."

"What about your thirty-eight? We can't leave it behind."

"Oh . . . yeah. It's in the Audi's center console."

Jack took out his penknife, sawed through the zip-ties around Effrem's wrists, and pocketed them. Effrem asked, "Souvenir?"

"DNA." Effrem's prints might be all over the inside of the car, but Jack wasn't about to leave behind such an obvious piece of trace evidence. "We need to go. Can you run?"

"A close imitation, at least," Effrem replied.

Jack had no specific plan aside from putting distance between them and the scene of the crash. Their best option was to head east, he decided, and try to make their way back to where Jack had parked his car near Kultfabrik.

They were a quarter-mile from the crash site, following the rail line north toward the Ostbahnhof and using the trees alongside the ballast embankment as cover. Occasionally a train would rumble past, its brakes squealing as it slowed for the station.

The chase and subsequent crash had attracted a lot of attention, Jack could tell from the flashing glow of emergency lights above the trees. He saw no sign of police helicopters, but that wouldn't last long. Jack was already assembling the worst-case scenario in his head:

After securing the crash site and letting the firefighters deal with the SUV's gas leak, the police had likely set up a perimeter, then begun searching the surrounding area for the vehicles' occupants. One man was dead and gunfire had been exchanged during a high-speed chase. If the first officers on the scene believed the lumberyard worker, one of Munich's finest had inexplicably disappeared from the scene, possibly the victim of a kidnapping.

Around them, the trees began to thin. Jack saw the glow of streetlamps.

"Wait here," he said, and kept walking until he reached the sidewalk.

A police car drove past, its spotlight skimming over the trees. Jack stepped back deeper into the shadows until the car was out of sight, then returned to where Effrem was leaning against a tree, massaging the side of his head.

Jack said, "We're at Rosenheimer Strasse. Not far to Kultfabrik."

"Let's hail a taxi," Effrem said.

"We can't afford witnesses," Jack replied.

If they hadn't already, the police would soon be contacting taxi companies, asking if anyone had done just what Effrem was suggesting.

"My head hurts. Bastard thwacked me with a gun."

"Möller?"

"Who else? Just because I tried to kick him in the head."

Courtesy of Stephan Möller, Effrem's head had taken a beating, first from a bullet graze, now from a pistol-whipping.

"I'm starting to not like the guy very much."

Jack couldn't help but laugh. "Don't blame you."

"What now? Which way?"

Jack checked his watch: less than twenty minutes since the chase had started. It seemed much longer than that. He wondered if the police had managed to identify Kultfabrik as the point of origin yet. He doubted it. Right now, drunken complaints from Optimolwerke people were probably low on the list of priorities for the police. It would take time to assemble the puzzle pieces.

Jack took off his jacket, pulled it inside out, exposing the red lining, and handed it to Effrem. "Put the hood up, too. You look like shit."

Effrem shrugged. "Thanks for coming after me, by the way."

Lights flashing, another police car raced down Rosenheimer Strasse, followed closely by a matte-black panel truck containing what Jack guessed was Munich PD's version of a SWAT team.

"How're we going to explain this, Jack? They'll find out the Audi's under my name."

Jack thought about it for a moment. "Go back to the hotel. The police will show up eventually. Your story is the car must have been stolen. You must have left the keys in it. Stick with that story and keep it simple. Just like you did with the Alexandria cops. Be curious but not too curious. Ask them for a report number so you can call your insurance company and the rental car agency—"

"Yeah, I get it," Effrem said.

Jack's cell phone chimed. He dug it out of his pocket and checked the screen. It was a text from Belinda Hahn—or at least from her cell phone. She wasn't using the burner he'd given her. **Jack, I think there are people outside.**

Effrem was looking over his shoulder. "A trap, you think?"

Jack texted back to Belinda, **Blue.**

She replied with their agreed-upon confirmation code: **Little Boy.**

Effrem said, "Still not proof."

"It's as close as we're going to get. We don't really have a choice."

"They could have gotten it out of her. Or she could be involved—"

Jack cut him off: "Effrem, we're not ignoring this." Even so, the timing of Belinda's call for help wasn't lost on Jack. Möller had three loose ends—Jack, Effrem, and Belinda Hahn—and the German had just tried to wrap up Jack and Effrem. Why not go for all three on the same night?

Jack texted her: **Where are you?**

Belinda replied with an address, then asked, **What do I do?**

Lock doors, windows. Hide, he answered. **If anyone tries to force the door, call the police. Have pepper spray?**

Yes. I'm scared, Belinda texted.

I'm on my way.

25

NORTH OF MUNICH, GERMANY

Jack turned off the highway and headed north. His headlights illuminated a sign that read MARZLING 3 KM. According to his dashboard clock, almost an hour had passed since Belinda had first texted him.

"Damn it."

He checked his phone. It had been almost fifteen minutes since Belinda had responded to his last text. To his dismay, she had simply said, **Please hurry.**

The day before, when he'd advised her to find someplace else to stay, he should have been more specific, "someplace nearby." According to Google Earth, the address she'd texted him from belonged to what looked like a farmhouse-turned-cabin twenty-five miles north of Munich, just outside the village of Marzling and on the banks of the Isar River.

It had taken him and Effrem a precious fifteen minutes to make their way back to Kultfabrik, and then another fifteen for Jack to drop Effrem at the hotel and reach the highway leading out of the city.

Following his phone's navigation cues, Jack drove into Marzling proper, then turned south onto Isarstrasse, which took him past a mile of farm fields and homesteads to a bridge spanning the Isar. Once across this, he turned left onto a dirt road that followed the river's meandering banks. During his drive north, rain clouds had thickened and the wind had picked up, rippling the river's surface. Fat raindrops spattered against his windshield.

When he was a half-mile from the cabin, he reached a fork in the road. To the right was Blaue Forelle Strasse, the cabin's de facto driveway. He drove fifty feet past it and pulled over.

Part of him wanted to hurry, to find out why Belinda had gone silent, but he resisted the impulse. At Kultfabrik he'd rushed his clearing of the building's third floor and had almost paid for it. If Belinda was already dead or had been taken, a headlong charge at the cabin would do nothing to change that.

He texted her again: **What's happening?**

After nearly a minute of silence, the phone chimed with her response: They had been in the house.

Red, Jack texted.

Baron, came Belinda's reply.

Gone now?

I think so, she replied.

How long ago?

Twenty, thirty minutes, Belinda texted.

How many men? asked Jack.

Don't know! Afraid to move! Hiding in closet.

There were two possibilities, Jack decided, both plausible, and one perhaps the product of overthinking on his part: He'd gotten Belinda's text within ten minutes of the crash at the lumberyard. If Möller's men had been sitting on Belinda's cabin, Möller might have ordered them to spook her, in hopes that she would send out a call for help, and then to hunker down and wait for Jack's arrival. They had nothing to lose but time on a fruitless ambush. The second possibility was more straightforward: Having failed to kill Jack and Effrem, Möller had decided to minimize his exposure and ordered his men to withdraw. As for Effrem's suggestion that Belinda was in league with Möller, Jack's gut said no.

He called up Google Earth and zoomed in on the property. Sitting as it did in the river's valley, the cabin was surrounded by trees in full bloom, fed by the Isar's spring melt. While the terrain ruled out ambush-at-a-distance with long guns, the thickness of the foliage offered plenty of places for bad guys to hide and wait for Jack's approach.

Nothing's perfect, he reminded himself. *No plan survives first contact with the enemy.* He'd deal with whatever came.

Jack texted Belinda, **I'm just passing Eching. Be there asap.**

If this got passed on to Möller's men, it might give Jack an advantage.

Jack spent the next thirty minutes picking his way through the forest until his legs were numb from crouching, his elbows and knees were raw from crawling, and the batteries in his off-brand NVGs were so weak that it was like staring into a static-filled television. The rain clouds had so far failed to open up, but rather spit droplets that struck the ground like hurled pebbles. Jack could feel a bone-deep cold settling into his limbs.

When the rear wall of the cabin finally came into view he forced himself to lie still in the undergrowth and watch for another five minutes. The cabin had indeed once been a Bavarian-style three-story farmhouse, with a cedar mansard roof, whitewashed exterior, and dark green shutters. It wasn't far from what Jack's younger self would have imagined a gingerbread house to be like.

Nothing was moving and he saw no lights.

Jack crawled ahead and wormed his way underneath the wraparound porch, then got out his phone and texted, **Almost there. Turning onto Blaue Forelle.**

This was the road leading directly to the cabin. Now to see if his impending approach got a reaction.

Belinda didn't respond.

Another five minutes passed. Either he was alone or Möller's men were too damned good for him to spot. Next, the house.

Before he even reached the front door he could smell the stink of gas. Jack holstered his gun; its muzzle blast would be more than enough to ignite the gas. He pulled the collar of his T-shirt up over his nose and tried the doorknob. It was unlocked. He pushed through, then sidestepped left, clear of the backlit doorway.

Belinda had said she was in a closet. *Where, though?* He texted the question to Belinda and again he got no response. Depending on how long this gas had been flowing, she could already be dead.

Led by his penlight, Jack moved through the cabin as quickly and quietly as possible, opening windows and stopping at every door that might be a closet until he'd cleared the first floor. He climbed the stairs and repeated his search.

At the end of the hall, in a bathroom linen closet, he found Belinda curled into a ball. Clutched loosely in her hand was a cell phone, not the burner he'd given her. He checked her pulse. She was alive. He shook her. "Belinda!" No response. He rubbed his knuckles hard against her sternum and she let out a moan.

Downstairs, a door slammed.

Jack froze. Listened.

He crept to the bathroom window and looked out. The pane beside his head exploded. He ducked, dropped to his belly, crawled back to Belinda. He grabbed her wrist and dragged her into the hallway.

Think, Jack. Get shot dead or burned alive?

Belinda's cell phone beeped. Jack grabbed it, checked the screen. It was a text.

Come out. You come with us, she goes free.

Beyond the obvious—that someone preferred him alive for the time being—this text message told Jack something: If they planned to blow the house, the ignition source was probably already in place and remotely controlled.

How and where?

Buy some time, Jack. He texted back: **She's almost dead. Can't move her until she's awake.**

Come out now. She will be tended to.

This was a lie, of course.

When I know she's okay, I'll come out. Need fresh air. Breaking window. Don't shoot.

No response.

Jack crawled back into the bathroom to the window and used the butt of his HK to shatter the remaining panes.

The phone beeped: **No more windows. Five minutes. Be smart.**

Was the cabin close enough to Marzling to be on city gas? Jack wondered. Maybe not. Propane, then. He hadn't seen a tank outside, so where was it? The most likely place was the basement.

He pulled Belinda close to him, scooped her onto his shoulder, then crouch-walked back down the stairs to the kitchen. He found the basement door set into the wall behind the dining table. As quietly as he could, he slid this aside and opened the door, revealing a set of stairs leading down into darkness. The stench of propane washed over Jack, almost doubling him over. He coughed and bile filled his mouth; he swallowed it. His vision was sparkling. Though all the windows on the first floor were open, propane tended to settle, so he was likely standing waist-deep in the gas.

Go out the front, Jack. Surrender, take your chances, play for time. That might work for him, but not for Belinda, he knew. They would kill her regardless. The other option, to go out shooting, was also a nonstarter. In Hollywood blockbusters this desperate gambit was glorious to behold and almost always successful, but it rarely worked in the real world. He and Belinda wouldn't make it off the porch before being cut down.

Root cellar. Unbidden, the words popped into Jack's head. *Maybe.*

Another text: **Three minutes.**

Jack replied, **She may be dying. Not coming out until she's awake. You want me, you have to wait.**

No, came the reply.

Send someone in here to help me.

There was no response, which was no surprise. For all he knew, his capture was a secondary priority. If he pushed too far they might simply blow the house.

Jack laid Belinda on the kitchen counter, dug his knuckles into her sternum, then flicked her eyeballs with his fingers. She winced, then let out a groan.

"Belinda! Do you hear me? Belinda, it's Jack!"

"Jack," she murmured.

"Is there a root cellar?" he asked. He wasn't going into the basement, where the propane would be the thickest, without knowing there was an escape route. Jack kept rubbing his knuckles against her chest bone. "Belinda! Root cellar! Is there a root cellar?"

Her eyelids fluttered open and focused on Jack. "Root cellar?"

"In the basement! Is there one?"

She nodded feebly. "Behind water heater."

The phone beeped. **Two minutes,** the text said.

Jack didn't reply. They weren't bluffing.

He threw Belinda over his shoulder, walked to the nearest window, spent thirty seconds inhaling fresh air, then clamped the penlight in his teeth and headed down the stairs, the beam dancing wildly over the walls. At the bottom was a narrow brown-brick passage. Now the stench of propane was almost acidic, like a chunk of manila rope being snaked through his sinuses. Jack turned right. Belinda's head bumped against the bricks. She let out a yelp. *A good sign.*

The passage opened into a twenty-by-twenty-foot rectangular space with a dirt floor. Sitting against the left-hand wall was a long propane tank. Jack headed that way, playing his flashlight over the piping until he found a cluster of gauges. Zip-tied to one of the pipes was a pencil detonator bundled to a cell phone with duct tape. Simple and effective. The number of wraps on the duct tape made getting to the phone's battery time-consuming. More important, the accelerometer that was likely built into this phone could also serve as an ideal anti-tamper switch.

Forget it, move on.

Belinda's body, draped limply over his shoulder, started convulsing. She retched. Jack felt the gush of warm vomit on his neck. He turned his head, shining the beam over the space. Ahead, sitting beside a line of wall-mounted wooden shelves, was the cylindrical water heater. Jack headed that way. Nausea washed over him and his stomach heaved. He kept putting one foot in front of the other.

The cell phone beeped again. He didn't need to look at it. One-minute warning.

He reached the water heater and followed its curve to the rear wall. His knee bumped against something hard, but not brick. Wood. He looked down and his flashlight illuminated a waist-high hatch.

He dropped to his knees, grabbed the handle, and jerked. The hatch swung open. He bent at the waist and let Belinda slip off his shoulders, then wriggled past her into the tunnel. He reached back, grabbed her wrist, dragged her toward him. On hands and knees, he repeated the process until the tunnel opened into an alcove. Set into its opposite wall were four wooden steps that ended at a set of angled swinging doors; down their center Jack could see a slice of faint light. He crawled up the steps, put his back against the doors, and pressed until he was certain they weren't locked.

He crawled back to Belinda, dragged her up the steps, her head thumping against each of them in turn. Jack removed the penlight from his mouth and clicked it off, then drew the HK. On his phone he texted, **Okay, coming out. Don't shoot.**

He didn't wait for a reply but instead slowly pushed the doors, keeping his body as close to the ground as possible. If they were seen now and the alarm was raised they'd start taking fire. Death by bullet or death by explosion, it didn't matter.

Once he got Belinda onto level ground he started his crawl-drag routine again, aiming toward a cluster of trees ahead. Ten feet to go.

He rasped, "Belinda, help me, crawl!"

She muttered something incomprehensible, but his words must have registered. She started clawing at the ground and churning her legs.

Five feet.

Jack's cell phone beeped. He glanced at the screen:

Time's up.

He heard a whoosh. The air around him flashed orange. And then heat.

A voice shouting in German filtered into Jack's subconscious. He forced open his eyes but remained still. His brain was playing catch-up, assembling imagery and sound into something tangible, familiar.

Cabin, he thought. *Explosion*. The air was thick with the smell of burning wood and the sound of crackling flames. A few inches from his eyes a leaf was smoldering, its edges glowing orange. His scalp felt hot.

Jack heard a rustling. It was feet crunching through

undergrowth, he decided. *Don't move.* There were no friend-lies out here, he reminded himself. Only hostiles. He squeezed his right hand and felt the solidity of the HK's grip.

The crunching came closer, somewhere to his front and left.

He tracked his eyes back along the ground until an arm came into view; this he followed back to a head of short brown hair. Belinda.

"*Etwas?*" a voice called in the distance. Anything?

"*Nein.*"

The reply came from very close.

Very slowly Jack lifted his head, rotated it, and pressed it back to the earth. Eight feet away, a man illuminated by the flames crept from behind a tree trunk. His eyes scanned the ground ahead and to his sides. He held a compact assault rifle—similar to the FAMAS models carried by the men at Kultfabrik, Jack guessed—across his chest.

Belinda groaned, then stirred, rustling the leaves.

The man froze, then slowly pivoted toward the sound.

Slowly Jack rolled right, sweeping his gun arm under his body as he went until it was fully extended along the ground. He lifted the HK slightly and laid the front sight on the man's chest. He fired. The man went down. Jack rolled back onto his belly, then wriggled sideways until he was facing the ruined cabin. All that remained of the structure was a burning heap of debris sitting atop the foundation-turned-crater. The heat from the flames stung Jack's face.

He suspected the propane's heavier-than-air density had worked in their favor. Most of the gas had settled on the first floor and in the basement, and Jack's opening of the windows had dissipated some of the former. Sitting as far below-ground as it did, the basement had funneled most of the blast vertically. In fact, the ground nearest the house was almost pristine. Farther out, the terrain was littered with smoldering chunks of wood and wreckage, some as big as Jack himself.

Lucky or good? Which was better? In this case, luck.

He reached out, found Belinda's hand, and pinched and twisted the soft skin of her wrist. She jerked her hand away. Jack whispered, "Belinda, if you can hear me, don't speak. Flex your fingers."

She did so.

"We're in trouble. Can you crawl?"

Belinda lifted her head and looked at him. The hair encircling her face was singed and crinkled. "I can crawl," she whispered.

Jack took it slowly until he'd put a screen of tree trunks between them and the cabin. He rose to his knees and helped Belinda do the same and held her steady as she got her bearings. She looked back at the cabin. Her eyes glittered in the flames.

"Bastards," she whispered. "Rotten bastards."

"Payback comes later," Jack replied. "Right now we need to keep moving."

Jürgen Rostock had declared war on them. Jack wanted to be far away by the time Rostock realized he'd missed his targets yet again.

26

As far as Jack was concerned, Munich was a closed door to them, and he wanted to spend as little time in Zurich as possible. They were prey, and their only advantage right now was mobility.

Jack wanted to accomplish two things in Zurich: one, investigate the villa to which Effrem had tracked Eric Schrader; and two, do some digging into Alexander Bossard, the owner of the plane that had rescued Stephan Möller from the airstrip in Vermont. For Jack the question wasn't so much whether Bossard was connected to Jürgen Rostock, but how exactly.

It was an hour before dawn, and ahead Jack could see the glow of Zurich's skyline on the horizon. They'd made the two-hundred-mile trip from Munich in just over two hours; Jack had been on the autobahn before, but never at night. He'd found the experience at once exhilarating and exhausting.

After escaping the cabin and reaching the car, Jack had driven south to Munich, where he'd picked up Effrem and their luggage; they'd then gotten on the autobahn and headed west at top speed. Belinda, still suffering the effects of either the propane exposure or the shock of the incident or both, lay curled up in the Citroën's backseat, a sweater tucked under her chin. Here and there, singed hairs jutted from her head like bent electrical wires.

Effrem was also asleep, his head resting against the passenger-seat window.

Jack hit a bump in the road and Effrem bolted forward, hands reaching for the dashboard. He blinked rapidly and looked around.

Jack said, "You're okay. We're a few miles outside Zurich."

"Thank Cronkite," Effrem said.

"Pardon?"

"Something I picked up from my mother. She's an atheist. Walter Cronkite is as close to a God as she allowed in her life."

"Were you dreaming about Möller?" Jack asked.

Effrem nodded. "I was still in the SUV. It was on its side and Möller was pouring gas through the sunroof."

Jack decided to use this as a segue. "We need to talk about what happened at Kultfabrik."

"About what?"

"I told you not to get out of the car. You got out of the car."

"So? I was trying to help, Jack. I wasn't about to let Möller—"

"What you did was hand yourself to him, and now we'll be damned lucky if the Munich police aren't hunting for us. If Möller had gotten you alone—"

"But he didn't, did he? Things turned out okay."

Jack felt a knot of anger forming in his belly. "That's not the point, damn it. The point is I had a reason for telling you to stay put."

"Which was?"

"One, to keep you out of the line of fire; two, to have you as another pair of eyes; three, as backup in case I needed someone followed."

Effrem took a few seconds to answer. "I hadn't thought about two and three."

The irony of this conversation wasn't lost on Jack. Change the words and the setting and it could have easily been an exchange between him and John Clark or Gerry Hendley. Plenty of times Jack had acted on well-intentioned impulse, but in tight spots good intentions didn't make either you or those around you bulletproof. The difference between "Things turning out okay" and catastrophe often sat balanced on a knife's edge waiting for that Guatemalan butterfly to flap its wings.

Now, suddenly seeing himself from the outside looking in, Jack felt his stomach churn. My God, how many times had he come close to getting someone killed without realizing it? Or almost blown an operation because he refused to pause, take a breath, and listen to someone else? Effrem was young and eager, and perhaps only now was he realizing the deadly seriousness of what they were doing. Jack had no such excuses. He'd had years to outgrow his impulsivity and yet he hadn't. Why?

In fact, wasn't this one of those times he should be pausing to reassess the situation? They were flying by the seat of their pants and Jack was at the stick. Was it time to make a call to Clark or Hendley? he wondered. And tell them what, exactly? The truth was, beyond being able to make a marginal case that Stephan Möller was a murderer, he had nothing but hunches and an ever-growing list of questions.

And now it was too late to call a halt. He had two lives in his hands. If he went home, Effrem and Belinda were as good as dead. The only help Gerry Hendley would—and could—offer was an escort to get them back to the United States safely, and a few well-placed phone calls to a higher authority. *And then what?* he thought. *Hope someone else solved the problem? No.* They were in the thick of it now.

They had to keep moving and keep digging until Jack found a way to end it.

He realized he was gripping the Citroën's wheel so tightly his hands were shaking. He was one of those idiot swimmers who paddle into the ocean only to realize they've gotten caught in a riptide.

Jack said, "Listen, Effrem, a lot of this is my fault. You shouldn't be here. Back in Alexandria, I should have said no."

"It wouldn't have stopped me."

"Maybe not." Jack shrugged. "Either way, you need to hear what I'm saying: These people have tried to kill both of us, and they're going to keep trying. We either stop now and call for help or we get our shit together and do this right."

"I vote for that, the shit-together option."

"Fine, but that means listening to me and doing what I tell you. If there's time to explain, I will. Otherwise, just do it."

Effrem nodded, then grinned. "So, when you say 'Jump,' I ask 'How high?'"

"When I say 'Jump,' you do it, then ask when you can come back down."

From the backseat Belinda called groggily, "What stinks in here?"

"Your hair," Effrem replied.

"Right. And who are you again?"

"Effrem." He jerked a thumb toward Jack. "I'm with him."

———

Jack drove around the northern outskirts of Zurich until he found a suitable hotel, mid-priced and transient-friendly near the airport, then booked a room and put Belinda inside with a stash of food and water.

Her facial expression told Jack she wasn't happy about the sequestration, but neither did she argue. Belinda Hahn had taken some body blows recently: her father murdered, a stranger arriving on her doorstep to suggest her own boss may be involved, and her cabin blown out from under her. Whether she herself recognized it, Jack knew she was still in shock. Sleep was the best thing for her right now.

Once satisfied with her promise to stay in the room, Jack drove the Citroën into downtown Zurich, where he picked up Alfred Escher Strasse and followed it to Lake Zurich. The sun was fully up and the lake's flat surface acted as a mirror. Jack pivoted the Citroën's visor to block the glare coming through his side window. In the hills surrounding the city, the pine trees were sprinkled with snow, and the lake ice had melted, save for a few car-size bergs.

The villa to which Effrem had tracked Eric Schrader sat on a stub of land jutting into the lake about halfway down its western shore and was sandwiched between two gated yacht clubs. With the exception of the latter, the location vaguely reminded Jack of his condo in Alexandria. That, and a price difference of five or six million, he estimated.

At Effrem's direction, Jack turned right on Seestrasse, or Lake Road, then followed its meandering tree-lined course south until they reached the outskirts of the village of Wädenswil. Two more turns brought them to a frontage road not twenty feet from the shoreline.

"Out your window," Effrem said. "See the stone pillars and the black wrought-iron gate?"

Jack did, but just barely. The villa's driveway was obscured by tall, tightly packed hedgerows and overhanging pine boughs. Without slowing the Citroën, Jack scanned the entrance for signs of security but saw only a card reader mounted on a stone pillar. No cameras, no post for an attendant, and the ivy-covered wall on either side of the entrance was barely six feet tall, its crest made of smooth stone. Nor did Jack see any address placard. Ten feet through the gate, the driveway curved out of view.

Jack kept driving and the villa's entrance disappeared in his side mirror. "And this is where Schrader stayed?" he asked.

"Like he owned the place," Effrem replied. "Used the card reader to get in."

"Have you done anything to find out who it belongs to?"

"Tried. When it comes to places like this, the Swiss treat

property ownership the same way they treat their banking—with rigid privacy standards."

"Unless I missed seeing something, the perimeter is a piece of cake. Whether there's a security system on the house itself is another question."

"I can't believe I'm the voice of reason on this one, but what would we gain from breaking into the place? I'm guessing our hunch is right and it belongs to Alexander Bossard. What would we hope to find inside?"

It was a good question, and Jack didn't have an answer to it. They were unlikely to find a cardboard box labeled "Clues" in one of the villa's closets, but they had few leads, and only two in Zurich: this villa and Alexander Bossard. He wasn't going to brush aside either of them without some due diligence first.

That reminded Jack of something: "Have we heard back from Hacker Mitch yet on his hunt for Gerhard Klugmann?"

"Hold on," Effrem replied. He pulled out his cell phone and sent a text. The reply was immediate. He read it, then said, "He's getting close. Today or tomorrow, he hopes."

"Push him a little bit."

After Zurich, unless they decided to knock on the front door of Rostock Security Group's headquarters and ask to see Jürgen himself, they were out of leads. Getting to Klugmann was the kind of break they needed.

To kill time before nightfall Jack drove into Zurich's Altstadt, or Old Town, to put eyes on Bossard's office building. The Altstadt, also known as District 1, was a collection of perfectly restored medieval buildings, Romanesque churches, postage-stamp parks, and boutique shops and restaurants all contained within a maze of alleys and streets sitting astride the Limmat River. The place reminded Jack of a real-life Santa's village. Jack saw few cars, but the sidewalks were crowded with what looked like locals and tourists alike, the former hurrying about their business, the latter stopping every few feet to take pictures or gape at their surroundings.

They found Bossard's building near the Grossmünster—Great Minster—church, one of the city's oldest and most recognizable landmarks.

"Built by the very hand of Charlemagne himself," Effrem read from his phone's screen. "Or at least he commissioned the original church on the site. It's almost a thousand years old, if you can believe it."

The bright morning sun highlighted a façade and stonework that were obviously well cared for. Jack replied, "Doesn't look a day over eight hundred."

"Turn left here."

Jack made the turn, then one more, and pulled onto

Limmatquai, which ran abreast of the river. As they approached it, Jack found himself surprised. Rather than a model of imposing medieval architecture, Bossard's eight-story office building was just one among a line of unremarkable structures with cream or white façades and sharply pitched red-tiled roofs. If he hadn't known better he might have mistaken them for hotels. The entrance to Bossard's building was a lone bronze door beneath a green awning. A small gold plaque beside the door read 94 LIMMATQUAI.

"Did you ever go inside?" Jack asked.

"No, you want me to?"

"You feel up to it?"

Effrem nodded. "What am I looking for?"

Jack passed the building, found an open parking spot at the curb, and pulled in.

"Security cameras and/or guards, whether there's a manned reception desk and if so what's on it—computer, telephone, intercom, and so on. Are the elevators open or access-controlled—"

"You mean by key?"

"Or card. Same question if there's only a stairwell. Also, is there a visible emergency exit or any doors that look like they might lead to a utility room or closet? When you get inside, if there's a desk, just walk past it and head toward the stairs or elevators. See if you get a reaction, but don't push it. Don't be memorable."

"And while I'm collecting this plethora of intelligence, what's my excuse for being there?"

"Confused tourist."

"If there are cameras, do I hide my face?"

Jack shook his head and smiled. "No, don't do that. I also need a rough map of the lobby and its approximate dimensions. And if you see a business directory, find out which businesses are directly above and below Bossard's floor."

"Jeez, anything else?"

"No."

Effrem pursed his lips and exhaled heavily. "I guess it's a good thing I've got a stellar memory."

"Don't spend more than three minutes in there. Get moving."

Jack had chosen Effrem's time limit arbitrarily. He'd seen John Clark milk a first reconnoiter for twenty or thirty minutes and walk out best friends with the person he'd just subtly interrogated. In this case, Jack wanted to see if Effrem was going to follow orders.

Two and a half minutes later he emerged from the bronze door, walked back to the car, and climbed in. "Got it."

They drove a few blocks and found a café overlooking the Quay Bridge, which separated Lake Zurich from the Limmat River.

"Let's hear it."

As though he'd given a surveillance report a hundred times before, Effrem described the building's lobby: "Forty feet square, with a long horseshoe reception desk to the right, manned by a receptionist and a man in a business suit."

"Did he stand when you came in?"

"Yes."

"Did he smooth his tie or fiddle with his buttons when he stood up?"

Effrem frowned. "Uh, yes, actually. Why?"

"Habit. A lot of bodyguards pick it up. In a controlled environment, when someone unfamiliar pops onto their radar it's a way of having their shooting hand halfway to their weapon. Keep going."

"On the reception desk, there's two telephones, one computer workstation, and a key-card reader mounted on the raised counter. Past the desk, a bank of elevators, stairwell door, and an emergency exit. I counted three cameras: one overlooking the reception desk, one over the front door pointing inward, and one at the elevators."

The waitress returned with their coffee, then left again.

Jack asked, "Panning cameras or stationary?"

"Stationary."

"Exposed or shielded by a hood?"

"The latter," Effrem replied. "It didn't look like the elevators or stairs required a key or card, but I didn't get very close to them before the guard called me back to the desk. He was very polite, but very firm: This wasn't the place I was looking for; please leave now."

"Business directory?"

"None in sight."

Jack took all this in and nodded. "Good job."

"Thanks. What's all that info mean?"

"That unless we want to go in hard, breaking into Bossard's office after hours would probably get us caught, or killed, or both. Let's hope the villa pans out."

They sipped their coffee in silence for a while, watching the boats on the lake and soaking in the sun. Finally Jack asked, "What did that security guard look like?"

"Six-two, maybe, broad shoulders and blond hair. Why?"

"In the past ten minutes a green Opel cargo van has passed us three times. Now it's parked down the street and across from that Starbucks. No one's gotten out."

To his credit, Effrem resisted the urge to turn around and look. He asked, "Can you see anyone inside?"

"Just one behind the wheel, but the sun's on the windshield. I can't see his face." Jack wondered how many men could fit in the back of the van.

"What do we do?"

"Drink our coffee and wait."

Their shadow belonged to either Rostock or Bossard, but how had Jack and the others been tracked here? While their foray to Zurich wasn't unpredictable, the city was sizable and the bad guys had picked up their trail in record time.

Belinda. Jack dialed her cell phone, this one a burner she had no choice but to use, and waited through four rings before she answered. "Just checking in," Jack said. "Everything okay?"

"Yes. Why? When are you coming back?"

"Soon as we can. Just make sure the door is locked. Don't answer it for anyone but us."

Jack disconnected. *What now?* He wasn't about to lead this van back to the motel. The trick would be to either turn the tables on their shadow or shake him in such a way that it appeared unintentional. Once again here was a task where many hands would make short work, but Jack had limited hands, only one vehicle, and too little time for an elaborate plan.

He said to Effrem, "Get on your phone. I need a place that's remote, but within fifteen or twenty minutes of here. Preferably somewhere with dead ends."

"I doubt I'll find it on Yelp, but I'll have a look," Effrem replied. He browsed for a few minutes then said, "There are a lot of little villages in the mountains west of here. The roads up there look pretty snaky."

"That'll do."

They took their time finishing their coffee, then paid the bill and walked back to the Citroën. "Don't look for him,"

Jack warned Effrem as they climbed in and Jack started the engine.

With Effrem navigating again, Jack crossed the Quay Bridge, merged onto Bederstrasse with the rest of the lunch traffic, and headed west toward the foothills.

"He's with us," Jack said, glancing in his side mirror. "Four cars back, lane one."

"Anyone in the passenger seat?"

"No."

For the next ten minutes Jack kept heading west until finally they left the city behind and began climbing into the mountains. Almost immediately the van began losing ground. It pulled onto the shoulder, waited for a line of cars to go by, then did a U-turn and headed back toward Zurich.

"He's not playing," Jack announced.

"Or he wasn't following us," Effrem replied.

"Maybe."

27

At nine p.m. they left the hotel and retraced their southerly route along Lake Zurich to Wädenswil. Here, just fifteen miles outside Zurich proper, its night skyline appeared as a hazy dome of light on the horizon. Although it frequently passed through villages—there were fifteen on the left, or western, shoreline—the road south was dark and lightly traveled. Lake Zurich was more impressive than Jack had realized, reaching some twenty-five miles from Zurich in the north to Schmerikon in the south and, according to the fishing brochure at the hotel, more than five hundred feet deep in several spots.

As seemed to be par for the course, Jack had in his mind only a vaguely outlined plan. From their earlier reconnoiter,

Jack knew getting over the villa's wall would present no problem, but the house itself was an unknown. Google Earth's overhead view had shown little of the structure beyond a hip-and-valley roof that was barely visible through the canopy, a lush lawn, and an acre-size English-style garden on the property's western edge. For all Jack knew, the grounds were actively patrolled by a cadre of guards similar to the one Effrem had seen in Bossard's office building. If so, Jack would probably be scrambling back over the wall before the lawn had a chance to moisten his shoes.

Jack pulled into the Jachtklub Wädenswil parking lot and doused the headlights but left the engine running. The villa's outer wall was a quarter-mile south through a cluster of trees.

"Questions?" Jack asked.

"No, sir," Effrem replied with a mock salute. "Orbit a half-mile route between Horgen and Wädenswil and then wait until I hear from you. If you text 'evac,' I get back here at best speed. If I don't hear from you within ninety minutes, I pick up Belinda, move to the secondary hotel, wait another day, then leave, head to Brussels, and contact the U.S. embassy there."

"Right." This last bit of instruction would likely prove worthless if Jack's penetration of the villa went bad; more than anything else, it was designed to get Effrem and Belinda back to relatively safe territory. It would also have the added benefit of ruining Effrem's investigation. If there was no story left to pursue, he might live to see thirty.

"Why the Brussels embassy?" Effrem asked. "Why not the one in Bern?"

"They know my name in Brussels. You'll get more immediate action."

Though Jack had a hard time saying this with a straight face, the explanation seemed to satisfy Effrem. "Consider it done," he said. "Good hunting."

As Effrem pulled the Citroën out of the lot and back onto the road, Jack walked into the trees, where he paused to let his eyes adjust to the darkness before continuing on until the villa's stone wall came into view. The trees were thicker here and probably hadn't been trimmed for years; branches crisscrossed the top of the wall and jutted over the property. While the overgrowth lessened the likelihood of any surveillance cameras picking him up, it also surrounded him in almost complete darkness. Now he regretted his decision to not replace the night-vision goggles he'd lost in Munich.

Deal with it, Jack.

He turned right and followed the wall to its western corner. Here was the most likely place for a camera; corner-positioned cameras offered the most bang for the buck, but they also had built-in blind spots. Jack saw no camera.

Now came the less-than-glamorous part of being a special operator—the waiting and watching. Stealth was as much about stillness as it was about skulking. If his approach had attracted attention, he'd be getting visitors soon enough.

He sat cross-legged on the ground, his back against a tree trunk, and donned his portable radio's headset. He keyed the talk button. "Effrem, you there?"

"I'm here. Making the turn back north. I'll be driving past the gate again in about two minutes."

Ten minutes passed. Aside from some faint boat engine sounds coming from the direction of the lake, all was quiet. A rabbit hopped into view along the wall, spotted Jack, then sprinted away.

Long enough. He was anxious to get in and get out.

He approached the wall, grabbed its top with both hands, and hop-vaulted so his chin was level with the capstone. On the other side was a mulched planting bed interspersed with white tulips and cedar bushes.

Jack pulled himself up, flipped his leg over the wall's crest, then rolled over and dropped to the ground behind one of the bushes. Ahead he could see the curved black edge of the asphalt driveway. The main gate was somewhere to his right. He headed that way until the wrought-iron gate came into view, then crossed the driveway and ducked behind a hedgerow.

Jack continued like this for another fifteen minutes, partly to hunt for any patrolling guards, partly to get a better look at the villa itself, a two-story structure done in French farmhouse style. Switzerland was a country of four official languages—German, French, Italian, and a bit of Romansh—and the architecture and culture reflected this. The more expensive homes along Lake Zurich seemed to be a mixture of design styles, from old-world Tuscan to German neo-modern.

By the time Jack reached the villa's lake side he was convinced he was alone on the grounds. He'd seen no lights and no movement in or around the villa, so unless the occupants had turned in very early, no one was home.

Jack emerged from his hiding spot and strode across the lawn to the villa's rear patio, a slab of herringbone paving stones complete with a sunken grotto hot tub whose surface was choked with leaves and twigs. Jack switched his penlight to red, clicked it on, checked the patio doors and nearby windows for signs of an alarm system. Again, there was nothing. Apparently, Lake Zurich wasn't known for its high crime rate. Jack half wondered if the villa's doors were locked, but a quick check of the patio door answered his question.

Effrem's voice came over Jack's headset. "Jack, I've got a vehicle parked about a hundred meters north of the villa gate. I think it may be that green cargo van we saw earlier."

"Give me a percentage of certainty," Jack replied.

"Eight percent. This one's got an electrician's placard on the side, but it looked crooked. Might be a stick-on."

"Are you sure it wasn't there before?"

"No, not sure at all. Sorry. You want me to get closer and check the license plate? Or maybe see if someone's inside?"

"No, leave it." Effrem didn't reply immediately, so Jack asked, "Are you hearing me? Stay away from it."

"Okay, I hear you."

"Tighten up your loop so you pass the van every few minutes. If he starts following you, drive into Horgen and find as public a place as you can find and stay there. Keep me posted."

In turn Jack checked each of the villa's first-floor mullioned windows; all seemed to be bedrooms except for the corner room, which looked to be a study/library. A computer monitor sat atop the walnut desk.

Jack pulled a roll of masking tape and a glass punch from his rucksack, then taped an asterisk over the window's lower-left pane and pressed the punch into the glass until it shattered with a muffled tinkling. Carefully he peeled away the sections of taped glass, then reached inside and unlocked the window and climbed through.

He went still and scanned the room for blinking lights or the telltale soft clicking of a triggered motion detector.

There was neither. *Too easy*, Jack thought, a bit worried. In the United States, a luxury home of this caliber would be bristling with surveillance cameras and alarm systems.

Count your good luck and keep moving.

He pulled the window curtains closed, then sat down at the desk and powered up the computer. When the desktop appeared, a username/password dialogue box popped up.

Jack switched his headset plug from the portable radio to his cell phone and dialed Mitch, whom he'd asked to stand by, should Jack run into this very problem. When Mitch answered, Jack explained the situation.

"Well, there's no sense trying to brute-force the thing," Mitch said. "Permutations are in the billions. You got the flash drive I gave Effrem?"

"Yes."

"Let's try this first. Restart the computer, but hold down the command and R buttons as you do it."

"Recovery mode?" Jack asked.

"Yeah, you know what it looks like, then? Let's try the easy way first."

Once the computer's recovery-mode dialogue box appeared, Mitch had Jack navigate to the Utilities drop-down menu. "You're looking for 'Terminal,'" Mitch explained.

"It's there, but it's ghosted out. I can't select it."

"Worth a shot. Okay, insert that flash drive and do a force restart." Jack did this, and a black screen with a blinking orange cursor appeared. Mitch said, "Type 'run' into the command line, then sit back and wait."

"How long?"

"Depends on the size of the hard drive and whether the owner's running any third-party password or encryption protocols. Ten minutes, give or take. You should see a progress bar. The words 'run stop' will appear below the command line."

On Jack's belt the portable radio flashed. He told Mitch, "I'll call you back," then switched the headset over, turned up the radio's volume, and said, "Effrem, what—"

"—over the wall."

"What? Say again."

"Whoever was in that van just hopped over the wall! They're coming your way! Should I—"

"No, keep circling, but stay close to the yacht club parking lot. Just one, you're sure?"

"I only saw one."

"Stay off the radio unless it's absolutely necessary. I'll be in touch. Same thing applies: Two hours and you run."

Jack turned the computer's monitor so its light was shining away from the window, then peeked through the curtains in time to see a figure sprinting across the lawn and around to the villa's lake side. Jack checked the computer's progress bar: ninety percent to go.

Did he sit tight or go hunting? If this new player was responding to Jack's tampering with the computer, the chances were good he'd come straight to this study. Then again, why hop the wall rather than use the gate? Why post yourself outside the property rather than inside the villa itself? Those were questions for later. Right now he needed to be proactive.

Go hunting. He didn't want to be trapped in this room with only the window for an escape route.

He eased open the study door and poked his head out. To his left was a long hallway of dark tumbled stone tile. Beyond the hallway, he could see what looked like a living room decorated in robin's-egg-blue-and-white shabby chic. To his right, through an open arch, a winding stairway led to the second floor.

Jack heard what sounded like a burst from a dental drill followed by a soft double snick. He recognized the noise: an electric lock-pick tool known as a snap gun. Whoever was coming, they weren't wasting any time.

Jack raised the HK and crept down the hallway to the living room, where he paused to listen. He heard another sound, this one a door clicking shut. Somewhere to his right. He looked around the corner. Through an archway was the villa's kitchen.

As Jack watched, the back door swung open an inch, then went still.

Jack took aim.

The door moved again, just a few more inches, then clicked shut again.

Wind, Jack thought. *Probably*. Jack kept his gun trained on the door but let his eyes glide to either side of it, watching for movement. If the intruder had come through this door, what options did he have? Take cover behind the kitchen counter, or slip into the nook, or come through the living room arch toward Jack. Or . . . To the right of the back door was another set of stairs leading to the second floor.

As if on cue, Jack heard a floorboard creak above his head. If the intruder was familiar with the villa he might be crossing the second floor to the stairway behind Jack. Jack pivoted slowly on his heel, aimed the HK down the hall and waited for a five count, then pivoted back toward the living room.

From the second floor came a soft crash, as though someone had bumped a piece of furniture.

Move now.

With the HK raised and tracking, Jack paced through the arch and into the kitchen. A quick glance left told him the nook was clear. He circled behind the kitchen counter, saw no one hiding there, and continued toward the stairway door.

As he approached it, a semiautomatic pistol poked through the opening, almost crossing Jack's own weapon.

Startled, he stepped back. His heel rapped against the base-board. A figure rushed through the door, gun coming around to bear on Jack. The man's stance was straight-armed and overextended. Jack took advantage of this, batting aside the man's gun, stepping in close, and snapping the point of his elbow into the man's head. The man grunted but went along with the blow, using its momentum to coil his body for a counterpunch. Jack lifted his knee, slowing the strike, but not enough. The man's fist landed just below Jack's bottom rib. He gasped and bent sideways and felt his left leg buckle.

Strong and fast son of a bitch.

Jack drove his still-raised knee downward. His boot heel slammed into the tile, clipping the inner edge of the man's foot. The man yelped in pain. Jack repeated the maneuver, this time raking his boot's knurled edge down the length of the man's shin before stomping the man's foot a second time. Now the man collapsed sideways. Jack helped him, palming the side of his head and banging it against the doorjamb. The man dropped his gun. Jack kicked it, sending it twirling across the tile floor, then took a rapid step back and leveled the HK with the man's head.

"Are you done?" Jack asked, panting.

The man tried to get up, pressing himself off the floor with his left hand. Jack stepped forward and kicked it out from under him. He collapsed and his head banged against the tile.

"I said, Are . . . you . . . done?" Jack said.

"J'ai fini," the man replied. And then he added in lightly accented English, "I am done."

Jack clicked on his penlight. "Let me see your face."

"Why?"

"Show me your face," Jack growled.

Slowly the man lifted his head.

It was René Allemand.

28

W e've been looking for you," Jack said.

"Many people have been looking for me," Allemand replied. He sat upright and began massaging his shin and foot. "Can you stop shining that light in my eyes?"

Jack lowered the beam slightly. He keyed his radio and said, "What's happening out there? Do we have any more company?"

Effrem replied, "No. What's happening in there?"

"Everything's fine. Stand by."

Allemand asked Jack, "Who are you? Who are you talking to?"

Jack paused to consider his answers. While he tended to agree with Effrem that René Allemand was a victim in all this, there was a chance they were both wrong. "I can tell you who I'm not," he replied. "I'm not one of Jürgen Rostock's people."

This got Allemand's attention. He looked up at Jack with narrowed eyes. "What does that mean?"

"It means you're not the only one who's pissed off Herr General. Do you know a man named Eric Schrader? Very tall, German . . ."

"Perhaps."

"You met with him in Lyon."

Allemand didn't reply. Jack decided to go all in. "After you two parted company he flew to the United States and tried to slit my throat."

Allemand offered a Gallic shrug. "Well. It appears he didn't succeed."

"No, but it was close. He's dead now."

"You killed him?"

"Not exactly, but the result was the same. Captain Allemand, in case you hadn't noticed, you're still alive, and you're not zip-tied in the trunk of a car. If I was with RSG we wouldn't be talking."

"What you say makes some sense, but it doesn't explain why you're here and why you've been looking for me."

Jack was getting annoyed with their uneven information exchange. Then he reminded himself what René Allemand had been through. In fact, something told Jack he and Effrem probably knew only a fraction of the story.

"I know about Abidjan," Jack said. "At least part of it. I don't think you had anything to do with the attacks in Lyon. And I'd bet money there was a lot more to your kidnapping than anyone knows."

Allemand smiled. "And now this is the part where I unburden myself and we become fast friends, yes?"

"That's your call. As soon as I get done cloning the hard drive on the computer in that study—the one I believe belongs to Alexander Bossard—I'm leaving. You can either come with me and look at the data or go to ground again and pray you find a way to clear your name and get your life back. You decide."

Jack was reasonably confident he'd gained a sliver of trust from Allemand, but not so confident he would risk turning his back on the man. After collecting Allemand's weapon, a Walther P22, Jack returned to the study to find Mitch's flash drive had nearly finished its task. Jack sat down before the computer and watched the progress bar inch closer to one hundred percent.

Allemand appeared in the study's doorway. "Can I have my gun back?"

"I'll leave it beside the wall by the front gate," Jack replied. "Or you can join us for coffee and I'll give it back to you then."

"'Us'? It's not just you?"

"No. We come as a package deal, though. If you're going to trust me, you'll have to trust him."

"I do not think we're quite at trust yet, do you?"

Jack offered Allemand what he hoped was his best "couldn't care less" shrug. They desperately needed Allemand's cooperation, but Jack's gut told him playing hard-to-get was the smart move. "There's an all-night coffeehouse in Wädenswil, right off the Zugerstrasse and across from the police station. We'll be there for the next hour."

Jack removed the flash drive, powered down the computer, and stood up. "And you might want to retrace your steps before you leave."

"Pardon?"

"You're not wearing gloves. If you don't want your fingerprints found here, I'd wipe down everything you touched."

Jack and Effrem hadn't gotten through their first cups of coffee when they saw, through their booth's window, Allemand's van pull into the parking lot. The electrician's placard was gone. Jack said to Effrem, "Good call about that, by the way."

Effrem smiled. "I'm a learner."

Allemand walked inside and the hostess approached him. He gestured toward Jack and Effrem, then walked over. He grabbed a chair from a nearby table, plopped it down at the end of their booth, and sat.

To Jack he said, "This is your partner?"

"Yes."

"Do I get my gun back now?"

Jack nodded at the folded newspaper on the table. "In there. It's not loaded. Leave it that way until you're back in the van."

Allemand made no move to touch the newspaper. "You know my name, but I don't know yours."

Jack made the introductions, first names only. Allemand shook their hands and said, "René. Jack, you said Eric Schrader is dead. Is that true?"

"Google it. Alexandria, Virginia. Unidentified man walks into oncoming traffic and is killed instantly."

"That's unfortunate. I was hoping to catch up to him. We were overdue for a chat."

Allemand smiled when he said this, but there was none of it in his eyes. Jack suspected that if Schrader hadn't died in Alexandria, he wouldn't have survived his run-in with Allemand. Jack assumed their "chat" would have involved power tools and electricity. If so, Jack wondered, had Allemand already had that kind of brutality in him, or had his experiences since Ivory Coast taken him to that dark place?

The waitress appeared and asked if Allemand wanted anything. He waved her off. Once she was out of earshot he said, "So, how do we proceed, the three of us?"

Jack and Effrem had discussed this. They'd decided to lay everything out for René and hope they were bringing something valuable to the table.

Jack said, "Effrem tells you his story, then I tell you mine."

"And if I do not want to share my own?"

Jack answered with a little steel in his voice: "Then that's on you. Get in your van and leave, but stay out of our way. Effrem, tell him."

Effrem took Allemand through his story, starting with Fabrice the café owner in Abidjan, then his tailing Eric Schrader after Allemand's meeting with Madeline in the Parc de la Feyssine, then finally his encounter with Jack and Stephan Möller at the nature preserve.

"That was you in the Parc de la Feyssine?" asked Allemand. "I thought I might have picked up a tail, but after I left it was gone. Madeline brought you to our meeting? Truly?"

"She's worried about you. She's trying to help."

Allemand frowned; it was almost a snarl. "I shouldn't have called her. Sentimentality is weakness. So. You followed Schrader to Virginia, then found this Möller person . . ."

Jack asked, "You've never heard the name?" When Allemand shook his head, Jack showed him a screen capture from the West Haven gas station's surveillance camera. "He's since lost his beard."

"Doesn't look familiar. You think he's with Rostock?"

"We have no evidence of a connection—to Möller or Schrader. Do you?"

"Nothing that would suffice in court."

This statement surprised Jack. Was Allemand merely using a colloquialism, or did he really believe this situation could be resolved on the white side of the law?

"Please go on," Allemand said. "After the nature preserve . . ."

Jack continued the story, but first backtracked to the attack at the Supermercado before recounting their hunt for Möller, his escape at the Vermont airstrip, their foray into Munich, then their meeting at the villa.

Effrem asked Allemand, "You were tailing us this morning. How did you know we'd be here tonight?"

"Like you, I had to leave Munich in a hurry. The only other trail I could follow was the same one that brought you here: Alexander Bossard and Schrader. I've been here for a week. I set up real-time game cameras in the trees across from the villa, hoping either Bossard or someone else would show up. He's impossible to get to at his office or his apartment in the city. I saw you pass by the villa a few times, got curious, and drove down here. I picked you up on your way back to Zurich. Jack, why would Jürgen Rostock want you dead?"

"I was hoping you could tell me."

"I can't."

"Effrem has a theory about you," Jack said. "He thinks you were false-flagged. That's when a—"

"I know what it is. What makes you think that, Effrem?"

"It's what you said to Madeline—'He isn't who he claims to be.'"

Allemand shook his head, scratched furiously at his arm, then replied, "I don't recall saying that."

"Not good enough," Jack replied. He shoved the newspaper toward Allemand. "Time for you to go."

"Pardon me?"

"We've been straight with you. If you're not going to reciprocate, we've got no use for you. In fact, from what I can tell, you're more of a liability than an asset." Jack intended this last comment to sting, and the change in Allemand's eyes told him it'd worked. "We'll be better off without you."

Allemand said nothing for several seconds. "It's difficult, you must realize. I don't have a home, Madeline is the only person from my former life that knows I'm alive, and a good portion of my fellow Frenchmen think I died either a deserter or a traitor and therefore got what I deserved. Jürgen Rostock is a powerful man. I've been walking on a razor's edge since Abidjan. I feel like I'm sometimes in a dream, other times not. And now, to find out my Madeline confided in a . . . reporter. Is it hard to see why trust is hard for me?"

"I get it, I do," Jack replied. "But here's what I know, René: Whatever your connection is to Rostock, it's a miracle you're still alive. I don't think you'll last out here on your own much longer. You've got to trust somebody sometime. Whether that's us, only you can decide."

Allemand, who'd been staring at his hands, clasping and unclasping them while Jack was talking, now looked up. He held Jack's gaze for a long five seconds; Allemand's eyes were twitching slightly. He said, "What do you want to know?"

29

L et's go back to the start," Jack replied. "What happened in Abidjan?"

"The night they took me I was going to meet a girl, a Red Cross worker from Strasbourg. We met when her orientation group came to get some basic first-aid training before going into the field."

"What's her name?" Effrem asked.

"Uh . . ." Allemand thought for moment. "Janine Pelletier. No, Périer, that's it.

"Do you have a picture of her?" Jack asked.

"Perhaps in my OneDrive account . . ." René got out his phone, tapped a few keys, then handed it to Jack.

He studied the photo and returned the phone to René. "Go on," he said.

"Not long after I got there, a van pulled up. Five men in balaclavas poured out, swarmed me, put a hood over my head, and shoved me into the van. It happened so fast . . ." Allemand shook his head. "I barely put up a struggle, I was so shocked. After that, it was all something of a blur. We drove for hours, I don't know in which direction, but it was almost dawn when the van stopped. I was put in a basement, I think, in a small brick room with no windows."

Effrem asked, "Did anyone speak to you, ask you anything?"

"No, and that made it all the worse. No one said a word, not from the time I was taken to the day I got free. Once a day, every day, someone would come into the room wearing the same balaclava, give me food and water and change my waste bucket, then leave. A couple times a day two or three of them would come in, beat me and kick me until I passed out. Every few days another one would come in, put a gun to my head and pull the trigger, but the gun was always empty. Several times they had me stand on a chair with my head in a noose, and they would simply watch me. For hours. There were other . . . things, too, but I can't . . ." Allemand's words trailed off.

"How did you get free?"

"I was rescued. One night, very late, I heard two explosions. I recognized them as flash-bangs—you know, stun grenades—and then there was a lot of automatic weapons fire. About ten minutes after it started, the door to my cell opened and a pair of men in camouflage came in. They told me they'd come to rescue me. They took me somewhere by vehicle, maybe Abidjan, but I can't be sure. It was a private home, some kind of compound. Waiting for me were a doctor and a nurse. I had broken bones, torn ligaments and muscles, contusions on my liver and spleen. Even with the medication, the pain was indescribable. A few days later Jürgen Rostock showed up. It was his men who rescued me, he told me.

"From there we moved around a lot. Rostock told me my life was in danger, that people were hunting for me, that it had something to do with my father and the Army Defense Staff. I never quite understood it. I was fuzzy, you know, from the drugs, but eventually, after about six weeks, Rostock said they'd eliminated the threat."

"Which was what?" asked Effrem.

Allemand shook his head. "I'm not sure. I'm sorry, it's, uh . . ."

"That's okay," Jack said.

Was René a junkie? he wondered, René's demeanor suggested a narcotic addiction, perhaps to oxycodone. His injuries certainly warranted such a prescription.

Pieces began falling into place for Jack: What kind of group, terrorist or otherwise, kidnaps a soldier—a soldier from a famous family, no less—but claims no credit for it and asks for no ransom? His captors had tortured him, but had neither asked him questions nor tried to coerce him into some trumped-up, inflammatory confession.

And what about after his rescue? Rostock had made no effort to return René to his loved ones. And then there was the constant moving about, the vague, looming threats to René's life, the insinuations about his father. And through all of this, Jürgen Rostock and his men were the only ones looking out for him, the only ones who could keep the boogeymen at bay.

Seeing it now with fresh eyes, Jack recognized René Allemand's odyssey for what it was: an elaborately choreographed brainwashing program. But to what end? To answer that question, Jack had to first determine whether René understood the true nature of what'd happened to him. There was a larger worry as well: How reliable was he at all? He'd been kidnapped, that much was fact, but they had only his account of what happened after he was thrown into that van in Abidjan.

"What happened next?" asked Jack.

René replied with a proud grin, "Rostock offered me a job."

Effrem leaned forward. "What? What do you mean?"

"A job in his company. He offered me a position as a field officer. I'd heard of RSG and knew of its reputation, but I'd always assumed my career would be in the French Army.

What happened in Abidjan and then what Jürgen and I talked about made me reconsider. I took the job."

"And you never thought to contact your father or the Army to let them know you were alive? Why, for God's sake?"

"At first, it was at Rostock's suggestion. I was going to be doing undercover work, he said, and the training and transition were going to be intense. Once I was past that, Rostock was going to help me get my old life back. Later, well, I'm not sure why."

Effrem's mouth was hanging open. He said, "Are you suggesting you participated in faking your own death to join RSG? That you were going to be part of some secret . . . what, exactly? What was Rostock asking you to do?"

Allemand stared vacantly at Effrem, his face a mask of frustration and confusion. Clearly he wanted to, and should have been able to, answer Effrem's question, but there was a disconnect somewhere in Allemand's brain, related either to his addiction or to his treatment at the hands of Rostock, or a combination of the two.

Effrem said to Jack, "Christ Almighty, this guy is out there—"

Jack cut him off. "We're just having trouble following this, René."

"Yes. Of course. These are not simple issues we're dealing with. The world, I mean. We're on the brink of a preci-pice." Again Allemand's words trailed off, as though he'd lost his place in a script.

Jack felt a wave of sympathy for René, but it was tainted by a gut punch of fear. He'd already felt he and Effrem had dropped into the rabbit hole. Sitting across from René, Jack now felt like he'd met the Mad Hatter. Or the White Rabbit. None of this was René's fault, of course, but Jack now real-ized they'd joined forces with a highly trained soldier who not only had lost touch with reality, but was probably suffer-ing from a narcotics addiction and PTSD as well.

Abruptly, Rene stood up. "I need the restroom."

"Down that hall and left," Jack replied.

Allemand walked away.

Effrem leaned across the table at Jack and rasped, "The man is insane, Jack."

"Hold on—"

"No! I've spent a long time on this story, maxed out my credit cards, and almost gotten myself killed chasing a luna-tic. We've got to get out of here. I'm done, Jack. Let's go." Effrem moved to stand up.

"We're not going anywhere," Jack snapped. "Sit down. You're not seeing it, are you?"

"What?"

"René was kidnapped and he was held and he was

rescued, but it's all Rostock." Jack spent the next two minutes explaining his theory until slowly Effrem's expression softened.

"Jack, brainwashing? That's *Manchurian Candidate* stuff. Science fiction."

"You'd be surprised. I think what happened to René is an extreme form of operant conditioning combined with drug therapy. Negative reinforcement, isolation, threat of extinction, desocialization, a skewed version of Stockholm syndrome—it's all there. It's what he went through, from the time he was kidnapped until Rostock offered him a job."

"If that's the case, why is he on the run from Rostock?"

"I think he knows something's not right about all this, but he can't pin it down. It's like trying to grab a fistful of water. One minute he's suspicious of Rostock, the next praising him. Allemand either saw or heard something that spooked him—something that contradicted his conditioning—so he bolted."

"Let's just assume you're right. Why him? Aside from his famous name, right now he's just another soldier. Why would Rostock go to all this trouble?"

"I don't think it's got anything to do with René. This is about his father, Marshal Allemand."

"In what way?"

"I don't know yet. But as a coercion technique, what

Rostock's done is brilliant. If you kidnap a child your leverage lasts only as long as you have control of that child. Same with threatening the child's life. But what happens when you take the child's mind and turn it against the parent?"

"A puppet," Effrem replied.

"A puppet whose narrative and fate you control," Jack added. "René is either a heroic French soldier who survived a horrendous experience, or he's a traitor to his country. To someone like Marshal Allemand, that's a powerful lever."

The question was, a lever to accomplish what?

Effrem's eyes had glazed over. "Kidnapping," he murmured.

"What?"

Effrem held up his finger for Jack to wait. He got out his cell phone, browsed for a minute, then said, "Son of a bitch! I knew I'd read something about this. René wasn't Rostock's first victim. Five years ago Alexander Bossard's daughter, Suzette, was kidnapped in Brazil. RSG rescued her."

"Save a man's child and you could own him for life."

"It's a hell of a debt to repay," Effrem said. "So what do we do with René?"

"In the long term, that's a question for a psychologist. In the short term, René's going to keep going until he assembles the puzzle in his head or Rostock kills him. If we keep him close we can at least steer him a bit."

Allemand returned to the booth and sat down. He drummed his fingers on the table and looked at each of them in turn. "You have more questions, yes?"

"You said you and Rostock talked," Jack replied. "About what?"

"What else? Islamic terrorism. It has to be stopped."

Jack didn't disagree, but René's tone had been condescending, as though Jack had asked what should be done with a lawn that needed to be mowed. *You mow it, idiot.*

"How?"

"Not the way we've been doing it here, or in the United States, for that matter. It's time to remove the gloves, as you might say. We root them out, wherever they are, and kill them all. If you help a terrorist, you are yourself a terrorist. If you sympathize with a terrorist, you are yourself a terrorist. We've been treating this like a conventional war. That's ludicrous. We need to go nuclear." As he'd been speaking, René's tone had become increasingly strident, and now he punctuated this last statement by jabbing the table with his index finger.

"You mean literally or figuratively?" asked Effrem.

"Whatever it takes. Nation-state armies are worthless in this kind of fight. Too many laws, regulations, rules of engagement. Governments come and go, as does political will. Terrorists don't bother with those things; we can't afford to, either. It has to stop, don't you see that? We have to stop them before it's too late. Rostock's approach is the only one that can work."

Jack thought: The looming threat, the ticking clock, and the savior. Three more operant-conditioning techniques.

"What approach?" asked Effrem.

Allemand was gazing out the window. After a couple seconds he snapped his head toward Effrem. "What?"

"I said—"

Jack broke in: "Maybe you can help me understand something. If you believe in Rostock's message, why are you running from him?"

"Schrader," Allemand replied simply. "I didn't trust him. He was my contact, my training officer, but there was something about him. I started following him."

"And?" asked Effrem.

"Did you follow the Lyon attacks?"

Both Jack and Effrem nodded.

"Do you remember the bomb maker's apartment they found a week later, near that pharmacy, and the makeshift shooting range outside Montanay? A few days before the attacks, Schrader visited both places."

Jack was stunned. Provided this wasn't a delusion of René's, Eric Schrader, one of Jürgen Rostock's operatives, had been involved in the Lyon attacks.

"But Schrader was working for Rostock," Effrem said.

"No, I think he turned. I was trying to get proof to take to Jürgen. I didn't know who else at RSG might be allied with Schrader, so I decided to handle it myself. And it's a good thing I did. Schrader and Alexander Bossard met a number of times with Rostock present."

Once again Allemand's reasoning was muddled. Schrader was a rogue agent and Rostock a terrorist-fighting savior who couldn't see what was happening under his own nose. Jack suspected part of René's mind was pushing him toward the truth about both Rostock and what had happened to him in Abidjan, but he couldn't yet make the leap. What would happen when the man had no choice but to face that chasm?

30

WÄDENSWIL, SWITZERLAND

Halfway through Allemand's revelation Jack had decided it was time to get Belinda Hahn out of harm's way. He'd been leaning in that direction already, but René's instability forced the issue. Plus, Allemand's trust of Jack and Effrem was tenuous. Belinda's presence might be too much for the soldier.

As it turned out, Allemand van had been serving as his command post and mobile living quarters. Jack convinced him to follow them back to the motel, then sent Effrem up to the room while he and Allemand sat in the van. During the drive Effrem had called his mother in Brussels to arrange for Belinda's safekeeping.

Effrem called a few minutes later. "She's ready to go.

There's a red-eye leaving in a few hours. I'll drive her, then come back. We're coming down now."

"Good. Drive safe."

Jack waited a few minutes to ensure Effrem and Belinda were gone, then led René up to the room. Jack ordered pizza, and then while René took a shower he plugged the flash drive into his laptop and uploaded the data to Mitch's private server. Mitch called a few minutes later as René emerged from the bathroom.

Mitch said, "Jack, there were no documents of interest on that computer, but I did find something interesting in the browser history—looks like a business portal. Is this guy an attorney? In Zurich?"

"Yes."

"Then, yeah, it fits. I don't know what kind of encryption and firewalls I'll find on the portal's server side, but I'll get started and keep you posted. Anything specific I should be keying on?"

"For starters, any mention of Jürgen Rostock or Rostock Security Group, or similar combinations. Throw my name in the mix, too." Jack lowered his voice, then added, "And any mention of a Janine Périer. She may have worked for the Red Cross."

"Got it."

Jack disconnected.

Allemand asked, "Who was that?"

"We've got a guy working on the data from the villa," Jack replied.

"Why are there three toothbrushes in the bathroom?"

"What?"

"There are two of you, but three toothbrushes," said René. "Is there someone else staying with you?"

"No," said Jack. "I must have packed two by mistake."

René considered this, then nodded. "Mind if I use one? I have no running water in the van. My teeth feel like they're wearing socks."

Effrem returned three hours later. René had fallen asleep in the armchair an hour earlier, which Jack took as a good sign. You don't sleep around people you can't trust, especially someone in Allemand's condition.

Jack was sitting at the table, willing his phone to ring. "There's a few pieces of pizza left," he whispered, nodding at the box. Effrem sat down, fished out a piece, and took a bite.

Jack asked, "What do you think about Lyon?"

"You mean about Schrader being involved in the attacks? If it's true, there's no way a guy like Schrader could orchestrate something like that. Rostock could, though."

"I agree." Rostock's kidnapping and rescue of Allemand was a type of false-flag operation. Staging a terrorist attack and then pinning it on another group, though more complex in scope, wasn't dissimilar in principle. "The group that claimed credit, the Sahrawi Islamic Liberation Army, dropped off the radar, didn't it?"

Effrem nodded. "Officials I talked to in both Lyon and Paris claimed to know nothing about SILA. Then again, it's not uncommon for smaller factions to dissolve, then reconstitute under a different name."

"True, but after the second-deadliest attack on French soil? I don't buy it."

"Me neither, come to think of it."

Jack wondered if there was a part of René's mind that had already come to a similar conclusion: SILA was a construct of Jürgen Rostock's, both fuel and another target for antiterrorist rage in Europe. There was, Jack thought, already plenty of that to go around—and rightly so. No Western nation would deny that the threat of Islamic terrorism was dire. Hell, the majority of the Muslim world felt the same way, so said all the intelligence he had analyzed.

If Lyon had been a Rostock operation, there had to be more to it than simple pot-stirring. What, though? And again, the as yet unanswered question that had been nagging Jack from the beginning: Why did Rostock want him dead?

M itch called an hour later. The ringing of Jack's phone woke Effrem and René. Jack put Mitch on speaker.

"I'm not calling about Bossard. But I can tell you where to find Gerhard Klugmann."

Allemand asked, "Who the hell is Gerhard Klugmann?"

"A hacker we think works for Rostock," Jack replied. "Where can we find him, Mitch?"

"You're not going to like it."

Effrem replied, "I haven't liked much of anything in the past few weeks, so what's the harm? Where is he?"

"In Windhoek, Namibia."

"Namibia," Effrem repeated. "What the hell's in Namibia?"

31

PARIS, FRANCE

A s for the deeper answer to Effrem's question, Jack had no idea, but a few minutes on Google offered a possible superficial answer: Namibia was home to almost thirty thousand German speakers, a holdover from Germany's almost two-hundred-year history with the country, which had even been called German South-West Africa from 1884 until the middle of World War I.

Rostock's possible presence in Namibia was no coincidence, Jack felt. Rostock had shown a preference for German employees. If Klugmann was there as part of RSG's operation, Namibia's German population would offer a deep pool of resources.

However, before he picked up his group and left Europe, Jack needed to satisfy his curiosity about the true reason for

René's kidnapping. To do this, Jack left Zurich a few hours after Mitch's call and landed in Paris shortly after noon. In his absence, Effrem would do his best to keep René occupied and even-keeled.

Marshal Hugo Allemand, though many years into retirement, was a fixture on Paris's social and political scene. As had Jürgen Rostock, Marshal Allemand had parlayed a celebrated military career into a civilian life of luxury and influence. Subsequently Jack had little trouble finding the Allemand estate, a working horse farm an hour north of the city near Montmorency Forest.

Jack pulled his rental car up to an iron gate festooned with stylized fleurs-de-lis and pushed the intercom. *"Oui?"* a male voice replied.

"Parlez-vous anglais?" Jack asked. His grasp of basic French was serviceable, but he'd found that outside the country's tourist hubs the locals preferred visitors either speak proper French or not try at all.

"Yes, I speak English," came the reply.

"I'm here to see Marshal Allemand."

"The marshal has no appointments scheduled for today. Please contact his secretary and she will—"

"I'm here about the marshal's son, René."

"The marshal has said all he cares to about his son's disappearance. All press inquiries should be directed to—"

"His secretary, I know." Jack placed his cell phone up to the intercom box and tapped the play button. After ten seconds Jack hit stop and said, "I made that recording less than eight hours ago. I'll wait."

The intercom was silent for a bit, then: "One moment, please."

It took five minutes. When the voice returned, Jack was directed to follow the driveway to the main house, where he would be met. Once through the gate, Jack did as instructed until he pulled to a stop before a ten-thousand-square-foot French-Georgian-style mansion. The colonnaded front steps were bracketed by a pair of bronze stallions rearing back on their hind legs.

A fit-looking man in a black suit was waiting on the walkway. By the time Jack climbed out of the driver's seat, the man was standing at his door. "I am Claude. Please raise your arms to shoulder level."

Jack did so. Claude ran a magnetic wand up and down Jack's body, then expertly frisked him before asking, "What is your name, please?"

"Jack."

"Your surname?"

"Smith."

Claude frowned at him. "Follow me, Monsieur Smith."

He led Jack through the front doors, across a white marble foyer, then through a set of French doors to a solarium filled with hanging plant baskets. Marshal Allemand was seated at a white wicker table. He gestured for Jack to sit, then nodded at Claude, who took up his post beside the doors.

"Do you know how many people have come to me with proof my son is alive? How many conspiracy theories there are out there?"

"No."

"Too many to count. If I find that you are playing that same game, I will do everything in my power to see you prosecuted. Do you understand?"

Jack had no doubt the marshal would carry through with his threat, regardless of whether Jack had broken any laws. "I understand," he said.

"You are free to leave if you so choose."

Jack turned in his seat so Claude would have a clear view as he took out his cell phone and held it up for inspection before placing it on the table before Allemand. "The recording is cued up. Just tap the play button."

Allemand neither looked at the phone nor reached for it but rather kept his eyes fixed on Jack. "You told Claude this recording is from eight hours ago? Where were you at the time?"

"In a motel outside Zurich. Marshal Allemand, your son is alive. And he's in trouble. I'm trying to help him. Watch the video. If you're satisfied that's René, we'll talk. If not . . ." Jack shrugged. "I'll sit here until the police arrive."

Allemand placed his index finger on Jack's cell phone, pulled it toward him, then leaned over the screen and tapped play.

For the next two minutes the marshal watched as Jack and René chatted over their pizza the night before. René hadn't been aware of the recording. Marshal Allemand played the video twice more, then sat back in his chair. His eyes were moist.

"That's my son," he said, his voice cracking.

Jack nodded but said nothing.

"He looks different. Older."

Jack replied, "He's been through a lot, and he's going to need a lot of help."

"Explain, please."

Worried about overwhelming the already shell-shocked Allemand, Jack gave him a condensed version of the story René had told them at the Wädenswil coffeehouse. He added his theory that René had been brainwashed. He left out any mention of the Lyon attacks and Jürgen Rostock until the end. At the mention of the German's name, Allemand leaned forward, his face hard.

"Jürgen Rostock—René told you this himself?"

"He did."

Allemand paused for a moment. Then, in a voice heavy

with conviction, he said, "This much I know: René did not have anything to do with the Lyon attacks. That's not in him, and I know my son."

"I agree with you. I don't think the kidnapping was about René at all. I think it's about you. Is that possible?"

Allemand didn't reply, instead asking, "Why hasn't René contacted me?"

"He thinks you gave up on him. Rostock insinuated your business dealings led to René's kidnapping."

"That's nonsense! You believe Rostock did this to gain leverage over me? If so, why hasn't he approached me?"

"René went on the run. Rostock doesn't have control of him. There's a part of your son's mind that knows it's not seeing reality. He's been trying to work it out for himself and I think the shock of being involved with anyone remotely connected to the Lyon attacks pushed him over the edge. You didn't answer my question: Would Rostock have anything to gain over you by kidnapping René?"

"Possibly. What do you know about Rostock?"

"Just what I've read in the papers. He's powerful, that much seems clear."

Allemand half smiled. "Power is influence, and Rostock has that—far beyond German borders, and in wide circles. Do you know what happened to Rostock in Afghanistan?"

"No."

"I'm not surprised," Allemand replied. "Rostock has

worked very hard to keep it out of the spotlight. In the spring of 2005, Rostock and his wife were visiting a reserve *Heer* battalion in Kabul. A suicide bomber rammed into their vehicle, killing Rostock's wife and two of his aides. In fact, everyone in the vehicle except for Rostock died. He lost his left leg below the knee and most of the mobility in his right arm. It crippled him and cost him his career."

"How so?" asked Jack. "He wasn't a ground soldier. Those kinds of injuries wouldn't disqualify him from service."

"It's what the attack did to his mind. He became erratic, politically belligerent, insubordinate. The Bundeswehr put up with it for almost a year and then quietly ushered him out the door."

"Politically belligerent," Jack repeated. "What does that mean?"

"Rabidly and publicly anti-Muslim. Not simply anti–Islamic terrorism, mind you, but a more all-encompassing, less discriminating mind-set, if you understand my meaning."

Jack did. The anti-Islamic rhetoric René had used back in Zurich was similar to the political timbre of what Marshal Allemand was describing—essentially a kill-them-all-and-let-God-sort-them-out approach.

Allemand continued: "Rostock wasn't without his supporters, of course, but to have someone of his stature and influence speaking out as he did wasn't something the German government could tolerate.

"So he was forced out. Shortly after that, he formed RSG and backed away from the spotlight. When he was interviewed or asked about military affairs he was circumspect. Not a trace of his earlier belligerence."

"A night-to-day change," Jack replied.

"A remarkable transformation," agreed Allemand. "But it was superficial. About five years ago Rostock began a campaign, a very quiet one, mind you, but a campaign nevertheless. I was, I believe, his first visit."

"What did he want?"

"To wage war. Privately. His way. Of course, at the start he was more subtle about it, but that was the essence of his proposal."

"Why come to you?"

"It was his belief that Western governments don't have the stomach to deal with terrorism, at least not in a definitive way. I didn't necessarily disagree with his assessment, but democracy is what it is, and for all its faults there's no better form of government. If you're going to claim to be a democracy, either you accept it warts and all or you don't. What Rostock was proposing was antithetical to democracy."

"You said, wage war 'his way.' Did he define that?"

"Private armies answerable to no government," replied Allemand. "No laws, no rules of engagement, and a simple mandate: Root out terrorism and all its support structures by any means necessary."

On its surface the concept had its appeal, Jack had to admit, but it was only practical if the laws you were willing to break were those at the very foundation of Western society. Without the checks and balances built into democracy, the dictate of "by any means necessary" was ripe for all manner of sins. It was a slope that would likely be slippery with blood in no time.

Jack suddenly realized what Rostock had proposed to Marshal Allemand was in broad terms not unlike The Campus's own mission. The difference lay in scope and intention. To fight terrorism you sometimes had to get into the gutter. That was ugly reality. At its most basic, it was a matter of target discretion. Terrorists kill indiscriminately. Once the good guys started down that road with purpose and intention, the war was lost.

"What did he want from you?"

"To 'sign on,' as it were, to start softly ringing the warning bell and recruiting allies. For his plan to work he needed advocates in Europe and the United States, both civilian and martial. And money, of course. With those two things he believed he could prove his theory, starting small at first, making headway where governments had failed, establishing and running networks that would provide actionable intelligence, destroying cells and training camps. Don't misunderstand me: I never had any intention of going along, but his presentation was impressive, right down to five-, ten-, and twenty-year plans and public relations strategies. Rostock was in it for the long haul, and I could see the fire in his eyes. He's a true believer, Jack, and the most dangerous kind—someone with means and motivation."

"I assume he didn't quit his campaign after you said no?"

"Of course not. Since then he's approached me a number of times, along with dozens of others across the EU and in the United States. I don't know if he's managed to gain any supporters, and if so how many."

"Why is all this a secret?"

"Rostock is very careful about whom he approaches and how. Nothing is recorded and nothing is written down. If you're going to accuse someone like Rostock of campaigning to be a private warlord, you'd better be ready for a fight, not just a legal one but a public relations one as well. Or worse. So far no one's been willing to take him on."

"Including you?"

"Sadly, yes. I assumed Rostock would eventually give up. Alone, the funds required for what he was proposing would be in the hundreds of billions of dollars."

Jack said, "We think it's possible Rostock was behind the Lyon attacks. What do you say?"

"Of course it's possible. It's an old trick, Jack, manufacturing the will to wage war. It happens more than people know. At its most benign, an organic, violent event is capitalized upon and used to massage national policy. At its most malignant, the event itself is fabricated. The fact that Lyon took place on my home soil, not long after the Paris attacks, is"—Allemand paused, considering his words—"disturbing."

"Had René not run, Rostock would have him under his thumb."

"Yes, I see that now. And don't ask me whether that leverage would have been enough to change my mind about Rostock's plan. I don't know the answer, and I'd prefer to not think too much about it. Jack, can I ask you: Why are you involved in this?"

"You can ask," he replied with a smile.

Allemand nodded. "I see. Where is René right now? Still in Zurich?"

"Yes. I have someone with him."

"I will send a plane for him."

"He won't get on it—not willingly, at least. And if you try to force him it'll make things worse. For him and for you."

"So I do nothing?"

"For now. Marshal Allemand, what would it take for you to come forward and speak out against Rostock?"

"Jack, I'm not worried about the repercussions I would face, but we would need more than my voice."

"What if I can bring you proof?"

"You bring me that, even the smallest thread I can tug on, and I'll start calling every name in my address book, from here to Washington, D.C."

32

WINDHOEK, NAMIBIA

While it was spring in Switzerland and Germany, it was late summer in Namibia. Having envisioned the country as nothing but a vast desert, Jack was surprised to see great swaths of lush grassland and scrub forest outside the plane's window. According to their flight attendant, April was the end of Namibia's rainy season, and this one had been wetter than normal. It showed. Watering holes and lakes dotted the terrain; interspersed among them, milky-brown rivers.

The plane touched down and Jack trotted down the stairs to the tarmac, followed by Effrem and René, who appeared more at ease, Jack thought, relieved. Though Namibia and Ivory Coast were separated by three thousand miles of coastline, he was concerned merely being on African soil again might throw Allemand for a loop. For similar reasons Jack hadn't told René about his trip to Paris. The soldier already had enough on his fractured mind.

"I thought it would be hotter," said Effrem.

The sky was a cloudless blue, the temperature in the mid-seventies. At the edge of the tarmac a light wind swayed the chest-high grass.

"Actually, it rarely gets over ninety Fahrenheit," René replied. "It's the garden spot of Africa."

Along with the rest of the plane's passengers, Jack and the others headed toward the terminal. Jack said, "Okay, guys, eyes open. We're looking for a single-engine Pilatus PC-12 NG, tail number HB-FXT." Both Jack and Effrem had seen Bossard's private plane in Vermont, but René had not, so Jack showed him a stock photo on his phone.

"What makes you think it's here?" asked René.

"I don't, necessarily." Bossard had used the plane to rescue Möller; it wasn't a big leap to imagine that the lawyer made it available as needed to Rostock. It was just as likely Gerhard Klugmann had arrived by a commercial airliner.

"I don't see it," Effrem said.

"Neither do I," René added.

"Three strikes," Jack said. He powered up his phone and

saw a text message from Mitch. In all caps it read, **PROGRESS. CALL ASAP.**

O nce through customs, they picked up their rental car, a white Toyota Land Cruiser, and set out for Windhoek, Namibia's capital, some twenty-five miles to the west. Effrem drove, with René seated behind him gazing at the passing landscape.

If Jack hadn't already known about the country's Germanic connections, the various place-name and other town signs along the two-lane highway would have given him a clue: Herbost, Kapps Farm, Hoffnung, Neudamm Railway Station . . . The combination of the mixed terrain with these distinctly European words strengthened the landscape's otherworldly feel.

Effrem, too, seemed fascinated by the scenery. "Have you ever seen *The Boys from Brazil?*" he asked. "You know, Nazis in South America?"

Jack laughed. "I've seen it."

"Déjà vu, only desert instead of rainforests."

Jack called Mitch. Munich was an hour ahead of Namibia. Mitch asked, "Where are you?"

"On the road," Jack replied. He had no reason to mistrust Mitch, but Jack had over recent years become habituated to the need-to-know rule. It was the norm in their business. "You have news?"

"Yeah, a couple things: I've got Klugmann's exact location nailed down. He's staying at the Hilton Windhoek, somewhere near the top floor. Give me a little time and I can give you the floor."

"Windhoek has a Hilton?" Jack asked.

"Based on the pictures, it's beautiful—something you'd see in Chicago or New York."

"What's the other news?"

"The name of the woman you gave me, Janine Périer, didn't match any of the Red Cross rolls for Africa, but there was a Janine Pelzer assigned to Abidjan for about six weeks last year. Her home country is listed as Germany—Munich, to be exact. I'm sending you her picture now. It's from her official ID card."

It took a minute for the image to arrive. Immediately Jack saw it was the same woman René had gone to meet the night of his kidnapping. Jack had hoped to be wrong about this, but it seemed clear Janine had been working for Rostock as a honeytrap.

"Current location?" Jack asked.

"I have no idea."

"Where are you with Bossard's company portal?"

"I'm into it. There's a lot of data, some of it encrypted folder by folder, and since I'm hijacking idle user logins I can only work in spurts. The system doesn't allow multiple terminal logins."

"I'm not following you."

"When one of Bossard's staff goes to lunch or the bathroom they log out of their terminal. I get an alert, then use their login to gain access to the portal. When they come back and log in again I get kicked out, so I have to find another idle username. And repeat ad nauseam."

"Got it," said Jack. "How long until you've got it all?"

"I should have everything collated tonight after they shut down the office. By the way, you got the FedEx I sent?"

"Yes, before we left Zurich."

"If anything needs explaining, call," said Mitch.

Jack hadn't bothered making hotel reservations in Windhoek, but now that they knew where Gerhard Klugmann was staying, Jack searched his phone for whatever was closest to the Hilton, which turned out to be AVANI Windhoek Hotel & Casino, one block north of the Hilton.

After handing their Land Cruiser over to the valet, Jack and the others collected their bags and went through to lobby reception. Jack asked for and got a top-floor suite, a multi-bedroom space of one thousand square feet with a walkout balcony overlooking the downtown district.

"I went to Las Vegas once. That's what this reminds me

of," René said, hands braced on the balcony railing. "If there was anything like this in Abidjan, I never saw it. Then again, we never saw much outside the base."

"Make yourself at home and relax," said Jack.

They chose bedrooms, then parted company for a couple hours of rest and decompression. Jack was exhausted; he couldn't remember the last time he'd gotten more than five hours of sleep in one stretch. Effrem likely felt the same; as for René, there was no telling the last time the soldier had any real peace, let alone untroubled sleep. He'd been on the run for a long time, made even more grueling by his mental state, Jack guessed. Part of Jack wondered if he should have taken Marshal Allemand up on his offer to fly René back home. On the other hand, the man had already been kidnapped once. Who knew what a second time might do to him?

As agreed, at five-thirty they met back in the suite's main room. Jack ordered room service, baked salmon and crab-and-orzo salad for him and Effrem; prime rib, roasted asparagus, and spring potatoes for René.

As they waited for the food, René sat on the coffee table

before the flat-screen television and surfed channels until he found a game show, what looked like the Namibian version of *Wheel of Fortune*, then sat down on the couch to watch. The host and contestants were speaking Oshiwambo.

Effrem looked over at Jack and shrugged; Jack reciprocated. He doubted it was the show's content René enjoyed, but rather the normalcy of the activity.

Their food arrived and they ate in silence and watched *Wheel*. When the credits rolled, René used the remote to shut off the television. "Thank you for the meal, Jack."

"You're welcome."

"What is the plan? Are we going after this Klugmann?"

As he'd been with Möller, Jack was of two minds about their best course with Klugmann. Grab him and squeeze him for information, or play the waiting game and hope Klugmann led them to something significant?

"Right now I'm more interested in Bossard's plane. There's only one airport aside from Hosea Kutako—Eros. It could have landed there—"

"Actually, if you count airstrips, there are dozens of places within fifty miles of here," Effrem said. "I couldn't sleep. I did some research. The Wi-Fi here is excellent."

"Dozens of airstrips," Jack repeated.

"But only six with runways long enough to accommodate a Pilatus PC-12. Subtract from that three that lie within state-controlled game preserves, and you're left with three airstrips Bossard's plane could put down at—Midgard, Pokewni, and Osona."

"I'm impressed," Jack replied.

"It was either this or Minesweeper."

"You made the right choice. Okay, we're going to split up. René, I want you to stay here—"

"Why?"

"Because I need someone to stay close to Klugmann's hotel."

This was a white lie. Even if Klugmann was there, without the exact location of his room they had no way of knowing whether it was visible from their suite. Jack was more interested in giving René more decompression time.

"If we get word that he's moving, you'll have to follow him," Jack added.

René nodded. "I can do that."

"Effrem, you're checking Eros Airport. Take a taxi there and have a look around. From what I could tell, all the onsite hangars are reserved for repairs. If the Pilatus is at Eros, chances are decent it's sitting outside."

"And what's my excuse for loitering about?"

"You'll think of something. I'll take the Land Cruiser and check the other three airstrips. Can you send me their locations—"

"Done," Effrem said, thumbing keys on his cell phone.

Of the three airstrips in question, Osona and Midgard not only were the closest to Windhoek, but also were within thirty miles of each other and a straight shot north from Windhoek, so Jack chose to investigate these first.

Knowing his phone's signal coverage was likely to be nonexistent much beyond Windhoek's outskirts, Jack took several screenshots of his phone's navigation screen, then used these to get on the four-lane Western Bypass highway toward the town of Okahandja.

It was night by the time Jack put the capital's lights in his rearview mirror. As before, the sky was a cloudless black backdrop sprinkled with pinpricks of light. The moon was so bright Jack almost found his headlights unnecessary.

Forty minutes later the Land Cruiser's headlights illuminated mile marker 17 and Jack began coasting. According to his map, there were no official signs for Osona Airstrip, but rather a faded wooden one pointing toward the now abandoned Bergquell Farm about a half-mile northwest of the runway.

The sign was so small that Jack overshot it and had to do a U-turn. He guided the Toyota off the highway, down a dirt driveway, then onto a broad frontage heading east. He had covered several hundred yards when he realized that he was actually on the airstrip's mile-long runway. He killed the

Toyota's headlights and drove on using only the moonlight to guide him.

There was nothing here, Jack realized. The head of the airstrip was nothing more than a large cul-de-sac, a turn-around for departing aircraft. When he reached this he turned left onto another dirt road, which led him to Berg-quell Farm, nothing more than a cluster of rusting sheet-metal huts, none of them large enough to hide even the smallest of planes.

One down.

The second airstrip, Midgard, was thirty miles east of Osona, but the only route there took Jack first north to Okahandja, then on a looping road that followed the edge of Swakoppoort Dam Reservoir. On Jack's phone the satellite view of Swakop looked like a giant starfish crushed flat, the reservoir's waters a startling blue against the otherwise brown landscape.

For twenty miles Jack followed the wide gravel road as it wound deeper and higher into the hills, until finally he saw a sign that read MIDGARD AIRSTRIP—KHORUSEPA LODGE. The latter didn't appear on his map, but he suspected resort lodges came and went around Windhoek, failing under one owner before being renamed and revived by another.

Jack made the turn, followed the road for another half-mile as it wound its way through a series of ravines to a fork in the road divided by another sign. To the left, Midgard Airstrip; to the right, Khorusepa Resort Lodge. Jack turned left and after only a few hundred yards found himself at the edge of a runway. He shut off the headlights.

Parked opposite him at the edge of the tarmac was a white single-engine airplane. The tail number read HB-FXT. It was Bossard's Pilatus. The plane's windows were dark, its wheels chocked, the side door closed.

No one was home. Or so he hoped.

He grabbed his rucksack from the passenger seat, climbed out, and walked across to the plane, where he ducked beneath the nose cone. He rapped his knuckles against the aluminum fuselage. Nothing stirred inside the plane, so he knocked again, this time louder. He then walked to the side door, lifted the latch, and twisted. With a hiss of hydraulics the door swung downward, extending the built-in steps as it went. Jack climbed inside and paused to look around. *Did it matter?* he wondered. The instructions Mitch had included in the FedEx package made no mention of where to place the GPS tracker.

Jack found the bathroom just aft of the cockpit. He removed the tissue-paper box from its cubby, dropped the tracker inside, then replaced the box and left.

---

ack in the Toyota, he retraced his path to the fork in the road and turned down the road to the resort. Abruptly he rounded a corner and found himself on a palm tree–lined cobblestone avenue at the end of which a thatched entryway spanned the width of the road. Through this he glimpsed a circular driveway, lighted brick pathways, and what looked like individual bungalows.

He braked to a stop and doused the headlights.

This was unexpected.

He checked his watch: It was one-fifteen. He saw no one moving about, no lights in the bungalow windows.

"The hell with it," Jack said.

He drove down the avenue and through the entrance, then eased the Toyota under the lobby awning. Through the windshield he saw flames rising from a circular stone fire pit. Seated around it were eight people. Jack pulled the binoculars from his rucksack and zoomed in on the group. All were men. Three of them had their backs to him; the five facing him he didn't recognize, and he wondered if one of them was Gerhard Klugmann.

Something tapped against Jack's window. He turned his head and found himself looking into the face of Stephan Möller.

Ah, shit, Jack thought.

"Kann ich Ihnen helfen?" Möller called. His tone and posture were relaxed. *"Haben Sie Sich verlaufen?"* Are you lost?

Jack didn't give himself a chance to think. He rolled down his window an inch, put a little gravel in his voice, and replied in Spanish, *"Estoy perdido. Hablas español?"*

"Nein, Deutsch."

Jack said, *"Onjala Lodge?"*

Möller was shaking his head now, getting annoyed. *"Nein. Sie sind an der falschen Stelle. Gehen Sie weg!"* Go away!

"Lo siento, lo siento," Jack replied.

He put the Toyota in reverse, did a U-turn, and drove off.

I t was almost four a.m. when Jack pushed through the door to their hotel suite. Effrem was sitting cross-legged on the floor, the only illumination coming from the glow of his laptop screen.

"Hey," he whispered.

Jack turned on a table lamp and plopped down in an armchair. "Hey."

Without looking up from his screen, still typing, Effrem said, "I struck out at Eros. You?"

"The plane's sitting on the tarmac at Midgard. I found Stephan Möller staying at a lodge nearby." Jack gave Effrem the details of his night, then added, "There were about eight of them, all German I'd be willing to bet." *And all with a similar skill set*, Jack guessed. "Möller was the only one I recognized."

"I'll be damned," said Effrem. "Good job. Mitch hit the motherlode with the Bossard portal, by the way. I forwarded you the link to the server. I've been going through the documents for the last couple hours."

"Anything interesting?"

"A lot, actually. For starters, I know why Rostock wants you dead."

33

WINDHOEK, NAMIBIA

Jack didn't respond immediately. Though he'd started all this with the sole intention of finding the answer Effrem now claimed to have, Jack realized it hadn't been on his mind for days. He'd stopped wondering why someone had tried to kill him. It was an odd feeling.

"Tell me," Jack replied.

"Last year you did a financial audit on a German company called Dovestar Industrial Machinery."

Jack recalled the job. As part of Hendley Associates' white-hat cover, he and several other analysts took on consulting contracts, usually having to do with mergers and acquisitions. As Jack recalled, Dovestar was one of five audits he did that year.

"I think I remember," he said. "It was routine. A couple days in Aachen, then back home."

"There was a little more to it than that."

"Refresh my memory."

"A Dutch company offered to buy Dovestar. By all measures it was a good offer. But Dovestar declined. For whatever reason, both the Dutch and German press got ahold of the story and started asking questions. The rumors were that Dovestar was in financial trouble, considering layoffs, and maybe on the road to bankruptcy. So why turn down the buyout? everyone asked. That's where you came in."

"To assuage fears, Dovestar contracted Hendley to do an audit."

It was coming back to Jack now. "It was essentially a financial-soundness report. I don't recall any red flags."

"That's because they were buried very deep, and it wasn't that kind of audit. The long and the short of it is this: Through a number of cutouts, Dovestar is ultimately owned by Rostock Security Group. That kind of subterfuge is what Alexander Bossard's firm specializes in, and as far as I can tell, RSG had been their only client for the past six years. Dovestar's a legitimate company, but RSG has been using some of its accounts as hidden piggy banks."

"For what purpose?"

"If I had to guess, an off-the-books operational fund.

Your audit, routine though it was, triggered an automatic review by BaFin."

Jack knew the abbreviation. It stood for Bundesanstalt für Finanzdienstleistungsaufsicht—the Federal Financial Supervisory Authority. In essence it was Germany's version of America's Securities and Exchange Commission.

Effrem went on: "The hearing was scheduled for next month. You're supposed to testify as to your audit findings."

Jack shrugged. "I hadn't heard about it. It might be sitting in my in-box."

"Without your sworn testimony the chances that RSG's relationship with Dovestar and the disposition of those secret funds will be exposed drop to almost zero," said Effrem.

"If I go away, the problem goes away," Jack added.

"That's what Rostock was probably hoping for. From what I gather, it's German boilerplate law: Without you present to certify the audit and be examined by Dovestar's counsel, the audit is worthless."

Jack suddenly realized the solution to all this might be as simple as his showing up for the audit hearing next month. Or maybe not. Everything they had on RSG and Dovestar's relationship had been obtained illegally. None of it was admissible, and if he tried to get around that, BaFin would find his hands dirty and his audit suspect.

He asked, "What's the status of the Dovestar funds now?"

"According to Bossard's memoranda, they were cleared out and buried about a month after you filed your audit, but as I said, it's a permanent legal record. A snapshot, if you will. If BaFin managed to trace Dovestar to RSG, Rostock would end up in the hot seat."

Jack smiled. "Effrem, you continue to impress me."

Effrem shrugged. "I spent most of my childhood sitting at the kitchen table watching my mother dissect financial and political puzzles. It must have rubbed off on me."

"What we need to know is how and where Rostock was spending that money."

"According to Mitch, through Dovestar, Jürgen Rostock's paid Klugmann almost four hundred thousand dollars over the past five years for 'IT consulting.'"

"That's a lot of hacking," Jack replied. "Or a few select, high-level jobs."

Jack now had his long-awaited answer, but as was par for the course, it only led to more questions. Klugmann was in Namibia and Möller was in Namibia. Therefore, by proxy Jürgen Rostock was in Namibia.

Jack tried to grab a couple hours' sleep. His mind wouldn't quiet, so after twenty minutes he got up and returned to the main room. René was in the adjoining kitchen, making coffee. Effrem still sat on the floor, laptop resting on his crossed legs.

"Good morning," René said with a smile. "Coffee?"

"Morning. Sure."

"Effrem told me about the plane. You're sure it was Möller?"

"Yes."

"Was there anyone else you recognized?"

Translation: Was Rostock there? Jack replied, "No one who looked familiar."

Jack walked away from René, sat down in the armchair, and whispered to Effrem, "Did you tell him about Dovestar?"

"No. It's your call whether he can handle it."

"Let me give it some thought."

Jack opened his laptop and downloaded Mitch's Bossard files from the server. All were searchable PDFs. According to Mitch's attached note, the only mention of Jack was in relation to the Dovestar audit, but Jürgen Rostock and RSG appeared in the files hundreds of times, which made sense as RSG was Bossard's only client.

"Effrem, start a spreadsheet. I want you to track the dates and amounts Klugmann was paid by Dovestar. He was paying Klugmann a lot of money, which suggests whatever Rostock needed him to do was significant. Based on what I'm seeing, Bossard handled a lot of overseas logistics, shipping, and procurement for RSG, but the details are ambiguous. I want to know if any of Klugmann's payments match them."

"Match them how?"

"Amounts, locations, permit applications, and transport arrangements . . . Anything."

Over the next two hours they went about their individual tasks, Effrem building a payment profile for Klugmann, and Jack a history of possible RSG overseas operations. Once done, they compared data. Jack said, "Okay, over the past five years I've got four RSG projects Bossard spent a lot of time on: one in Canada, one in Panama, one in India . . ."

"And most recently Namibia," Effrem added.

"Right." Jack gave Effrem the date ranges. "Any close matches to Klugmann?"

Effrem traced his finger down his screen. "Six payments from Dovestar. Looks like a couple for each date range you gave me. What do you think? Down payment and final payment for services rendered?"

"Possibly."

"There're no payments for Namibia, though."

"The Dovestar fund was shut down after my audit. They must be paying Klugmann through another source. Let's look at what was going on in those countries at the time. I'll take Canada and Panama, you take India."

"What am I looking for?" Effrem asked. "The phrase 'going on' is a little vague."

"Anything that might fall within RSG's wheelhouse—terrorist incidents, major crimes, assassination attempts. You get the idea."

Their task was challenging. Each of these countries had its fair share of problems—fringe political factions, terrorist groups, drug cartels, attempted coups, as well as frequent instances of random violence in the larger metropolitan areas. Even having restricted their searches to Jack's date ranges, there were hundreds of incidents that might have something to do with Rostock Security Group.

"I'm not getting anywhere," Effrem said after an hour.

Jack sighed and rubbed his hands through his hair. "Same here."

They knew Bossard was doing legal work for RSG in these countries at these times, and they knew Gerhard Klugmann had been paid for services rendered during these times. The correlation was there, but not the common thread.

René, sitting on a stool at the kitchen counter, said, "This Klugmann is a computer expert, a hacker?"

"Right," Effrem replied.

"Then clearly that's what Klugmann"—René hesitated, then finished—"was being paid to do. What you're looking for aren't incidents, but rather incidents related to computer malfunction."

Jack smiled. He and Effrem had overlooked the obvious. "Smart, René," Jack said. He did note, however, that René had shied away from naming Rostock as Klugmann's paymaster. He wasn't quite there yet.

"Effrem, let's try this again but narrow the search even further."

René's tweak made an immediate difference. Effrem called from his laptop, "I may have something. Two years ago, a waste reclamation plant in Mumbai dumped fifty thousand gallons of sewage into the Ulhas River. Cleanup is ongoing. Multiple lawsuits against the Japanese company responsible for the plant's operation. Suspected cause: sitewide system malfunction.

"Here's something in Ontario from three years ago: Control systems for two oil refineries malfunctioned and vented thousands of barrels into a nearby fishery."

René asked, "Private company?"

"Yes," Jack replied. "I've also got two incidents in Panama last year, both at sugarcane storage facilities. One, a malfunction in the climate control system that led to fungus infestation. Estimated loss was sixty million. The other was a fire control system that failed to detect a fire. Estimated loss was thirty million. Both facilities were privately managed."

"I'd call that a pattern," said Jack.

"What are we saying, though? That Klugmann cyberattacked those facilities and caused those catastrophes? For what reason?"

"Who stood to benefit from those companies' losing their contracts?" Jack asked. "Did these countries nationalize the failed facilities, or did they hire another company to take over?"

Effrem surfed on his laptop for a few minutes. "Mumbai's reclamation plant stayed private, but another company is managing the facility."

"Same with Ontario," Jack noted. "And Panama."

"This is unbelievable," Effrem said. "We can't be looking at this right."

Jack wasn't so sure. Economic espionage was a booming business, with hundreds of billions of dollars at stake. Rarely did a week pass without a new story about one company trying to sabotage a rival's market research or financial position. Gossip was spread, media campaigns launched, and legal battles fought, all as an economic cold war. Was direct-action sabotage that much more of a stretch?

The Panamanian sugarcane business was probably $4 billion a year. With those kinds of profits, hiring someone like Rostock to oust a rival company and be installed in its place could be seen as both a reasonable expense and a sound investment.

Marshal Allemand had mentioned the immense coffers Rostock would need to fund his private war on terrorism. Having failed to find either advocates or investors, had the

German developed a niche side business as an economic mercenary?

Talk about aggressive market development. Through disaster Rostock creates an economic vacuum and then arrives to save the day for his client. Jack wondered how many times Rostock had done this. They'd found three possible instances, and perhaps one in the making here in Namibia, but could there be others they had yet to find?

René, who had been following the exchange closely, walked over and sat down on the couch opposite Jack. "All this that you're suggesting, you believe Alexander Bossard is involved?"

Jack and Effrem exchanged glances. Jack hesitated, then replied, "Involved, yes, but he's secondary. We think Jürgen Rostock is at the head of it."

René nodded thoughtfully. "And why would he do all this?"

"To fund his war on terrorism," said Effrem. "René, you said it yourself: Rostock is convinced governments can't do the job and that his approach is the only one that has a chance of working. Does he believe that? Is he truly committed?"

"Of course."

Jack said, "Then how do you know how far he's willing to go? If you need to make a little mess to clean up a bigger one, isn't it a fair trade?"

René was frowning, shaking his head. "Stop. Just please stop."

Jack and Effrem went quiet. Finally René said, "Earlier you were talking about Dovestar. What is that?"

"Are you asking?" said Jack.

"Obviously."

"Just wanted to make sure. Effrem, tell him everything."

Effrem did so, starting with Jack's audit of Dovestar, RSG's connection to it, and the secret operational fund. He ended his recap with the evidence that Dovestar had been paying Klugmann.

"It sounds like there is a better case against Bossard," René said.

Jack did his best to keep the frustration from his voice. "Here're the pieces of the puzzle. Follow me on this: Without knowing it, I uncover evidence that Rostock is hiding money at Dovestar; Eric Schrader tries to kill me, Schrader works for Rostock, Schrader and Möller know one another, therefore Möller likely works for Rostock. There's evidence Schrader was involved with the Lyon attacks. Finally, there's evidence that it was Rostock who kidnapped you, held you, and tortured you."

"What evidence?"

Effrem answered: "Janine Périer."

"What about her?"

"She doesn't exist," said Jack. "Her real name is Janine

Pelzer. She's German. She lives in Munich, the same place RSG is headquartered. Rostock used her as a lure, René. She helped set up your kidnapping."

"No. I don't believe you."

Jack replied, "There's a part of you that does."

"Why would Jürgen do that?"

Jack decided they'd pushed René far enough for now. "We don't know yet. We're working on it."

René waved his hand dismissively. "Until you have an answer for me, I refuse to buy into any of this." He stood and stared down at Jack. "Do you really believe I could miss seeing all this? I'm going for a walk to clear my head."

With his belly in a knot, Jack took the elevator down to the lobby, then out the doors to the valet desk. It was two hours since René had left.

"Can I help you, sir," the valet on duty said.

"I'm looking for a friend. He came down a couple hours ago." Jack described René's face and clothing.

"Yes, I remember, sir. He asked for a taxi."

"To where, do you know?"

"Hosea Kutako Airport. I hailed the taxi myself."

34

Jack's choice of Zurich was based on little more than a gut call. If his reason for leaving was what Jack suspected, René's destination could be only one of three locations: Khorusepa Lodge to find Möller; Munich to confront Rostock; or Zurich to force answers from Alexander Bossard. René had already suggested Bossard, not Rostock, was the driving force behind all this, so in René's mind Bossard was not only the juicier target but also the easiest, for he'd already spent weeks stalking Bossard.

Fifteen hours later and six hours behind René, Jack's plane touched down at Zurich's Kloten Airport just after midnight local time. Having left Zurich in a hurry, Jack had told Effrem to not return their rented Citroën, but rather to leave it in the airport's long-term parking. Jack went straight there, then drove to the level on which he and René had left his van.

The van was gone. For the sixth time since finding René gone, Jack dialed his cell phone. As with each time before, the phone went to voice mail. Jack disconnected before René's greeting began. He called Effrem, who answered immediately.

"Any luck?"

"His van's gone, so at least we know this is where he came," said Jack. "Is the Pilatus still at the Midgard airstrip?"

"The GPS tracker hasn't moved. That doesn't mean Möller and his men are still there, though. Jack, I can—"

"Forget it, Effrem."

They'd already had this conversation a few times, Effrem pressing for permission to stake out Khorusepa Lodge and Jack demurring. Effrem had come a long way since their first meeting at the nature preserve in Alexandria, but the kind of surveillance mission Effrem was proposing would have been risky even for Jack.

"So I just sit here?" Effrem asked.

"No, you sit there and keep working the Bossard material. Look for flaws in our thinking, details we overlooked. Sift it all through your journalist's brain."

Marshal Allemand had promised action against Rostock if Jack offered evidence to support his allegations, and the information in the Bossard material went a long way to doing that.

But not far enough, Jack thought.

Rostock's people had come to Namibia for the same reason they'd gone to Mumbai, Ontario, Panama, and who knew where else, and Jack wanted to catch them in the act. That might not happen if René succeeded in grabbing Bossard—or if he failed in the attempt, for that matter. If either news reached Rostock, Namibia would be called off. But would that outcome be so bad? he wondered. In the short term, no, but Rostock wasn't going to stop. If not Namibia now, where next?

Effrem made one last attempt: "If they don't take the Pilatus, we're going to lose them. Let me go—"

"No," Jack replied. "Stay put. I'll be back as soon as I can."

How to find one van in a city with hundreds of thousands of vehicles? Jack wondered. René had told Jack he'd been living in the van. Where in Zurich could he park overnight and not be ticketed or harassed? No, that was the wrong approach. Jack didn't have time for that. It all depended on one factor, he decided: Had René already managed to grab Bossard? If so, then René could have taken him anywhere. If not, then René would have to ambush Bossard at either home or work, or, between the two, deal with Bossard's bodyguards, and get cleanly away. Objectively, it was a tough tactical problem, but perhaps not so to René and his dangerous blend of training, experience, and brittle mental state.

Where, though? René had landed in Zurich after Bossard's office on Limmatquai had closed for the day. Unless René was willing to wait until morning, that left him one target: Bossard's home. According to René, Bossard lived in one of the city's wealthiest neighborhoods, Zürichberg, a forested hill rising more than two thousand feet above the city's eastern edge.

Jack punched the address into his phone's navigation app and started driving.

As the crow flew, Bossard's home was fifteen minutes from the airport, but the exclusive neighborhood could be reached by only one road, so Jack had to circumnavigate the base of Zürichberg and pick his way through the city before starting his climb up the hill, which added another twenty minutes.

Finally his navigation app told him to turn into a driveway entrance lit by a lone faux gas lamp and hemmed in by tightly packed spruce trees. As they closed in around him, Jack rolled down his window, doused the Citroën's headlights, and let the car coast to a stop. Outside his window, night insects buzzed softly and Jack could hear the distant trickling of a creek.

He called up his Google Earth application, entered Bossard's address, then zoomed in on the two-acre property. The overhead view showed Bossard's house as a white rectangle sitting in the middle of a clearing of green grass. It wasn't until Jack changed the angle of the view that he realized the rectangular roof hid a five-thousand-square-foot house that looked like a cross between Frank Lloyd Wright's Fallingwater and an M. C. Escher print come to life. The structure was all right angles, glass, hidden wraparound balconies, and zigzagging exterior stairs.

Jack drove ahead until the home's lawn came into view, then pulled over and shut off the engine. He walked around to the trunk and removed the spare tire, under which he'd tucked his HK nine-millimeter. He walked the remainder of the driveway, then stepped left into the trees and maneuvered until he could see the house.

Unsurprisingly, the house was dark. Either Bossard and his wife were simply asleep or René had already been here and was gone. Or was still here. He'd seen no other cars on the drive up, either moving or parked, but that meant nothing. René Allemand had become adept at playing cloak-and-dagger.

Jack pulled out his phone and dialed René.

A few seconds passed.

Faintly, almost imperceptibly, came the sound of René's marimba ringtone.

Oh, God. Jack's heart was pounding. René was here, in the house, either lying in wait for Bossard or having already captured him. What of the man's wife and his bodyguards? *Damn it, René.*

The marimba tone went silent. René's phone went to voice mail. At the beep Jack cupped his hand over the microphone and whispered, "René, call me back. We've got activity at Khorusepa Lodge. We could use your help." Jack disconnected and set the phone ringer to vibrate-only mode.

Jack doubted he'd get a return call, but if René had been worrying about Jack pursuing him to Zurich, perhaps Jack's message had bought him a slight tactical advantage. The problem was that the home's vast windows and darkened interior made any approach route dangerous. Would René open fire on him? Jack wondered.

From the house came a woman's scream, then a lone gunshot.

No choice now.

Jack stepped out of the trees, raised the HK, and sprinted across the lawn to the house's nearest wall, which he followed to a sliding glass door. Through it he could see a kitchen and dining alcove; the decor was modern industrial: hard angles, straight lines, and brushed stainless steel. A body lay on the polished concrete floor. It was a man in a suit. Bodyguard, Jack guessed.

With his gun trained on the interior, he reached out and tried the door. It was locked. He moved on until he reached the building's next corner, where he found a set of zigzag steps that led him to the second-floor wraparound balcony. He stopped on the top step and crouched. Ahead was another wall of glass. On the other side was what looked like a home office. The interior door was open, and through it Jack could see a carpeted hallway lit by a green outlet nightlight.

Jack stood up, walked down the balcony until he found the office's heavy exterior glass door. He tried the latch. It was unlocked. He eased open the door. With a soft hiss of hydraulics, the door swung open. Jack stepped through and, as the door hissed shut, paced to the doorway and looked down the hall. There were three doors, two on his right and one at the end of the hall. This one was partially open, and through the gap Jack could see what looked like the moving beam of a flashlight.

A woman cried in German, *"Hör auf damit! Bitte!"* Stop that! Please!

Jack heard the sound of a scuffle, feet shuffling on carpet, followed by a thump and a grunt of pain.

"Er kann nicht atmen!" the woman shouted. *"Bitte!"* Her voice panicked, partially garbled, but Jack caught two words: *can't breathe.*

Jack murmured, "The hell with this." He zipped his anorak all the way up so the cowl was covering the lower half of his face, then stepped out and trotted down the hall. He stopped at the door. Through the gap to his right was a bed. A woman with long gray hair and wearing a nightgown lay facedown on the bed. Bossard's wife. Her feet and ankles were duct-taped. Her head was facing Jack, but her eyes were fixed on something out of sight.

Jack pulled out his phone and again dialed René.

The marimba ringtone started.

Jack eased open the door, raised the HK, and stepped into the bedroom.

To his left, René—or so Jack assumed, as the figure was wearing a black balaclava—stood before Alexander Bossard, who was bound to a hard-back chair. His right eye was swollen shut and blood trickled from his mouth. René had his Walther P22 pressed against Bossard's forehead.

René dug his phone from his pocket and checked the screen. "Damn it," he muttered.

Bossard's wife saw Jack in the doorway. She screamed. René glanced in her direction, saw where her eyes were pointed, then started to spin around. Jack was already moving, charging forward. Using the butt of the HK, he backhanded René across the temple. He stumbled sideways, then slumped to the carpet, unconscious.

Mrs. Bossard was still screaming. Jack pointed his gun at

her. *"Ruhe!"* he barked. She went quiet. He added, *"Ich werde nicht wehtun. Verstehst du?"*

"Ja, ja," she replied, nodding emphatically. *"Ich verstehe!"*

Jack turned to Alexander Bossard; his head was lolling to one side. His eyes were half closed. Jack said, *"Keine Sorge. Ich komme wieder."* Don't worry, I'll be back. *"Verstehst du?"*

"Ja," he mumbled.

Jack glanced at Mrs. Bossard and got another nod.

He reached down, pocketed René's gun, then grabbed him by the jacket collar and dragged him out of the room and down the hallway. He removed René's balaclava.

"Idiot," Jack whispered.

The door to Jack's right was a bathroom; he soaked a towel in the sink, then wrung the cold water over René's upturned face before dragging his knuckles over René's sternum.

René's eyes fluttered open. He tried to sit up. Jack pushed him back down and held the HK before his eyes. "Understand?"

"Oui."

"What the hell were you thinking, René? Is that man downstairs dead?"

"No, of course not."

"This was very stupid. How did you think this was going to play out?"

"Bossard would talk, and then we would know."

"Know what?" asked Jack.

"If you and Effrem are right about Rostock."

Jack squeezed the bridge of his nose between his index finger and thumb. "I should hand you over to the police. In fact, that's what I'm going to do." He pulled out his cell phone.

"You wouldn't do that, Jack."

"I'm doing it right now."

"Please, don't. Just listen. For a moment." Jack shrugged his agreement and René said, "I wasn't going to kill him, or his wife."

"You beat the shit out of him and terrorized his wife."

"He deserves it. And worse."

"Maybe," Jack replied. "But you're not seeing the big picture. Right now, whether we're right about Rostock and about what happened to you isn't the point. Something bad is about to go down in Namibia. We have a chance—or had a chance, for all I know—to stop it. Instead, I'm back here. All because you can't keep your shit together and act like the soldier you should be."

René didn't reply, but rather squeezed his eyes shut. He lifted his head and banged it against the carpet. "I want this to be over, Jack."

"Then go back to France. I went to see your father in Paris. He wants you home. He never gave up on you, and nothing he did led to your kidnapping. It's Rostock, René, and you know it. He tortured you, messed with your brain, got you addicted to drugs. He's behind the Lyon attacks and the incidents in India, Canada, and Panama. And maybe others."

"Why would he kidnap me?"

"He asked your father to support his neo-warfare plan and your father turned him down, as did many others. Rostock reasoned that getting a Marshal of France on his side would be the first domino."

"That's delusional," René said. "He's delusional."

He's made the leap, Jack thought. He said with a smile, "Takes one to know one."

René smiled back. "Are you still going to call the police?"

"Are you going to stop acting like a dickhead?"

"Yes."

"Then we're good."

Jack helped René to a sitting position. René sighed. He gave himself a slap on the head. "God, what have I done? Idiot! Is Bossard hurt badly?"

"I'll look him over, but I don't think so. Did you ask him anything?"

"No, not yet. After I started beating him, I froze. I realized that beyond getting my hands on him, I didn't have a plan."

"Did you speak to either of them?" René nodded. "In French or German?"

"German. Why?"

"We might be able to turn this to our advantage," Jack replied, then spent the next few minutes explaining what he had in mind. "Is your German good enough to pull it off?"

"*Ja, sicher!* Much better than yours."

"Good. Follow my lead."

René got to his feet. Jack grabbed him by the collar and marched him down the hall into the bedroom. Jack positioned him between Bossard and his wife, then cuffed him in the head. *"Los!"*

In German and with some decent acting skills, Jack saw, René apologized to the Bossards. He'd overstepped his authority, had misunderstood his instructions. The people for whom they work want Jürgen Rostock, not Bossard. Millions have been spent and promises have been broken. They were supposed to get a Mumbai or an Ontario. We know you've been helping him. If you choose to help us instead, you'll come to no harm. If you call the police or Rostock we will know. We will come back.

When René finished speaking, Jack jerked him by the collar and shoved him out of the room. Then Jack squared off before Bossard. The man's one undamaged eye was wide open and he was sitting erect, alert. Their piece of theater had had its desired effect. Bossard would play along, but how thoroughly, only time would tell. At the very least they had stuck a wedge between Bossard and Rostock. Now Jack wanted to drive it home.

He walked behind Bossard's chair and cut his hands free of the duct tape.

Jack said, "Do you speak English?"

Bossard rubbed his wrists and stared up warily. "Yes, I do."

"Five years ago your daughter Suzette was kidnapped in Brazil, correct?"

"Yes, what—"

"And Rostock rescued her. Shortly after that you took RSG on as a client. That was no coincidence. He's done it since. It's a recruiting technique. *Verstehst du?*"

"*Ich verstehe*," replied Bossard. "I understand, but I have trouble believing Jürgen would do such a thing."

"Then you haven't looked hard enough. You can believe me or not believe me. It changes nothing. You're either with us or against us. Someone will be in touch. Have your answer ready."

35

Effrem hadn't answered his phone since René and Jack arrived at the Zurich airport for their return flight. Almost eighteen hours and no contact. Jack had a sinking feeling what that meant, and he hoped he was wrong. According to Jack's phone, the GPS tracker on the Pilatus hadn't moved an inch from its spot at Midgard Airstrip. If Effrem had disobeyed Jack's orders and gone to Khorusepa Lodge to keep an eye on Möller, his silence might mean nothing. That far outside the city, cell coverage was spotty at best. Or it could mean he'd been caught and Möller was getting another chance at interrogating Effrem.

As he and René stepped onto the tarmac and headed toward the terminal, Jack dialed Effrem's phone one more time and again got his voice mail.

"You try," Jack told René, who dialed and then disconnected. "No joy."

Jack's phone beeped. It was a text from Mitch. The time stamp was from eight hours earlier. **Call me.**

Jack did. Mitch said immediately, "Klugmann moved. He left the Hilton."

"How long ago?"

"I texted you as soon as it happened. When I didn't hear back I called Effrem."

"Where's Klugmann now?"

"I have no idea."

Jack had a fair idea where, which meant Effrem did as well. "Mitch, I'm going to text you an e-mail address. If you don't hear from one of us in five days, send all the Bossard docs to that address. Can you do that?"

"Five days, no problem. Should I include an explanation or a—"

"No, they'll figure it out. Thanks. See you."

Jack disconnected. He recounted his conversation with Mitch to René. "Let's get back to the hotel."

The suite was unoccupied, but some of Effrem's clothes were missing, as were some items from Jack's go-bag he'd left behind: binoculars, digital camera, multi-tool, duct tape, and first-aid kit.

"Idiot," Jack said.

"At least I've got company," René replied. "What do we do?"

"We go after him. Do you have any idea where we can get some weapons?"

René had no specific ideas, but, he said, having lived and worked in Africa for years, he knew generally where and for whom to look. "Weapons dealers here use a lot of the same survival strategies," he said. "They're often not so frightened by the police but by rival dealers."

"To cull competition?" Jack asked.

"And to increase their own inventory. Plus, it's a matter of pride. If you're going to be a merchant of death in Africa, you can't be shy about using violence. You must walk the walk."

At least Effrem hadn't taken the Land Cruiser, Jack thought. With Jack behind the wheel, they toured the city. Though he occasionally glanced at the foldout map in his lap, René spent most of the time gazing out his window, telling Jack to turn in here, circle back there, pull to this curb or under this tree, where they would watch the people for a while before moving on. At open-air markets and cafés

René would leave Jack behind in the Toyota, then walk around and chat with locals. Though Jack didn't understand what exactly René was seeing or asking, it was clear the soldier was getting a feel for Windhoek's pulse and rhythm.

"Do you think he'll be there?" René asked after a while.

"Who, Rostock?"

"Yes."

"I doubt it. Rostock's a general. As much as they may want to, generals know better than to go into the field. Möller is his captain. We'll be dealing with him and however many RSG operatives he brings along. At least eight that we can count on."

"So be it," René murmured, staring out the window.

After another hour of scouting, René declared that Katutura Township Central, the heart of Windhoek's worst slum, was their best chance for finding what they needed.

Jack took the Western Bypass highway north to the edge of the city, where he turned west onto the perhaps sadistically named Independence Avenue, which took them into the slum proper. Everywhere Jack looked there was nothing but dirt and rolling, rock-strewn hills, all packed tightly with sheds and huts made from a mishmash of materials, from cardboard to aluminum to massive highway signs that had been bent into open lean-to or A-frame shelters. Everywhere smiling black children ran and played while women waited in quarter-mile lines at a water pump.

"Seventy percent of Windhoek lives right here, Jack," said René. "About a hundred and forty thousand people."

Jack had the urge to stop the Land Cruiser, get out, and empty his pockets, but he knew it would likely cause more harm than good. A problem like Katutura wouldn't be changed by simply throwing money at it. Jack didn't know what the larger solution was, but looking at the faces of the kids waving as they passed made his heart ache.

After a few brief stops to ask for directions they found the neighborhood they were looking for, the aptly named Soweto. Given the conditions here, Jack imagined most of its occupants would prefer living in its South African name-sake.

The road took them over a hill and down into a shallow valley whose slopes had been tiered into lots for huts. Soweto's business district was a hundred-yard-long stretch of mom-and-pop businesses that offered food, repairs, and medicines. At René's direction Jack pulled the Toyota to a stop beside a brick building painted bright red. The sign over an open garage bay said SMARTY'S REPAIRS.

They got out and went into the cool of the garage. In German, René asked one of the mechanics something. The man pointed to an open door to their right. Inside, they found a potbellied middle-aged man sitting at a desk. His head was shaved. He was rubbing lotion into his scalp. He raised a hand in greeting, then wiped his hands on his pants and walked up to the counter.

"English?" René asked.

"Some good, some not."

"Tell him what you want, Jack."

"Just like that? Can we trust him?"

René chuckled. "You think he's an undercover cop, so dedicated he chooses to live here year round and run a business? No, this is Smarty, the owner, and the most honest arms dealer in Windhoek."

"Who told you that?"

"Everyone . . . no one," replied René. "Go ahead, tell him what you want. If he has it, he'll give you a price. There's no haggling. His prices are fair."

Jack had been assembling an equipment list in his mind. He shrugged. When in Rome . . . As Jack spoke each item, Smarty would say either "yes" or "no." He had eighty percent of what Jack requested, including a trio of AK-47s and a thousand rounds of ammunition.

Smarty wrote a price on a strip of paper and slid it over to Jack, who said, "That's fair. You take dollars."

"Everything but Discover card," Smarty replied.

It was late afternoon by the time they put Windhoek in the Land Cruiser's rearview mirror and began the two-hour journey up the Western Bypass. Assuming that at some point he would be returning to Khorusepa Lodge, Jack spent some extra time studying the area's topology and road systems, if they could be called that. As he'd learned during his first reconnoiter, once off the Western Bypass the roads were all dirt and often little wider than a vehicle. Still, looking at the Google Earth screenshots he'd stored on his phone, he counted at least four ways in and out of the Khorusepa Lodge area.

They were twenty miles south of Osona Airstrip when the sun began dipping behind the mountains to the west. René, whose window had borne the brunt of the afternoon sun, said, "Thank God," and returned the visor to its overhead position.

Jack's phone chirped. "What's the screen say, René?"

"It says 'tracking.'"

"That's the GPS I planted on the Pilatus. The app icon is on the home screen, lower-left corner. Call up the map. The tracker will show up as a pulsing blue dot."

"Yes, I have it."

"Tell me where it's going."

"South."

South. That was wrong. Midgard's runway ran east to west. "Let me see. Take the wheel."

René grabbed the wheel and Jack studied the phone's screen. The tracker was indeed moving south, away from the runway and onto the same road he'd taken into Khorusepa Lodge. When the dot reached the fork in the road, it turned left toward the lodge itself.

Clearly it wasn't the Pilatus taxiing down that narrow ravine road. Someone found the tracker and planted it on a vehicle. Who? It had to have been either Effrem or Möller—Effrem in an attempt to aid Jack's pursuit of Möller; Möller hoping to make it look that way and lure Jack into an ambush. Here was another classic "Damned if you do, damned if you don't" scenario. Either Effrem was aboard this vehicle or he was still at the lodge.

Jack watched the dot until it came to a stop in what he estimated was the lodge's lobby turnaround.

Jack retook the Toyota's wheel and handed the phone back to René, who asked, "Well? What do we do?"

"Nothing's changed. We keep going."

They drove in silence for five minutes before René said, "It's moving again, back the way it came . . . Now turning north toward Swakoppoort Dam Reservoir."

"It's heading for the Western Bypass."

"Can we intercept them?"

Jack checked his watch and did a quick calculation. "Maybe. It's going to be tight."

Jack pressed harder on the accelerator.

The miles and minutes ticked by as Jack and René kept heading north and the blue dot west toward the Western Bypass. The sun's upper rim finally slipped behind the hills and Jack turned on the Land Cruiser's headlights. Bugs began to strike the windshield with rapid, overlapping clicks.

The sign for Osona flashed past the windshield, followed soon after by the sign for Okahandja. Ten miles to the turn-off. Jack asked René, "Where is it?"

René turned the phone so Jack could see the screen. "Still heading west, closing toward the Western Bypass. He's got maybe four miles to go."

"Too close . . . too close," Jack murmured.

René said, "We don't even know if he's in that vehicle, Jack."

"I know that. If he isn't and we lose it, that tracker won't last forever. Beyond fifty miles the signal will be too weak. If he's still at the lodge . . ."

René finished his thought. "There's only one reason Möller would leave Effrem behind."

Because Möller was finished with him.

And if Effrem was aboard that vehicle it was as a captive, in which case he was still alive, but on borrowed time.

Lose-lose.

Jack stomped on the accelerator. The Toyota's speedometer swept past 146 kph. The headlights picked out a sign ahead: OKAHANDJA 3 KM.

"The turnoff to the lodge is well before that," René said. "It'll come up fast. You might want to start slowing."

Jack kept his foot on the accelerator. "Get the AKs from the backseat and prep them." Their best opportunity to ambush the vehicle was before it traded the narrow dirt road for the broad blacktop.

Another sign: D2102 500 M.

Jack let his foot off the accelerator.

René had his face pressed to his window, hand cupped around his eyes. "I see them! Headlights. They're very close, Jack."

Jack doused the Land Cruiser's headlights. "I'm going to have to turn hard right, so hang on. As soon as I come to a stop, open fire on the vehicle's engine block. Get it stopped, but keep your shots low. I'll go for the occupants."

"Jack, hit the brakes!"

"What? Why?"

"I count three pairs of headlights—no, four! It's a convoy. We can't handle four at the same time, Jack, you know that! Get us out of sight!"

"Damn it!"

Jack stepped on the brakes. The Land Cruiser started fishtailing. Jack eased right and the tires bumped onto the shoulder.

Ahead, the lead vehicle was coming to a stop, its right blinker flashing in the darkness. It was a Toyota Hilux, Jack saw.

He braked again, jerked the wheel harder right, and pointed the hood toward the drainage ditch. The front tires thumped over a berm, and the nose vaulted upward, then dropped again. Jack braked and the Land Cruiser ground to a halt beside a boulder.

Jack climbed out and, using the boulder as cover, maneuvered until he could see the turnoff. The fourth and final vehicle in the convoy turned onto the highway and sped north into the night.

36

WESTERN BYPASS, NAMIBIA

"Y ou have to decide, Jack," René called from the Land Cruiser. "What's it going to be?"

Jack turned and sprinted back to the Land Cruiser. "The lodge."

He backed out of the ditch onto the road, then pulled ahead and turned onto the dirt road. Jack covered the ten miles to the airstrip-lodge fork in twenty minutes. Headlights off again, he turned left until he saw the edge of the runway. The Pilatus was still there, wheels chocked and windows dark.

Wherever that convoy was headed, it was either too close to justify the flight or located too far from a landing site.

Jack turned around, made his way back to the fork, and turned toward the lodge. When he reached the cobblestone entrance, Jack said, "Rostock rented out the entire lodge; there's no staff. Anyone with a gun is fair game."

"I understand," said René.

"We'll check the bungalows first."

"I'll follow your lead."

Jack braked to a stop ten feet before the arch and shut off the engine. René handed him one of the AKs and a pair of magazines. Jack inserted one of them into the AK, cycled the bolt, then made sure the safety was on. They climbed out of the SUV.

With Jack in the lead, they headed through the arch. He pointed right, toward the lobby doors. René nodded and checked the doors. He shook his head. They continued on. When they reached the lawn, Jack pointed across to the line of eight bungalows, then gestured to René and mouthed, *Spread right*. Twenty feet apart and walking abreast, they crossed the lawn. No lights were visible in the bungalows.

Jack angled toward the one on the far left. René adjusted course to match him, his AK raised and tracking back and forth. When Jack reached the first bungalow's walkway, René stacked up behind him and gave him an "I'm here" pat on the shoulder, and together they approached the door, then split, one on either side of the door.

Jack crouched, leaned sideways, and peeked through the

window. The interior was tidy, with no signs of occupancy. He looked at René and shook his head.

They retraced their steps to the sidewalk and moved on to the next bungalow. Here, too, Jack saw nothing to indicate it had been used recently. At the third and fourth bungalows, same result.

As they approached the fifth bungalow's walkway, Jack caught a whiff of something in the air. It was the acrid stench of overseared meat. He glanced at René, who tapped his nose, pointed at the bungalow's front door, and mouthed, *Coming from in there.*

Jack stopped at the door. His check through the window revealed the bungalow's interior was in disarray. The beds were unmade and food trays were stacked on the dresser. Beer bottles overflowed the garbage can. In the center of the room was a hard-back chair. Dangling from its front legs was what looked like duct tape.

Jack signaled to René, *Going in,* and got a nod in return. Jack tried the knob. The door was unlocked. They went through and quickly cleared the bungalow. Jack and René clicked on their flashlights and looked around.

On the floor beside the chair was a bloodstained white towel, and balanced on the closest corner of the dresser was a curling iron. Its chrome surface was splotched with a dark, flaky material.

"It's charred skin," René whispered. "Fresh."

Ah, Christ, Jack thought. "Let's keep moving."

At the sidewalk they turned left and headed to the next bungalow.

Jack froze. René followed suit.

Noise.

What was it? A muffled clang, a scraping sound. It was familiar. It took Jack a few more seconds to pigeonhole the noise: a shovel in dirt.

A male voice shouted, *"Beeil dich!"* Hurry up.

"It's coming from behind the bungalows," René whispered.

Jack started running. At the last bungalow, the sidewalk turned left. Jack followed it down a tree-lined path to an oval-shaped dirt parking lot fronted by a split-rail fence. When Jack reached its edge he stopped and dropped into a crouch. The lot's far edge was made up of overgrown bushes. There was a vehicle in the lot: a black Hilux.

Through the bushes came a flicker of light.

Jack looked at René, who nodded his readiness. They stepped over the fence, crossed the parking lot, and split up, each taking one side of the Hilux. They met at the front bumper.

"I'm done!" a man called. It was ragged and weak, but Jack recognized the voice: Effrem. "If you're going to do it, just do it! Assholes!"

In German-accented English a voice replied, "Suit yourself. Rolf, get the gas can."

The bushes rustled. Rolf stepped into view. Dangling from his right hand was a semiauto pistol.

"René, take him," Jack ordered.

René lifted his AK and put three rounds into the man's chest. Even as the man fell, Jack sprinted past him and crashed into the bushes. He burst into a small clearing lit by an LED lantern sitting on the ground. The other German stood at the head of a pit. Effrem was in it, stripped to the waist and slick with blood and dirt and sweat.

Jack shot the German in the side, and he stumbled and dropped to his knees. Jack shot him in the side of the head. He toppled over.

Jack called to Effrem, "Anyone else?"

"No, just the two of them." Effrem lifted the shovel above his head and hurled it at the German's body. He turned to Jack. "Jack, will you please get me out of here?"

They put Effrem in the Hilux, then drove it around the fence and onto the lawn, stopping before the last bungalow. After shouldering the door open, René stood watch while Jack helped Effrem inside and sat him on a bed.

René called, "I'll have a look around for other stragglers

and then get the first-aid kit." As he left, he shut the door behind him.

Jack closed the curtains and turned on the bungalow's overhead lights.

Effrem's appearance momentarily paralyzed Jack.

Scattered across Effrem's torso were at least ten cylindrical burn marks from the curling iron. The tips of his pinkie and third finger on his left hand were pulp, probably the work of a hammer, Jack guessed. Effrem's bottom lip was split and his right eye socket was so badly bruised and swollen it looked like a smashed plum.

"Fucking hell," Jack muttered.

"Is it bad?" Effrem said.

"Pretty bad."

"It's starting to hurt, Jack, really bad. For a while I was numb, but now it's—" Effrem winced, then exhaled heavily. He cradled his shattered hand in his lap. "He didn't ask me anything. Not one question!"

"Möller?"

"He just did it. For no reason. For fun." Effrem's eyes brimmed with tears. "Möller told those two to get rid of me. I thought, *Well, how much can a bullet to the head hurt?* And then they told me to start digging. They were going to set me on fire . . . bury me in that hole. Why? Why that way?"

Because Möller's a psychopath, Jack thought but didn't say.

Effrem was crying now, his chest heaving with sobs. Jack sat down on the bed and pulled Effrem's head onto his shoulder. "You're alive, Effrem. Just keep repeating that in your head: I'm alive."

René returned with the first-aid kit and went to work on Effrem, checking him for any obvious signs of brain damage or internal hemorrhaging, then having him down four ibuprofen followed by two miniature bottles of whiskey Jack found in the dresser.

Once the battered journalist had stopped shaking, René turned his attention to Effrem's burns and wounds. He left Effrem's hand for last.

"Hammer?" René asked him.

"Plumber's wrench," Effrem replied.

Jack asked, "What's the diagnosis?"

"The burns are superficial. As long as they're kept clean, they'll heal. Same with his eye and lip."

"What about my hand?" asked Effrem. "I'm going to lose those fingers, aren't I?"

"Only if they get infected. The tips of the bones are broken, but the blood flow is still there. You will, unfortunately, never attain your dream of being a hand model."

Effrem smiled faintly. "Guess I'll have to stick with journalism. Jack, I'm sorry. You said 'Jump' and I didn't jump. I was worried we were going to lose Möller. I had a gut feeling that Pilatus wasn't going to move, but Möller was. I thought if I could at least follow them for a while we'd have a direction to follow."

"You moved the GPS tracker?" Effrem nodded and Jack said, "You're forgiven."

They covered him in blankets and gave him another mini-bottle of whiskey. He was asleep within minutes.

"He's fighting shock," René said. "He needs at least four hours of sleep before we move him. We need to get him back to Windhoek."

"Good luck with that. He's stubborn."

"And you're okay with him coming with us?"

Jack said, "Not really, but he's earned the right to decide for himself. Even if he just wants to go along for the ride, I'm going to let him."

René shrugged. "You're the leader. These are some terrible men we're dealing with, Jack. What they did to him—what they were going to do to him . . ."

"I know."

"And they belong to Rostock."

This wasn't a question, Jack realized, but rather a statement. The only emotion he heard in René's voice was one of cold resignation. He'd cleared the chasm, Jack knew.

———————

Seventy-five minutes after they arrived at the lodge, the GPS tracker's signal faded with the convoy still heading north on the Western Bypass. Jack told René, "We lost them."

"Maybe not," Effrem said from his bed. He reached out and turned on the nightstand lamp. "I heard Möller say something about GPS and the Hilux. Maybe its nav system was programmed so they could catch up to the main group."

René was already on his feet. "I'll check." He returned to the bungalow a few minutes later. "He's right. There's a destination programmed into the system."

"Where?"

"Someplace called Kavango Dam."

37

KHORUSEPA LODGE, NAMIBIA

René monitored Effrem's condition through the night and shortly after dawn proclaimed him fit to travel. To assuage his conscience, Jack tried to convince Effrem to take the Hilux back to Windhoek for medical treatment, but Effrem dismissed the idea even before all the words had left Jack's mouth.

After stripping the two dead Germans and their Hilux of anything of use, Jack and the others piled back into the Land Cruiser, left the lodge, and made their way back to the Western Bypass.

According to the coordinates in the Hilux's navigation system, Kavango Dam lay 110 miles to the northeast, but neither Jack's phone map nor René's paper map showed any sign of the structure, or of any body of water. Worse still, though the dam lay just thirty miles west of the Western Bypass, the only access road snaked its way through 150 miles of Otjozondjupa Region's most rugged terrain.

By mid-morning, having traveled as far north as possible on the Western Bypass, Jack turned off the blacktop and headed east on a dirt track that was little more than twin wheel ruts worn into the earth. After four hours they'd covered only eighty miles and the road was worsening as it zigzagged deeper into the hills. By nightfall they were still forty miles from their destination. The road narrowed until the view out Jack's window was blocked by a sheer rock face.

From the backseat Effrem said, "The other side's even worse, Jack. About three feet from our tires there's a drop-off. I can't even see the bottom."

René asked Jack, "Push on or stop and set up camp for the night?"

"Push on," Jack replied. "Möller has a good eight-hour head start on us. For all we know, they're already at Kavango."

"Yes, but doing what?" asked René.

"Effrem, check your phone," Jack said. Since they'd left Khorusepa Lodge, their reception had been wildly sporadic. Any headway Effrem made into researching Kavango Dam was maddeningly short-lived. Despite the pain, he had been working hard to assemble these information snippets into something cohesive.

So far all they knew was that the Kavango Dam had

been completed just two months earlier at a half-mile-wide section of the Omatako River. Since then a massive reservoir had been filling behind the dam. Downstream from the dam were nearly twenty villages and farms.

Effrem said, "I've got a bit of signal. Let me see what I can do with it."

After another ninety minutes and ten miles the road widened and began descending. Jack was able to pick up some speed. By midnight they were within eight miles of the dam.

"It turns out Kavango's a regulator dam," Effrem said from the darkness of the backseat.

"Which is what?" asked Jack.

"Regulator dams are built upstream from hydroelectric dams. They're designed to control the volume of water flowing into a hydro."

"Is there a hydro around here?" asked René.

"Not yet. Evidently Kavango's a sort of trial balloon for something called the Otjozondjupa Renewal Project. By 2028, the Namibian government wants to be exporting electricity to its neighbors. If Kavango works, they're planning to build a hydro a mile downstream."

René said, "What's that mean, 'works'? Either it holds back the water or not, yes?"

"No. Apparently, regulator dams require some pretty sophisticated hydraulic control systems. They're due for a 'proof of concept' test in two days."

Effrem's words struck a chord in Jack's brain. "Systems," he repeated. "As in computer-controlled systems?"

Effrem was silent for a few seconds. "Shit, that's it."

"What?" René said. "I don't understand."

"Effrem, who installed the Kavango control systems?"

"Uh . . . a British company called Mondaryn Engineering."

"Was it an open-bid process?"

"I don't know for sure. Probably so."

That was the connection, Jack realized. Rostock had been hired by one of Mondaryn's competitors to sabotage Kavango's flow-control systems. Jack explained it to René, who asked, "Effrem, how many people live downstream from Kavango?"

"Hundreds, maybe a thousand."

Jack steered the Land Cruiser over a rise and stopped. He shut off the headlights.

Below them, running from east to west, was a curved line of pole-mounted sodium-vapor lights. Beneath these Jack could make out the dam's faded ochre-colored concrete parapet. Rising from its midpoint was a bunkerlike structure that Jack assumed led to the dam's interior.

Jack got out his binoculars and scanned the length of the parapet. At the far end, barely visible in the shadows, was a trio of black pickup trucks. Jack handed the binoculars to René, who looked and then nodded: "Möller's Hilux."

"Yes, that's them. I don't see anyone about."

"You think they're already inside?" asked Effrem.

"I'd put money on it. Klugmann has to work his voodoo from the control room or else he wouldn't be in Namibia."

Jack put the Toyota in neutral, took his foot off the brake, and let gravity carry them down the hillside to the dam's access road. When they were fifty yards from the parapet he braked to a stop.

René said, "I wish we had more time to plan this, Jack."

"If wishes were horses we'd have an Apache providing air cover for us. Effrem, get out and come around to my side. You're driving."

"What?"

"You're going to find some high ground and start video recording."

"What good will that do?"

"Maybe none, but you're doing it. If René and I don't come back out, you need to get to Windhoek and contact Mitch. He's got an e-mail address you're going to need. Tell the person on the other end the whole story and they'll take it from there."

Jack felt a vibration rising through the Land Cruiser's floorboards.

"What is that?" asked René.

Down the length of the dam, red strobe lights began flashing.

A pair of men emerged from the parapet's access bunker and began jogging toward the Hiluxes at the far end.

"Time's up," Jack said.

38

With Jack in the lead, they sprinted onto the parapet.

"Keep an eye out for Klugmann," Jack called to René.

"How will I know it's him?"

"Whoever hasn't got a gun doesn't get shot."

"Right!"

Jack glanced over his shoulder. Effrem was standing beside the Land Cruiser's open driver's door. Jack stopped, turned back.

"Get moving, damn it!" he shouted.

He waited until Effrem climbed into the Toyota and started backing down the access road before he started running again. René was fifty yards ahead. Two more men emerged from the control bunker's door. Neither one was Möller, but Jack had no way of knowing whether one of them was Gerhard Klugmann. Both were carrying FAMAS assault rifles.

René opened fire. One of the men went down. His partner ducked back through the bunker's door and swung it shut behind him. René peppered the door with his AK. The rounds sparked on the steel.

Jack caught up with René and jogged the remaining distance to the door. It suddenly opened and a FAMAS barrel emerged. Jack dodged right and René dropped flat. Jack dropped to one knee and sprayed the door's gap. The FAMAS disappeared back through the door, which swung open to reveal a body lying across a steel catwalk landing. Jack sprinted toward the door. He called, "René, you good?"

He got no answer. He glanced over his shoulder. René was lying facedown on the concrete. He wasn't moving. A pool of blood spread beneath his body.

I'm sorry, René, Jack thought, and kept running.

At the door he pressed himself against the bunker wall, took a breath, then peeked through the door in time to see two men rushing up the steps. Jack shot the first one twice in the chest, then dropped to one knee, and stitched the second man's legs out from under him. The man tumbled back down the steps. Jack followed him. The man was stunned as much by the fall as by the damage to his legs. He had lost his rifle, but Jack frisked him anyway. Once he was sure the semiconscious man posed no further threat, Jack turned down the next set of steps to a concrete alcove. To his left and right were two royal-blue steel doors.

Jack flipped a mental coin and opened the door on the left, revealing a maintenance tunnel no wider than his shoulders and dimly lit by overhead fluorescent bulbs. Electrical conduits lined the concrete wall. The hum of machinery was thunderous and rhythmic; Jack could feel it in his belly.

He shut the door and tried the other one, which opened onto a catwalk lit by pendant lights. Jack stepped to the handrail and looked down. He saw nothing but blackness and billowing mist. He could hear the roar of gushing water. The air smelled of ozone.

To his right the catwalk ended, so Jack turned left and jogged fifty feet until he reached a set of steps that took him down to another catwalk. At its far end, a set of short steps led to a glass control booth. Through the windows Jack could see flashing red and orange lights.

He started down the catwalk.

In the control booth two figures rose up and began shattering the glass windows with the butts of their rifles. Moving at a sprint, Jack opened fire on the booth. The two men ducked out of sight. Jack reached the steps. He crouched so his head was below the door's lower edge, then ejected the AK's magazine and inserted another. He then reached forward, tapping the AK's barrel against the door.

A horizontal line of bullet holes appeared in the steel.

Jack rolled back on his heels, then onto his back, and took aim on the control booth.

Wait, Jack. Wait . . .

A figure appeared in the window. Jack pulled the trigger. The man's head disappeared in a halo of red mist.

There was at least one more man on the other side of this door, and unless Jack was willing to backtrack and look for another way into the control booth, his only option was to suck it up and go.

He stood up and pressed himself as tightly against the handrail as possible, then mounted the steps and grabbed the doorknob. *Stop.* He needed a little misdirection. He pointed the AK up at the control booth window, fired a short burst, then swung open the door and charged through. He found himself in a short passageway of white-painted cinder blocks. At the end was an open door. He headed for it. Halfway there, a figure dashed past the opening from right to left. Jack almost opened fire, but caught himself. The man hadn't been armed. Klugmann, maybe?

At the door Jack peeked left, saw a set of steel steps that led to what he guessed was the control room. To his right

was a yellow door with black lettering that read MAINTE-
NANCE LADDER. Jack stepped left, crept up the steps to the
control room door, where he paused.

Don't stop, don't think, he told himself. Giving himself a
chance to weigh the odds and rethink tactics would con-
sume time he didn't have.

He swung himself through the door. The room was
empty.

The wall to the left of the windows was dominated by a
long control console, its buttons and built-in screens a sea of
flashing warning lights.

Too late, Jack thought.

Whatever was happening was beyond his abilities to control. Clearly the dam's flow control systems had already
fallen prey to Klugmann's virus. Hundreds of thousands of
gallons of water were already gushing down the Omatako
River toward the farms and villages downstream.

If he couldn't stop it, he needed to at least be able to
prove who started it.

Jack left. As he turned onto the stairs, he saw a rifle butt
plunging toward his face. He jerked his head to the side,
and the butt slammed into his cheekbone, then slid down
the side of his head and clipped his ear. He heard rather than

felt the tearing of cartilage. Blood gushed down his neck. He stumbled sideways. His AK fell through the railing and crashed to the floor below. Blind in his right eye, Jack reached up, bear-hugged the figure standing there, then pushed off, sending them both down the stairs with the man's rifle sandwiched between them. As they fell Jack caught a glimpse of the yellow maintenance door swinging shut.

Still entwined, he and his attacker smashed into the floor, with Jack on top. He raised himself, gaining some maneuvering room, and slashed the point of his elbow across the man's nose, breaking it, then into the side of his neck, and continued punching until the man went still. His face was a mask of blood.

Jack got up, grabbed his AK, and headed toward the yellow door. On the other side was a ladder leading up to a fluorescent-lighted opening. He was at the opposite end of the tunnel he'd found on his way in.

At the top of the ladder he crawled into the tunnel. He stood up and started running. Ahead of him, two figures disappeared around a curve in the tunnel. Jack was there a few seconds later, just as the second man stepped left through a door. He was unarmed.

Jack lifted the AK, took aim, fired. The bullet punched into the back of the man's right thigh. He collapsed through the door and out of sight. Jack sprinted ahead and peeked around the corner. A stocky, bald man with a pasty face lay on his back, both hands clutched around his bleeding hamstring.

The man was wearing a black T-shirt. Emblazoned across the chest in red German Fraktur-style letters were the words *Game of Thrones. Winter Is Coming.*

"Gerhard Klugmann," Jack said. "I've been looking for you."

Half dragging, half carrying Klugmann, Jack hurried up the steps to the parapet.

René's body was gone.

"Over here," Jack heard.

He turned to see René sitting with his back against the bunker. His left arm was bloody and bent backward at the elbow. Jack dumped Klugmann onto the parapet and asked René, "Möller?"

"That way, toward the Hilux."

Jack walked to the center of the parapet. Stephan Möller, still bearing the limp from Jack's bullet at the Alexandria nature preserve, had only gotten a hundred yards toward the Hilux.

"Möller, stop!" Jack shouted.

Möller kept going.

Jack lifted the AK to his shoulder and fired. The bullet smacked into the concrete to the left of Möller's feet. The

German glanced over his shoulder, shouted something at Jack, and then tried to pick up the pace, his limp now a penguinlike hobble.

"Last chance," Jack yelled.

René said, "Just kill him already."

"We can use him. He can hand us Rostock."

Jack laid the AK's front post over Möller's legs and fired a short burst. Möller went down. He writhed, then rolled onto his belly. Jack started walking down the parapet toward him.

He'd covered half the distance when he heard the roar of an engine. A horn began blaring. Jack turned, raised the AK. He lowered it.

With Effrem behind the wheel, the Toyota Land Cruiser swerved around Jack, straightened out, and sped toward Möller, who'd managed to get to his knees.

"Effrem!" Jack shouted. "Don't. We need him!"

The Toyota eased left as Effrem aimed the hood at Möller, then began picking up speed. Möller, apparently hearing the approaching engine, looked over his shoulder.

Effrem never hit the brakes.

EPILOGUE

PARIS, FRANCE

True to his word, the same day Jack appeared at the front gate of Hugo Allemand's estate with René in tow, his arm in a wrist-to-shoulder cast, the marshal opened his black leather-bound address book and started making phone calls.

Though Effrem, now back in Brussels and working with Mitch via phone, was still weeks away from fully assembling what Jack suspected would be more than enough evidence to prompt a German and EU investigation into Rostock Security Group, René Allemand's account of his ordeal at the hands of Rostock had been more than enough to spur his father into action.

Despite the fact the marshal had retired from the military and withdrawn from the social limelight, his clout was significant. By midafternoon the first reports of anonymous allegations against Rostock Security Group and its founder were surfacing on European news networks and radio stations. The beating of the drum had begun. Marshal Allemand would soon be calling a press conference. He assured Jack he would not be the only person of influence standing before the microphones. Apparently Rostock had visited his hardball tactics on other VIPs across Europe: From Italy to Great Britain, Marshal Allemand had little trouble convincing his peers of what Rostock had been up to. Those who had balked at supporting the German's endeavors but had failed to speak out were now only too happy to join the growing coalition. And before Allemand was done, Jack guessed, those who had covertly supported Rostock would have to choose between coming forward of their own volition and being exposed by the looming investigation.

Jack had gladly accepted Marshal Allemand's invitation to stay at the estate for as long as he wished. With a deadline looming, he needed the time to think—but not about his decision, which he'd made even before they left Namibia. Playing shepherd to the impulsive Effrem and erratic René had been a brutal, eye-opening crash course in personnel management. Jack knew where he belonged.

While the choice was an easy one, the road he'd taken to it had been painful and costly.

Jürgen Rostock would fall, of that Jack was certain.

Taken alone, that was a victory that would save lives in the future, but it had also taken lives beyond those of Peter Hahn and Kaitlin Showalter.

Three hundred twenty-two, to be exact.

Jack's failure to stop Möller from sabotaging Kavango Dam's flow control system had cost the lives of three hundred twenty-two men, women, and children who'd been unable to escape the deluge before it engulfed their villages and farms. Inevitably and predictably, Jack found himself replaying the same question in his mind: If he'd been quicker or smarter, could he have stopped it? There was no answer, he knew, but he also knew it would be a long time before he stopped asking the question.

As he had for most of the past several days, today Jack slept until mid-morning, then jogged around the estate and swam laps in the pool before playing a game of tennis with Claude.

When he came back into the house, Jack found René and Hugo seated across from each other in the solarium. Smiling, the marshal waved Jack over to the table and poured him coffee.

Jack asked René, "When did you last talk to Effrem?"

"Not for a few days. I've left messages, but he hasn't responded. I hope that simply means he's busy digging Rostock's grave, and it's not the other thing."

"Other thing?" said the marshal.

"Möller," Jack replied.

Back on the dam's parapet, Jack had been expecting Effrem to swerve or brake at the last moment, but he'd done neither. Möller had died instantly, just as Eric Schrader had outside the Supermercado in Alexandria. For reasons he hadn't quite fathomed, Jack was finding it hard to enjoy the irony behind the two men's deaths. Jack suspected that whatever satisfaction Effrem had gotten from killing Stephan Möller had been fleeting and bittersweet. While Möller had tortured Effrem and ordered him burned alive in a hole in the ground, Jack believed Effrem was strong enough to get past that. But could he get past what he himself had done in retaliation?

On the positive side, whatever moral struggles Effrem might be facing, he wasn't doing it alone. At Marie Likkel's urging, Effrem had moved back home to the Likkel estate, where he and Belinda Hahn were, according to Marie, "getting to know one another." Jack was glad for them both.

René, too, had a long, tough road ahead of him. Coming to grips with the damage done to him by Rostock may have already cost René his relationship with Madeline. The wedding was on hold, as was René's future with the Army. Everything seemed tainted, he'd told Jack.

"Where do things stand with Alexander Bossard?" Jack asked.

Hugo Allemand answered. "One of my attorneys is in Zurich deposing him as we speak. Whatever you said to him, Jack, was more than enough to secure his cooperation. Once we have his deposition, we will make sure it reaches the proper authorities. It will be more than enough to tip the first domino. Jürgen Rostock, I suspect, is about to face a dramatic reversal of fortune."

Jack had little trouble believing this. Like Bossard, Gerhard Klugmann, now recovering from his gunshot wound and certain Rostock was hunting for him, had been debriefed by Marshal Allemand's legal team. The hacker was savvy enough to have realized that his former employer was no longer the winning team and that the best way to stay out of both Rostock's crosshairs and prison was to cooperate. According to Allemand's lawyer, Klugmann was a disturbingly immaculate record-keeper.

Jack checked his watch. It was three o'clock. Nine a.m. back home.

"Will you excuse me?" Jack said, and stood up.

He walked out the solarium's side door and onto the lawn. He sat down in the grass. He pulled out his phone and hit speed dial.

The line clicked open, and the voice at the other end said, "Gerry Hendley."

"Gerry, it's Jack. I think it's time we talk."